MARCORÉ

THE TEXAS PAN AMERICAN SERIES

MARCORÉ

By ANTONIO OLAVO PEREIRA

*Translated by Alfred Hower
and John Saunders*

ILLUSTRATED BY NEWTON CAVALCANTI

UNIVERSITY OF TEXAS PRESS
AUSTIN & LONDON

The Texas Pan American Series is published
with the assistance of a revolving publication
fund established by the Pan American Sul-
phur Company and other friends of Latin
America in Texas.

International Standard Book Number 0–292–70013–X
Library of Congress Catalog Card Number 75–111931
Copyright © 1970 by Antonio Olavo Pereira
All Rights Reserved
Printed by The University of Texas Printing Division, Austin
Bound by Universal Bookbindery, Inc., San Antonio

TO OSMAR PIMENTEL

Antonio Olavo Pereira's *Marcoré*, first published in Rio de Janeiro in 1957, won the coveted prize for fiction awarded by the Brazilian Academy of Letters and the Carmen Dolores Barbosa prize. Praised by many of Brazil's most exigent critics and maintaining favor over the years with the public, the novel is well on its way to becoming a modern Brazilian classic, having recently gone into its fourth edition. It has also been published and received with enthusiasm in Portugal. Adopting the intimist, introspective approach characteristic of such Brazilian masters of the past as Machado de Assis, Lima Barreto, Graciliano Ramos, and José Lins do Rêgo, and utilizing the setting of a small town in the interior of the state of São Paulo, Pereira tells a moving, bittersweet tale of family problems complicated by misunderstandings that lead to tragic consequences. The novel contains several dramatic scenes as well as tender and entertaining ones and introduces a set of very human, very credible characters. One of these—Dona Emma, the narrator's irascible mother-in-law—is especially well drawn and is not likely to be soon forgotten by the reader.

The central character of the novel is the narrator himself, a modest, somewhat introverted individual who tends to view life with pessimism and who, aware of his own human condition, tries not to judge others too harshly. He reveals his experiences and thoughts by means of a kind of diary that he writes at irregular intervals, usually at the end of the day in his office, over a period of about a decade and a half. His occupation is the prosaic but respectable and (unlike its counterpart in the United States) fairly lucrative one of notary public, a sinecure he has inherited from his amiable father-in-law. His office, where all important events such as births, deaths, marriages, and business transactions must be recorded, and the men's club that he frequents provide him with good vantage points from which to observe the activities of his fellow townspeople and speculate on the motivations that drive them. But the drama of his life unfolds mainly at home, where the forbidding figure of his mother-in-law dominates the scene and where unexpected complications develop after he learns that his gentle and affectionate but excessively devout wife, Sylvia, in her eagerness to insure the safe birth of their first child, has made a very strange kind of vow.

Brazilian critics have admired the construction of *Marcoré*, the purity, sobriety, and concision of its author's style, the credibility of his characters, his compassionate understanding of human nature, and the skill with which he unobtrusively sketches the background of a quiet little Brazilian town. Antonio Cândido called *Marcoré* "an impeccable novel, uniting power of observation with knowledge of mankind." Rachel de Queiroz described it as "a beautiful and tormented book." José Lins do Rêgo felt that its flow of life is "like that of life itself" and that it is a book "that makes one weep." Cassiano Ricardo called it "a masterpiece of psychological analysis" and "one of the purest and most convincing realizations of Brazilian fiction in our times." Paulo Rónai paid tribute to its author's admirable handling of language and his exact depiction of Brazilian characters, customs, and environment. Ricardo Ramos declared that "the author probes into the most intimate part of his characters with rare skill, provides them with flesh and tears, and makes the reader aware of their reactions, the hidden motivation of their gestures, words, and thoughts." Antonio Houaiss expressed the hope that Pereira would continue to produce more works as admirably human as *Marcoré*.

The author of *Marcoré*, Antonio Olavo Pereira, was born on February 5, 1913, in the town of Batatais in the interior of the state of São Paulo. The fifth of nine children in a family of modest means, he attended school in Batatais until he was fourteen, when his family moved to the city of São Paulo. There he briefly attended the Rio Branco secondary school and later the Ginásio do Estado (the state high school), but for reasons of health he had to leave before graduating and was never able to complete his formal education. He continued reading and studying avidly on his own and early developed a deep interest in literature, becoming an admirer particularly of the novels of Machado de Assis, Eça de Queirós, and Anatole France, and at about the age of twenty he began to contribute to various literary periodicals. He was employed for a while at the municipal library of São Paulo, under the direction of Rubens Borba de Morais, who was one of the organizers of the Modernist movement that so strongly invigorated and renovated Brazilian intellectual life in the twenties and thirties and who was later to become director of the United Nations Library in New York. Eventually Antonio Olavo Pereira became associated with the São Paulo office of the distinguished publishing house, José Olympio, which was established in Rio de Janeiro in the early 1930's by his oldest brother, José Olympio Pereira Filho. This helped bring Antonio Olavo into close contact with the literary world, for José Olympio published an extraordinary number of works by many of Brazil's foremost writers, including Gilberto Freyre, José Lins do Rêgo, Graciliano Ramos, Rachel de Queiroz, Jorge Amado, João Guimarães Rosa, Manuel Bandeira, Carlos Drummond de Andrade, Cyro dos Anjos, Lúcio Cardoso, Otávio de Faria, Amando Fontes, and Vinícius de Morais. Pereira found the novels of Graciliano Ramos and Lins do Rêgo particularly to his liking, and the introspective nature of their work (rather than their regionalistic interests) came to exert much influence on his own writing.

Antonio Olavo Pereira married Gulnara Lobato de Morais, a marriage that brought him a stepson, Rodrigo Monteiro Lobato, and a son, Antonio Olavo Pereira Junior. Together with Pereira's mother-in-law, the family has resided for some time in São Paulo, where he is now a director of the editorial department of José Olympio. The family lived for a few years, however, in the town of Tremembé, in the state of São Paulo, not far from Campos do Jordão, a tuberculosis sanatorium in the mountains that was to serve as the setting for one of Pereira's novels. In Tremembé he lived the life of a gentleman farmer, cultivating the plants on his small estate, translating, and writing. It was during this time that he wrote the final version of his first novel, *Contra-mão*, a work he had begun in his early twenties.

Contra-mão, published in 1950 by José Olympio (who also published his subsequent two novels), gave its author an auspicious start in his career as a novelist, for it was awarded the Fábio Prado prize. It is an interesting short work narrated in the first person by an exceedingly shy and sensitive young man (unnamed) who feels inferior and inadequate, unable to communicate meaningfully with his family or acquaintances. Trying hard to understand life and to discover his role in it, he feels that somehow he is out of step, that he is progressing "contra-mão" (literally, in the wrong direction on a one-way street). Rejected by his girl friend because of his timidity, he experiences anguish and frustration; life seems meaningless, tedious, monotonous. Eventually he decides to accept the suggestion of the elevator operator of the building in which he is employed as a minor clerk and approach another young lady who seems to be interested in him, and it is on this slight—very slight—note of hope that the novel ends. The story is told in short, staccato, often elliptical sentences, characteristic of the Modernist style of such writers as Oswald de Andrade, Antonio de Alcântara Machado, and Graciliano Ramos, and in this as well as in its general atmosphere and characterization *Contra-mão* seems to be a preparation for the more mature and finished work that Pereira's second novel, *Marcoré*, proved to be.

Marcoré did not appear until 1957, seven years after *Contra-mão*, and it was not until eight years later, in 1965, that the author pub-

lished his third and most recent novel, *Fio de Prumo*. The new novel
aroused much interest among Brazilian critics, who recognized it as
another strong, compassionate, well-written work by Pereira, a
worthy successor to his *Marcoré*. Although narrated in the third
person it is similarly introspective, for the point of view is solely that
of the protagonist (unnamed, and referred to only as "he") through
whose eyes and mind the novel is revealed to us. Like the narrators
of *Contra-mão* and *Marcoré*, he is an observant, sensitive individual
concerned about personal problems, family relationships, and the
meaning of life. The first twelve chapters of the novel show him as a
young man suffering from tuberculosis, forced to spend many long
months in a sanatorium in the mountains where he and several other
inmates lead melancholy and tedious lives, obsessed with the hope of
cure and longing for the day when they will be able to resume normal
lives. The young man is eventually cured and in a concluding chap-
ter of reminiscences and reflections we see him some twenty years
later, happily married, with two children, and successful in business,
a man who has achieved inner peace and feels he is part of a universal harmony. Unlike the frustrated protagonists of Pereira's earlier
novels, he has found a meaning and direction in life: God is the "fio
de prumo"—the plumb line. But even though he is a contented man
in his personal and family life, he is, like the narrator of *Marcoré*, constantly aware of the precarious and transitory nature of life and concerned about the petty differences of opinion, the materialistic
desires, and the many kinds of prejudices that erect barriers between
fellow human beings and prevent clear communication and full
understanding.

There is thus a strong note of compassion, a plea for mutual toler-
ance, that runs through all three of the novels of Antonio Olavo
Pereira, and this is a note that is especially evident in *Marcoré*.
"We're all poor devils," says one of the characters in the novel. Another one declares: "Life could be so wonderful, if only people
didn't have tempers and tried to understand each other calmly." The

narrator, seeing two friends bitterly separated by politics, wonders: "Why didn't people understand each other, why didn't they control their passions?" Examining his own character, he says: "I don't consider myself any better or any worse than others. I believe that in the last analysis we are all unhappy, each one in his own fashion." Later he adds: "Let everyone live in his own way and as best he can. Foolish to play the moralist." Near the end of his story, as he looks back in anguish at his experiences, he concludes that his life has been one of little value and that he has committed "a whole lifetime of mistakes." The reader of *Marcoré*, however, may well decide that the narrator is more deserving of pity than of blame, for while to err is human, Pereira indicates that to understand and to forgive should also be human.

ALFRED HOWER

Part 1 A STRANGER COMES INTO OUR LIVES

Chapter One

I hear Sylvia's footsteps in the dining room and I think to myself, annoyed: if she comes out here on the terrace she'll interrupt my reading. Sprawled in the wicker chair, I wait a second for her to walk to
the front door.

But Sylvia comes up to me, uncovers my face by pushing my newspaper to one side, sits down on my lap. Lively actions that she has not
performed for a long time. She rests her head on my shoulder, takes

one of my hands between hers. Probably some quarrel with her mother.

"Be nice to me. I feel so happy."

I can't restrain an impulse of bad humor, more evident in the tone of my voice than in my words: "Seems to me that you have always felt that way."

I'm worried that my father-in-law, Camilo, will suddenly walk in and snatch the paper away from me. He's out in the garden, watering the lettuce, waiting for me to finish reading.

Sylvia snuggles closer to me and sighs. Her heart beats beyond the breast that is squeezed against my arm. Our breaths mingle.

"Today of all days for you to be impatient with me!"

The silence that follows makes me feel ashamed, fills me with remorse. I have no right to treat my wife so rudely. Sometimes I have these flare-ups and offend her without any reason.

She remains motionless while her muffled heartbeats move faster.

I lift her hand to my lips and kiss it. Repeating ancient gestures mechanically, without the voluptuousness of old, I smooth her velvety eyebrows, pull the downy hair at the nape of her neck under the compact bun. Sylvia shows no reaction to my caresses. Perhaps she lives, as I do, on subjective impressions that will soon be ten years old.

I see her white throat, confined by the neckline that comes to a point over the division of her breasts. Her rounded arms, the right one with vaccination marks. Her rosy ears, formerly so sensitive. Her mouth, which is red even without lipstick. The curve of her legs and hips. Sylvia's warmth fuses with mine, but habit has limited our sensuality. Everything is calmness and reflection between us. Her heart beats through the breast which now and then rises with a deeper breath. This person belongs to me completely, to the extent that it is possible to possess someone's soul. I sense her submissiveness, her helplessness. My remorse increases.

"All right, then. What's it all about?"

My inflection shows that my annoyance has passed. Sylvia becomes animated, her entire body vibrates. She raises her head and whispers in my ear, "I'm expecting a baby!"

"Oh, come now, Sylvia. Not really! Are we going to have that non-sense again? Come on, let me read my paper."

I move my legs, as if to push her away. My impatience threatens to return. She sits up straight and looks right into my eyes.

"This time it's true. There can't be any mistake."

Her words do not perturb me as much as her look and her smile. There is a language in them that is rarely wrong.

"Absurd," I murmur without conviction.

"Don't say that, dear. Our dream is going to come true. Isn't it wonderful, after such a long time?"

She kisses my lips with a new emotion, an unknown purity.

I feel stunned, incapable of ordering the thoughts that occur to me. Down deep the hope prevails that this may be just another mistake on Sylvia's part.

"Why are you so sure this time?"

My voice fails me, revealing panic, confusion.

"I went to Dr. Leandro."

"What the devil kind of examination did he give you?"

The information does not please me. Doctors have excessive rights, too much liberty.

Sylvia smiles: "Nothing too much, silly. You'll see the prescription he gave me. I went there the day before yesterday, secretly, but the results just came today. Nobody knows anything about it yet. Isn't it nice having a secret like this?"

She kisses me again, wraps her arms around my neck.

"Didn't I always tell you that I would give you a child? It wasn't easy but it's going to happen at last."

I ask her to let me think it over, by myself.

She jumps up: "The only thing to think about is that our dream is going to come true."

And she goes out, almost running, her face all aglow. I tell her to be careful, so that she won't slip on the floor. I watch her disappear through the door of the breakfast room and her body really does appear to have grown a trifle bigger around the waist.

Her last words still vibrate on the terrace. "Our dream is going to come true." They seem to be pronounced by a distant voice, muffled like an echo, whose meaning I cannot grasp. What is the matter with me? Don't I share Sylvia's happiness? I allow myself to become wrapped in contradictory sentiments, with a vague fear predominating. I am unable to define it, and when I try to set it aside by thinking about immediate aspects of the problem it insinuates itself at the first opening to torment me. I don't know what it's all about, but I'm afraid of something. I try to visualize it in connection with the child, some deformity, some deficiency: my fear does not gain shape. I imagine terrible suffering for Sylvia, I even imagine her death, but I fail to gain any clearer understanding. Nevertheless, one fact is clear to me from the start: our lives will not be the same from this day on.

Lost in my thoughts I fail to notice Camilo's presence. It's too late when I reach out to salvage the newspaper. My father-in-law already has it in his grasp and is comfortably seated in the hammock near me.

"Much news?"

His usual question when I read the paper before he does. His excitement, the renewed gleam in his small eyes, are also part of the routine.

"I stopped halfway through."

I see now that I have lost interest in the broad sheets in which words trample each other. They have taken up a good portion of my time in my required everyday conduct. They have aroused various emotions in me, they have weakened some doubts, they have strengthened others. I look at them with indifference, as if my psychological axis had become dislocated, removing me from that world of print. Confused thoughts daze me, in unbridled succession. Camilo unfolds the paper to the political section, as always, and concentrates on his reading.

I get along well with my father-in-law, we have no disagreements despite the difference in our ages. We have been friendlier perhaps than I was with my father. Camilo is a man of different nature, he is understanding, easygoing. Our only discord is in connection with the newspaper. The right to read it first is disputed every inch of the way. We spend our mornings prowling around the front gate looking down the street, watching out for the yellow shape of the mailman—each of us alert to the other's vigilance. Priority goes to the one who sees him first. If we are at the table and Onofre suddenly calls out "Mail!" we jump up from our chairs and each one races out a different door to get hold of it. The winner returns to his chair, sits down on the edge of the paper until he finishes his lunch. A little later the loser places himself opposite him on the terrace, his eyes glued to the headlines, his legs quivering with impatience. The reading is done slowly, page by page, column by column. When the reader reaches the last news item, observing the other one's impatience, he often turns back to the first page for a general review. The other one goes back to his waiting position, without protest but with one more furrow in his brow. These are my moments of greatest intimacy and identification with Camilo.

Now the old man is there in the hammock, entrenched behind the paper. I can see only his fingers with their hairy knuckles and his crossed legs hanging motionless over the veranda. He does not know that the biggest news of the day is inside of me. Or, rather, inside of Sylvia, who is carrying it alive in her belly. I could give it form by calling it into our world. "You're going to have a grandchild, you're going to be a grandfather." This announcement has been made repeatedly for ten years, only to be followed each time by a biological refutation. Sylvia never abandoned the hope that it would be confirmed some day, sooner or later. Perhaps it has come too late: the idea of fatherhood no longer excites me; rather, it vexes me. At first I wanted a child, or two, to continue me and in whom I could see myself as I really am. A boy and a girl would have been just right, to serve as a perfect unfolding. None came, in spite of Sylvia's efforts and the vows she made. She lit candles to Our Lady of Perpetual Help, she said novenas that seemed interminable for she maintained continence while they lasted. All recourses had failed, our plan of multiplication had been forgotten. Now it suddenly reappeared with the news. "Our dream is going to become true." Dream, my eye. I no longer have any enthusiasm for the undertaking.

My uneasiness returns, still undefined. What if Sylvia needs an operation? What if the baby is born crippled? Dr. Leandro will take care of everything. The fewer examinations, the better. Let him go feel the devil's wife.

My fear comes and goes. Suddenly it becomes fixed, takes on meaning. Dona Emma comes into view in the back yard, her hands black with earth, a ringlet of hair falling over her forehead. A chill goes up and down my spine. What will my mother-in-law say when she finds out that Sylvia is going to become a mother? She'll raise the roof. Better to have lunch out, so that Sylvia can come to an understanding with her alone, at the table.

"Camilo, how about having lunch at Miguel's?"

Silence. Probably I haven't spoken loud enough to be heard. I repeat my proposal, my father-in-law lowers the paper. I seem to see printed letters floating on his fixed, faraway pupils. Little by little he comes to.

"What? Not today. Honorata is preparing a loin of pork with pumpkin sprouts."

I lack the courage to face Dona Emma's look when she finds out. It would be more prudent for Sylvia to leave a note for her under her pillow tonight, and let Camilo put up with the consequences.

A man is at peace with himself, and suddenly everything breaks up around him. My father-in-law's peace of mind is also hanging by a thread. Soon he'll start to worry, to make plans, to change habits. The old man has been longing for a grandchild, now he is going to have one. Maybe it's just another of Sylvia's mistakes. Dr. Leandro is not infallible. Others before him have been wrong.

Evangelina comes into the dining room with the tablecloth. The time is drawing close. Sylvia has remained calm, she must be in her room arranging clothes in drawers. Maybe Dona Emma will go there and perhaps they could come to an understanding, as mother and daughter, with explanations and embraces. The lunch would go along smoothly, Camilo would have his meal in peace. Surprises make Dona Emma tight-lipped. Her eye must always be the first to notice anything new or different in the house.

A frying pan sizzles in the kitchen. Honorata will soon have lunch on the table.

Camilo turns the pages of the paper, looking for passages he may have skipped. He's going to be a grandfather and he doesn't know it.

The figure of Faustino appears at the back gate, walking slowly, with his axe over his shoulder. He heads straight for the woodshed; at its entrance there is one pile of logs and another of pieces of firewood. I get up and walk over.

Faustino selects a piece of wood, sets it on the chopping block, aims a good blow at it with his axe. A crack appears, in it he places a wedge. A small mallet completes the job.

"Good firewood, Faustino?"

He stops his work, straightens up.

"First class. Special. A good buy, boss. This time they didn't cheat you on the length."

His eye with the cataract has the color of a clouded film and is always running at the corners. The other one, perfect, possesses profound vision and a gentle expression.

"A tree born during a thunderstorm is no good. It comes out full of knots and with an uneven grain. No axe can do anything with it. But this mimosa is nice and smooth."

The axe strikes. At each blow Faustino gives a little grunt.

"How are your children?"

Another pause. I feel a new, unusual warmth in this question that I have asked casually so many times before.

"Getting along, thank God."

And he takes off his hat, with its torn brim.

"How many grandchildren?"

"Eleven."

His smile is one of beatitude, of a man perfectly multiplied. Camilo and I have failed. If that tardy child makes it, it will be like winning a campaign.

"You are the one who ought to have a house full of kids. Didn't Dona Sylvia want any children?"

"It's not that. They just didn't come."

He takes off his hat again.

"It wasn't God's will. But you might be surprised all of a sudden. With women you never can tell."

I look at him suspiciously. Does he know about it?

"Nonsense, Faustino. They haven't come in ten years, they're not going to come any more."

He resumes his work, the axe gleams in the sun. The split wood has the good smell of resin. Chips fly.

There is a man with no problems. A good edge on his axe is all he needs for his life to go along without a hitch. His blood has been reproduced, it gives life to a whole series of hearts. His soul is no doubt also multiplied, looking at the world in different ways. Faustino is a man who has been completed. I envy him furiously.

I turn around, startled, in the direction of footsteps that approach. It's Evangelina.

"Dona Sylvia said to tell you that lunch is on the table."

She goes back to the kitchen, swinging her hips, her calves the color of brown sugar emerging out of her short skirt.

"Will you have some lunch, Faustino?"

He stops chopping.

"Some other time. I've just come from home. Enjoy your meal."

My footsteps reveal uncertainty. I must give the woodcutter the impression of an ox on his way to the slaughterhouse. Sylvia must have written to Dona Emma, the matter has probably been settled.

I meet her at the entrance to the terrace. She throws her arms around my neck, smiling, happy.

"Will it be a boy or a girl?"

Camilo sits up in the hammock, the hooks creak.

"What's this about a boy or a girl?"

He wears an anxious expression.

"Just another of Sylvia's crazy notions," I answer without looking at him. "The same old story."

Dona Emma appears in the doorway of the dining room, crosses the room, takes her place at the head of the table.

"This is no time for nonsense."

Her voice is commanding, imperious. The moon is unfavorable. If Sylvia blabs, we'll have a battle on our hands.

Camilo seats himself at the other end, Sylvia and I sit face to face, between the old couple. A pleasant aroma arises from the steaming tureens. I've no desire to eat. Camilo digs into his pork. Dona Emma has an expectant air. She keeps her eyes on Sylvia, alert.

Eating is impossible. I sprinkle some pepper sauce on the meat. Useless. My throat is tight, my tongue dry. I keep toying with bits of stew and rice.

The silence is getting on my nerves. I wish Sylvia would come out with it once for all. Better for Dona Emma to learn all about it right now, come what may. Camilo chews away noisily, aloof from the little drama that is being enacted around the table. Dona Emma thickens her beans with corn meal. Her look is distrustful, hostile. Sylvia seems to be defying her, remaining silent in order to increase the tension.

Camilo again helps himself from the platter of pork.

"So, Sylvia, what's all this about a boy or a girl?"

Dona Emma's nostrils quiver, her glance sharpens, moves from her daughter to me. I try to reach Sylvia's foot to signal her. A hot flush rises to my face. Cramps threaten my legs.

Sylvia smiles at me, stares at Dona Emma for a second, and turns to her father.

"Well, that's it. You're going to become a grandfather. And this time there can't be any mistake. All the tests were positive. Isn't that wonderful, Father?"

The tone of her voice, the brightness of her eyes, her radiant expression are incontestable arguments.

Dona Emma fulminates me with a mute query. I have to say something, contradict Sylvia, leave room for doubt, but my voice fails me. I take refuge in the pork, putting a forkful in my mouth.

Dona Emma crosses her knife and fork.

"What I've just heard is utterly ridiculous. I don't approve of such foolishness. Sylvia is too old for anything like that. I want you all to know that I won't even go near the child's cradle if such an absurd thing should actually happen."

And she goes off toward the door of her room. Camilo gets up, goes to Sylvia, whose face has clouded over. He embraces her, kisses her hair.

"Pay no attention to your mother's words, daughter. She wants a grandchild more than anyone. What she can't forgive is that she didn't make the discovery with her own eyes. You can understand that."

On his way back to his chair he pats me on the shoulder.

"What we need is to have a grandson, to carry on the family strain."

He finishes his meal with enthusiasm. Sylvia's plate remains almost untouched, like mine and Dona Emma's, scarcely begun. Honorata's unhurried footsteps make themselves heard. She approaches Sylvia and tilts her chin upward.

"Heaven help me, it's the pure truth! It's all clear in those mischievous eyes. Let Dona Emma talk. I'd like to see if she has the heart, when the time comes, to ignore the child. Now this house will be a happy one."

Honorata helped raise Sylvia and it is as if the grandchild to come were hers also. Her brown face seems to have a new luster, her mouth is less contracted. Silent, as obedient as a slave, she is the supreme authority in the house. A slow shadow that moves about all day long from place to place, keeping everything orderly and neat. Nothing is done without consulting her prodigious intuition, or listening to her measured and prudent words. Dona Emma is jealous of her, as she is of everyone around her. Every once in a while, when she is upset, especially on days when she is in a bad mood, she can't restrain herself and lets that feeling come to the surface. If Camilo asks her to sew a button on for him, she retorts furiously, "Go ask that 'silent efficiency.' Let her sew it."

It is Camilo's expression and he is often punished with it.

If, on the other hand, it is Evangelina who asks for orders about stocking the pantry, she shoos her out of the sewing room with shouts: "I have nothing to do with that. Go ask the manager of the kitchen."

And the manager takes care of it all.

Such scenes have been repeated for ten years at intervals that vary in duration. Honorata remains imperturbable, in her heart there is no room for quarrels. Under her protection the small storms unleashed periodically by Dona Emma's temper are calmed. The sensible hours are spent side by side. My father-in-law then observes, on the sly of course, with a delighted smile, "Good sign. Today we can stay at the club longer. The old ladies are on a honeymoon."

They converse on such occasions, in fact, for hours and hours, reliving common impressions of days gone by, while their crochet needles move lightly and swiftly.

Sylvia has never been considered the lady of the house. Her role in directing the affairs of the household is small. Unfairly, they do not recognize that she has any ability. She keeps our bedroom, her exclusive domain, spotlessly clean and in perfect order. The care she devotes to my clothes is almost an obsession. Now that she is going to have a baby, she will undoubtedly become more important.

Honorata has consoled her and has gone back to the kitchen, shuffling along in her slippers. Evangelina appears with a toothy smile, all excited, carrying the coffee tray.

"Congratulations, Dona Sylvia. I hope it will be a girl."

"A girl? Your grandmother!" Camilo breaks in. "You think I've waited so long just to have a granddaughter? Nothing of the sort. I want a boy."

Evangelina gets rattled, her face flushes as she starts setting the cups in place. Dona Emma's is left over.

"Go see if the door to her bedroom is open," says Sylvia.

She goes there, tries the doorknob carefully. Locked. She comes back with an air of relief.

Camilo takes charge of the coffee meant for his wife. His face is as animated as that of a child who has been promised something.

"If it's a girl, will you be unhappy?" inquires Sylvia, holding her hand out to me across the table.

Her eyes again have the expression they had before.

"Of course he will!" interrupts Camilo. "It can only be a boy. And he's going to be a giant, considering how long it's taken him to appear. That rascal has been on his way for ten years."

He laughs, pulls out a rolled cigarette. I look at my watch. It won't be long before it strikes noon. I have to get going.

I say good-by to Sylvia, I tell her to be careful and to take it easy. Down deep, I want to ask once more whether the tests can be right, whether all this can be just another hoax. I'm afraid of hurting her, of spoiling her day. Camilo picks up his hat.

"I'm going out for a little walk, daughter. Take good care of yourself, don't get upset over trifles."

He winks at her, nodding toward the bedroom.

We go out together. The sun beats down on the sidewalk. The

languor of the hour weakens the will, suggesting the comfort of a hammock. But my office is waiting, there's plenty of writing to do in those interminable books.

We proceed silently. Camilo walks more rapidly than usual. He is excited, undoubtedly eager to spread the news.

"Are you going to the office?"

"No. To the drugstore."

Domingos will be the first to know. That's as good as publishing it in the paper. Before long they'll get hold of the news at the club and will start discussing it. They may even wind up doubting that it's my child. Those bastards are capable of thinking anything.

"Camilo, you ought to keep it a secret for a while. The thing may go wrong."

He stops, looks at me in surprise.

"Dammit, you don't have much faith, do you? Why should it go wrong, after so many tests? After all, do you have what it takes or don't you?"

He takes a deep puff, starts walking again. Rapidly, with a vigor that I haven't seen in him for a long time. I begin to perceive that the hypothetical creature in the process of formation is going to change the course of our lives. Whether for better or for worse—that's the big question.

At the entrance to my office I see Aristides leaning against the door. I answer his greeting, I insert the key in the lock. The warm, musty smell of the room hits us in the face. It emanates from the books that enclose the past. Stacks and stacks of bookcases, containing the history of the city. The clerk throws open the windows, the air recirculates.

"There are some certificates to be done today. Shall I look them up?"

I nod affirmatively. From rummaging about among ancient things his face has taken on an aged expression. The years are weighing on him, his hair is turning white.

"Say, Aristides. How old are you, anyway?"

His head emerges from one of the bookcases with an air of surprise.

"Forty-three. Why?"

"Oh, nothing."

The search continues. He moistens his middle finger with saliva and turns the faded sheets.

"How many children do you have?"

Another look of surprise, although this time the question pleases him.

"Six, including your goddaughter."

The appended phrase seems intentional. It exposes a relationship that had never been taken seriously and that had been kept up only by means of little gifts I sent to the child with him as intermediary. I remember that he spent days, awkwardly embarrassed, getting up courage to invite me to the baptism. I finally did go to the sacristy and helped to hold the baby for the bathing. She kept crying and wriggling about desperately, threatening to slip into the basin. The salt made her quiet down as they dried her forehead.

Since that time I have seldom seen my goddaughter, who must be about four years old now. Good-for-nothing godfather. I should have refused the invitation. There would have been no shortage of decent godfathers for Aristides. What I feel is really not a lack of interest, but a sticky kind of laziness that doesn't allow me to make any greater effort. After all, he is a long-time fellow worker of mine, an important cog in this organization that has brought us a considerable amount of comfort. Fifteen years of daily association, almost ten years with Camilo. One living thing in this heap of antiques. I could act in a friendlier way toward him, treat him better. I don't make the effort, though, to leave my comfortable rut.

The routine work gets done, the day progresses slowly. Outside, the sultry weather resembles the breath of a furnace. No traffic at all. But sooner or later there will appear candidates for documents, for inscriptions in the books. There's never a blank day. There's always somebody getting born or kicking the bucket. Marriages, transactions concluded. Nothing is valid unless it is entered into the thick and grimy volumes. And so our lives are spent.

Aristides makes transcriptions, carefully, conscientiously. He is as proud of his artistic penmanship as he is of his children. In general, I think of him more as a working tool than as a human being. I make no distinction between him and the files, the stamps, the pad of certificates. A pulley, a bit worn out, but useful—that's all. And yet he's a good soul. A member of St. Vincent's and other religious brotherhoods. His life is more useful than mine, but I'm the one who is on top.

"Aristides, do you really believe in God?"

He raises his eyes, looks at me with an offended expression.

"What kind of question is that?"

My unreasonable interrogation about his personal matters must seem strange to him. His pen once again travels silently over the paper. His gray-patched head is undoubtedly sheltering some perplexed thoughts.

Gregorio enters, corpulent, gloomy, with an air of weariness.

"Good afternoon, Gregorio."

He gestures toward me with his hand, sits down, gathers his breath with an effort. Dark circles under his eyes, his beard unshaven, an expression of suffering. The master carpenter must be in some sort of trouble. After a few moments he takes a sheet of paper out of his pocket and puts it on my table. I pick it up: Dr. Leandro's handwriting.

"I'm very sorry, Gregorio."

I don't know if he has heard me or believed me. Aristides heard and did not believe me. He looks at me with an air, if not of censure, of resentment. He holds me in esteem but does not approve of my attitude. He considers me insensitive to the sorrows of my fellow man. A probable consequence of the nature of this job, from which

Camilo must also have come out hardened. Let a gravedigger get sentimental about his victims and none of them will get to rest their bones in their eternal abode.

The clerk makes the entry in the register. Gregorio's wife has left this world. She lived reasonably long: fifty-five years. Several children and grandchildren. A more complete experience than that of Dona Emma and Sylvia. The pen scratches the paper: Dona Anunciata, acute nephritis.

Gregorio receives the certificate, reads it with trembling hands, while his blue eyes moisten. He seems to obtain the confirmation of a real fact. That's the power of the papers that come out of this mill. Life, after all, is governed by it. And death also. The carpenter takes a while to get to the end. Before folding the proof that he is a widower, his lips tremble and he moans, "Miserable life!"

His words resound unpleasantly, with an anguished note. In his eyes there's a flash of revolt or of protest—I don't know which. Aristides gives him his change. Gregorio goes out without another word.

The clerk gets ready to resume his work, but first he says to me, pensively, "A fine woman, the deceased. She left at least half a dozen children, some of them small. I'll pray for her soul tonight."

Sylvia's child is smaller, I think to myself. He is sucking her blood in, drop by drop, in his eagerness to emerge into life. He will inherit his principal traits from her, the best of what there is in her character. He will be well endowed.

I wonder whether Dona Emma has calmed down. Honorata, almost certainly, has intervened with her abilities, her authority.

"Nonsense, senhora. Don't be stubborn. This house is a cemetery without a child."

Time drags on, until the church clock strikes twice. Aristides gets ready to leave. An idea occurs to me: "Oh, Aristides, I believe I'll have coffee with you. Let Sylvia know."

His expression reflects surprise and pleasure as he goes to the phone.

"If you had only told me earlier I would have had Augusta make some cookies."

"Nonsense. My comadre is busy enough as it is."*

I utter the title "comadre" spontaneously. Aristides transmits the message, hangs up, closes the windows briskly. I turn the key.

Side by side with the clerk along the broken sidewalks. The mournful houses doze in the sun. A train whistle sounds in the distance.

Gregorio has gone home, is preparing the departure of the funeral procession. His children must be in despair, crying, grieving the old man.

"How are your kids?"

"They weren't doing so well for a while, but they're fine now. Your goddaughter is getting to be quite a girl."

Good father. Talks about his children with pride in his chest.

Mine is brand-new, barely begun as yet. That damn Dr. Leandro. Getting too intimate, with the pretense of examining.

Father Bento crosses the square headed for the sacristy. He sees us, raises his hard-crown hat. His cassock rustles harshly.

"Tell me something, Aristides: does a child give a lot of trouble at night?"

"There are always some. But the joys of the other hours are greater."

To be forewarned is of course to be forearmed. If Sylvia brings a whining little boy into the world, I'll move out of the bedroom. You can't do any work after a sleepless night.

Suppose it's a girl? You never can tell what it's going to be. It may be a girl. I don't know, I don't know. The boy who asks for my daughter's hand will have to be someone special. She won't be handed over to any Joe that happens to come along. If any scoundrel makes her unhappy, I'll break him in half.

"And suppose it's a girl, Aristides?"

The clerk stops, his mouth open.

* "Comadre" and "compadre" are terms that express the relationship between a child's parents and his godparents.

"Don't tell me that . . ."

"Nothing of the sort. I don't know what I said. Come on."

Good afternoon to the passers-by. They appear now and then, un-hurried. They should have stayed at home. Nothing to do on the street in this heat.

Aristides' house has an iron gate. Façade painted blue, fading. He has me go up to the front door, then he goes around to the back, al-most running. In a moment he comes to open it.

"Come in, compadre. Don't look too closely. A poor man's house."

I don't know how long it has been since I visited here. Or did I come just once? His wife is slow in making her appearance. She is probably in front of the mirror straightening her hair. Colored litho-graphs on the walls, framed photos, a frightful calendar. The flock of kids appears at the kitchen door. Aristides brings my goddaugh-ter in by the hand. Round, surprised little eyes.

"Let your godfather give you his blessing," her father orders.

I step forward and pat her straight hair.

"She's grown up. It seems only yesterday that she was baptized."

Instead of a blessing, which I lack practice in giving, I give her a penny or two and the little girl runs out the street door. The others draw near, the oldest boy skinny, shy, sickly. A coin to each and they also dash out the front gate.

"They'll go to the store and spend it on junk."

"Let them go, Aristides. It's their money. By the way, what's the matter with the oldest one? He looks so yellow."

"He's had measles, like the others."

Comadre Augusta appears, drying her hands on her apron, com-pletely at ease. She breaks into a broad smile.

"What a pleasure to see you again, compadre. Let's sit down."

One question follows another about Sylvia, Dona Emma, Camilo, Honorata. Not even Evangelina is forgotten. I say nothing at all about the baby. It's better not to jump the gun. News of this kind makes it-self known in due time.

Comadre Augusta listens to my reports, expresses her sentiments about them, goes back to the kitchen.

"The water for the coffee must be boiling."

Aristides appears ill at ease, without anything to say to me. Neither do I know what to say to him. I'm surprised to note that outside of the office our relationship is limited, even strained. No intimacy, nothing in common. A consequence of this purposeless visit. The situation threatens to drag on, when the children come running back. Susana's fingers and face are smeared with chocolate. She comes up to me with a contented little expression on her face. Aristides cries out, "Go wash your hands, girl! Don't touch your godfather's clothes. And the rest of you, too. Don't you know any better?"

And he ushers them out through the kitchen door.

His wife's voice calls us inside.

The tablecloth is frayed and Aristides seems upset by my scrutiny. My comadre fills the cups as the children draw near again. Susana can't take her eyes off mine. A pretty little thing, chestnut hair, long eyelashes. Aristides' children appear to be neglected. The youngest one's nose is filthy with snot. Maybe he doesn't earn enough, has a hard time making ends meet. Six piranhas to feed is no joke.

"Is it too bitter, compadre?"

"It's fine."

It's terrible. Low-grade coffee, watery. Horribly brewed. The children devour the cornmeal cake. I share my piece with Susana and the boy who has had the measles. I win two smiles.

After I've finished my cup and refused a refill, comadre Augusta calls me aside, in the yard.

"Compadre, God must have sent you here. I wanted very much to talk to you."

A touch, no doubt. She will say that my goddaughter doesn't have a stitch to wear, needs clothes and shoes, and the oldest boy needs dental treatment.

"Don't be bashful, comadre."

She takes heart, her face turning red.

"Aristides needs a raise, compadre. The cost of living has gone up something terrible; we've been in a bad way. But that's the last thing he would talk to you about."

I feel as if I had been struck with a hammer, causing my muscles to go soft, my legs to weaken. The revelation astonishes me, and a feeling of guilt disturbs me. Why haven't I paid any attention to this problem of Aristides'? I've let him go so long without a word of inquiry, without any discussion about his financial condition. I had noted only that he was aging at an accelerated rate, and I kept attributing this to organic disorders. But there was only one reason for his pitiful condition: the man wasn't earning enough to get along on. And his timid nature did not permit him to be frank enough with me to ask for the raise he needed.

"All right, comadre. I'll see Camilo about it."

I hastened to leave. I was feeling remorse, a profound sadness that made me unhappy.

We entered the house. Aristides' eyes were cast down, guilty. The children were still around the table, looking for crumbs on the tablecloth. They stared at me as if I were a thief—or so it seemed to me. My goddaughter took my blessing, the others gave me their hands silently. I promised comadre Augusta that I would come back more often, and perhaps there was sincerity in that intention. I ought to try to make some amends.

Aristides went along, without saying a word. Poor devil. A timid soul, with no means of defending himself. Maybe it's my own soul that's worthless, maybe it's impervious and hard.

When we reach the square I give him my key.

"I'm going to my mother's house. I won't stay long."

"Give Dona Antonieta my regards."

We separate. Aristides cuts across the square, takes the street to the office. I turn the corner at the church, allow myself to walk along unhurriedly. Father Bento comes out of the sacristy, his hat moves up and down. He seems troubled, perhaps one of his sheep needs the last sacraments. It can't be Gregorio's wife, for she has become silent forever, unable to reveal anything about her afflictions anymore.

I walk along with some difficulty, my steps heavy, as if I were dragging chains. I can't explain this sudden feeling of fatigue, this oppressiveness that burdens me. Perhaps it's the case of Aristides, and, in a general way, the new situation to be faced.

The latch on the gate gives way easily. The jasmine shrub emits its odor from the shadow projected by the walls. I go around to the back, as usual, and find her seated next to the stove, sipping coffee out of a saucer.

"Alone, Mother?"

I don't see Marcilia, either inside or outside.

"Alone? No; with God!"

She gets up, takes a cup from the cupboard, fills it for me. I sit down on the little stool, near the door.

"Marcilia went to take some pomegranates to Sylvia. Didn't you meet her?"

"I didn't come from home. I had coffee with Aristides."

Her clear, cold eyes are turned toward the saucer. Her gnarled hands are thin, but firm. Her hair is turning white, evenly, unhurriedly. Extensive wrinkles line her face with its severe expression. Her harsh demeanor is a part of her nature that cost me many disagreeable raps on my head when I was a child, struck by knuckles that seemed to burn like a red-hot iron. My sister Claudia couldn't stand that method of punishment.

"Hit me anywhere but on my head!" she would scream, enraged, protecting herself with her arms. "That drives me crazy!"

Julieta, as sly as a fox, enjoyed a childhood that was free of punishment. She didn't experience the hardness of those long fingers or the biting suppleness of quince switches. I don't know what strange notion of justice led my mother to punish Claudia and me with cal-

culated severity and let my other sister go unpunished. Her partiality hurt us more deeply than her blows.

"What are you thinking about, son?"

Her voice does not have the harshness of her face, but it is far from being tender.

"Nothing. I was just thinking about the way you used to rap Claudia and me with your knuckles and how you always spared Julieta."

She turns her glance for a moment toward the yard.

"Julieta was more my friend, she never talked back to me."

Two episodes in our lives have deepened her bitterness: my father's death and, later, my marriage. If the first one has become diluted by time, the second one has continued and upsets her even today. She didn't dislike Sylvia, but she had already reserved me for her niece Adelaide, saying something about a family obligation. She had plans of living in the same house, giving orders, leading her daughter-in-law around by the halter. It all went down the drain. I didn't care for my cousin's bulging eyes: they were greedy, restless, with streaks of blood in their immense corneas. They frightened me. What was hidden behind them? What was the secret of that agitated soul? I didn't have the courage to probe its doubtful depths, even though from the time I was a child I had wanted to marry a cousin. I was fascinated by the romanticism of the word, the mystery that our very names seemed to contain. Adelaide herself, as a girl, excited my imagination, but she grew up, her eyes got too big, they bulged out for life. That was no adventure for me. We separated without any mutual sorrow, in time we each managed our lives in our own fashion. But my mother did not forgive me and at first she hurled a terrible insult at me.

"The reason you're rejecting your cousin is that you want to marry not only that pasty-faced girl but also the notary's office that her father has."

As I was no longer at an age to be afraid of her knuckles or switches, I shot an insolent reply back at her, but she was not entirely convinced by it. I can read in her face that the doubt exists even today.

Our eyes converge on the thrush that appeared on the wall and has perched on the guava tree. The yellow body seems fidgety, moves about restlessly. Suddenly it ceases its movements, and its melody, repeated at short intervals, pierces the afternoon silence.

> *Tira, tira,*
> *Sinhá,*
> *Paletó, sinhá . . .*

"That little bird comes to visit me every afternoon. It sings on the same branch, pecks at a piece of fruit, and flies away. I think it loves me more than my own children do."

Her complaint is involuntary, uttered perhaps out of habit. I am not surprised to hear it, for it is always present in our conversations.

Marcilia's slippers approach and seem to scrape an accompaniment to the song of the bird. There she is in the doorway of the kitchen, her dark face gleaming with sweat. She has been my mother's only companion since I got married. She takes care of all of the hard work and still has enough energy left to make sweets that she sells from house to house on nicely prepared trays.

"You here? I've just come from your house. Honorata told me everything."

Her smile is wide, good-natured. I look at my mother, embarrassed.

"Oh, yes . . . I almost forgot."

"That's the way it always is. I'm the last one to learn anything new that concerns you. But don't worry. Camilo has already stopped by here."

Her term of comparison is Dona Emma, it's in relation to her that my mother feels hurt. An implacable enmity keeps them apart and suspicious of each other. Dona Emma also had a son-in-law picked out and I spoiled her plans. She still has hanging in her bedroom, faded and almost indistinguishable from the leaden color of the wall, a portrait of her godson, whom she had selected as a mate for Sylvia. She keeps it for spite, as a mute protest. Lauro comes in from his farm from time to time, fat, prosperous, with his gang of kids. He maintains certain intimacies with Sylvia that their childhood spent together permits even today, but which annoy me nevertheless. He kisses her on the cheek, talks to her with his face close to hers, hugs her more tightly than necessary. What calms me down is the knowledge that Sylvia is pure and is truly in love with me. I am worthless, my merits are insignificant, yet I mean everything to her. Until now, at least, I've meant everything. I can be supplanted only by the stranger who is developing inside of her.

"Miss Sylvia is so happy! She has already begun to make little baby clothes. By the looks of it, Dona Emma didn't like the news at all. She was in her bedroom, grumbling."

Marcilia continues smiling, looking at me with approving indulgence. Her kinky hair is beginning to turn white, her cheeks are becoming sunken. Marcilia doesn't take care of herself, always at the stove, slowly wearing herself out. One of these days she'll have to face the mystery that she talks about so much. She contemplates it without fear, seated with my mother in chairs on the sidewalk, watching the night fall.

"Nonsense, senhora, the cares of this world don't come to an end. Not even after death does a body get any rest. It doesn't do any good to end up in heaven. The way it seems, you spend your life there putting up and taking down stars. Night comes, you have to decorate the sky; when day breaks, you have to gather everything up."

Images get confused in her mind—the real sky extending from one horizon to the other and the cardboard one, with paper stars, which appears as a background for the Virgin carried in processions. But she fears nothing, neither the eternal fire nor the embers of purgatory. Only good deeds have flowed from her hands, no refusal has ever been heard from her mouth. If she never had any children in her few years of married life, she helped my mother bring hers up, as well as those of Julieta and Claudia. Now, standing there, leaning against the door, she has the confident expression of one who is expecting another little master.

"Your mother-in-law couldn't approve at all of this. After all, she didn't even approve of your marriage."

"Don't harp on those old stories, Mother," I order her harshly.

Useless, because the old stories are always with us. They seem dormant and yet they spring to life at the slightest provocation, flare up, and burn. More than ever, the past thrusts forward at this moment and wounds like the point of a spear.

I don't know whether I can say that I have been happy these ten years. It is comforting to acknowledge Sylvia's love, constant, intense, approaching idolatry, at times excessive and irksome. Her constant vigilance to make certain that I should want for nothing and be happy with what she gave me, the passionate submission that made me her lord and master. Along with it, Camilo's friendship, the feeling of alliance that united us. But Dona Emma's temper ruined the smallest pleasures of my life. There has never been a perfect understanding between us. Nor between her and Camilo, nor even with relation to Sylvia. Her contrary nature, accustomed to jealousy and distrust, kept giving rise to misunderstandings that usually turned into quarrels. Sylvia was the one who suffered the most from this, because in our hours of intimacy, when I was most acrimonious, I would attack the old lady on the slightest pretext. "Your mother had no business having the branch of the myrtle tree that overhung the street sawed off. She thinks she knows something about plants but what she's doing is ruining our orchard." I knew less, but I acted grouchy just to mortify Sylvia. "That doesn't matter, dear. The branch will grow again. Didn't you yourself get involved with those urchins who used to come by and throw stones at the ripe fruit?" It was true, but my rancor would not yield. "And whose idea was it to move the tea rose from the flower bed? It is certainly going to wither." Sylvia would remain quiet, then smile sadly. "Mother isn't so bad. She has a temper, but at heart she is kind. You two are like stubborn children." She wasn't so bad, I knew. I had had firsthand knowledge of this, early in my married life. I had fallen ill with pneumonia and she insisted on taking care of me. She didn't allow Sylvia to help at all, she became impatient, biting her nails, when my mother tried to straighten out the bed-covers. She inspected the windows to make sure there would be no drafts, she prohibited anyone from talking or treading noisily in the house. The critical period of my illness cost her many sleepless nights. I remember her running back and forth between my bedroom and the kitchen, carrying mustard plasters and cupping glasses that felt like claws digging into my back. During my convalescence she worked away at the stove, seeking ways of overcoming my lack of appetite. She would spoon-feed me, she would get angry, treating me like a child, almost like her own son. Probably in her anxiety she was thinking about Lauro, confusing me with the son-in-law who never was. It's true that I owe her my life, but even so I do not consider my-self much indebted to her, for greater were the evils resulting from her jealousy.

I have never delved deeply into the roots of my life with the aim of making inner reforms. I do not consider myself any better or any worse than others. I believe that in the final analysis we are all un-happy, each one in his own fashion. The news about Sylvia's child forces me to take some unpleasant soundings. It's as if, having been awakened from a long hibernation, wrenched out of an opaque tor-por, I am beginning to see clearly into my past. More misses than hits, evil more often than good. I always was an egoist, I lived for my own comforts, indifferent to what was going on around me. Aristides is aging at his job, exploited, hard up, while his children go hungry. My mother just about considers herself abandoned. At the end of the month I give her a little something toward her support but I offer her no affection at all. She has to content herself with the daily visit of a little bird. As for Julieta, what greater contact do I have with her?

Her children grow up with no fondness for their indifferent uncle. Taking all in all, it's possible that the truth is in those clear eyes that at this moment are looking coldly at me: the notary's office must have played an appreciable part in my inclination toward Sylvia.

"You can expect a lot of trouble, my son. You two are not children any more, you could really have done without this new development. Your wife doesn't have any experience, and good will alone is not sufficient."

Well, the new development came unexpectedly, the thing to do now is accept it. I feel vague fears which, at the age of forty, arouse alarm. Dona Emma, undoubtedly, will have new motives for jealousy, will create new conflicts. Camilo will make his grandson the center of his greatest interest in life. Sylvia will be transformed, maybe she will assume command of the house. As for myself, I cannot predict anything, except that I'll be forced to modify some deep-rooted habits.

The thrush fulfilled its obligation, took off in a low-level flight in the direction of Ferreira's property. Perhaps it has someone else to visit. Not Paulo, certainly, for he would welcome it with a volley of lead. He is no man for sentiment, for mushiness. If he took a notion to eat it, that would be the end of it. I remember with some distaste, as I always do whenever his image crosses my mind, the episode of the theft of the loaf of bread. We couldn't have been any more than thirteen years old and we were still wearing short pants. On one of our daily trips to Humberto's bakery around dinnertime, Paulo had said to me, "One of these days we're going to swipe one of those round loaves."

We used to buy only coarse bread, which was cheaper, and the Italian bread made our mouths water.

I protested weakly.

"Swipe, no. Let's save up enough money to buy one."

His father was beginning life as a small farmer and mine was experiencing hard times. My resistance, nevertheless, had no moral foundation; the fact was that I lacked the courage to collaborate in the adventure. Paulo decided, as usual.

"Save, no. Takes too long. And in case you have any doubts about it, we're going to do it today. We'll make definite plans later."

We separated, he firm in his decision, I with my heart starting to pound. At night my sisters and I were listening to Marcilia's stories when his whistle sounded outside. I went out to meet him shaking in my boots.

"Let's go."

"But, Paulo . . ."

"No 'buts' about it. It's got to be today or never."

Spinelessly, I let myself go along. I was afraid of the consequences, perhaps we would end up in jail.

It was dark, there were distant, pale stars in the sky. We walked along in silence, and when we reached the corner that the bakery was on Paulo looked inside it. Deserted. On the counter, piles of wrapping paper and bits of bread. In the cabinets, the afternoon's production was arranged by variety. The pile of coarse bread had become smaller while that of the Italian bread seemed larger, both in the size of individual loaves and in the total number. Through the door that led into the interior of the house we could hear fragments of conversation. Paulo outlined the plan:

"You stay out here and watch. If anyone comes whistle."

And he entered, clapping his hands.

It wasn't long before Humberto himself came out, in shirt sleeves, a pencil behind his ear.

"My mother sent me to ask if you have any dry biscuits."

"Your mother picked the wrong day, boy. Tomorrow is the day we have them."

Paulo thanked him and started to go out. The baker went back through the open double door, as if interested in resuming an interrupted conversation.

He disappeared, Paulo looked at me, I signaled that he could go ahead. He climbed over the counter, went up to the cabinet that contained the Italian bread, turned the key with a deliberateness that froze me. The silence in the street was terrifying. I had the impression that invisible, accusing eyes were spying on us in the darkness, and that voices might shout out at any moment. Paulo opened the cabinet while keeping his eyes on the door that communicated with the rest of the house. He managed to make an opening big enough for the loaf at the top of the pile to pass through, in a slow and agonizing operation. At this moment footsteps sounded in the vicinity. I whistled feebly, not having the strength to do better. Without closing the cabinet, Paulo leaped over the counter, stuffed the stolen bread under his jacket. Just then, in the center of the light from the lamppost across the street, the form of Mr. Inacio, the schoolteacher, paused for a moment and stared at us. We took off, running toward the chapel of the Charity Hospital. One of the doorways was dark, so we sat down there, against the wall. We caught our breaths, each one reacting to the adventure in his own way. Paulo, composed, proud, and with his knife already open to slice the bread. I, feeling uneasy, cursing myself for my weakness. After all, Humberto was a friend of my father's and also of mine, for every time I went to pay the monthly bill he would give me some corn bread. I had no business betraying him like that. Still, the bread was there, and after all it was Paulo who had actually stolen it. My contribution had been very slight—nothing more than a weak and timid whistle. Having thus appeased my conscience, I accepted the first piece and ate it without any scruples. We consumed all of it, satisfying an old yearning. Stuffed, we talked for some time, having almost completely forgotten our excitement, and then noticed that someone was approaching quietly. Before we could make our getaway, Mr. Inacio appeared in front of us and stared straight into our eyes—first Paulo's, then mine. A fearful censure that I will never forget was contained in the pupils of those eyes that we knew so well and that glared at us in the darkness! He didn't say a word, then went back toward the bakery. Undoubtedly he had guessed our misdeed, had followed us at a distance, had spied on us, and had appeared in front of us with the mute reproval that we could translate perfectly: "ex-students of mine, transformed into thieves!" He was undoubtedly going to inform Humberto, our parents, and maybe even Mauricio the cop. We went home, worried. But the teacher kept our secret, nothing happened to us. I never again had the courage to face him in the light of day. I began to avoid him, turning corners when I saw him at a distance, until years later when, to my relief, he died, having drowned while fishing. Perhaps he has held back his denunciation, waiting for the day of the final judgment, to which he used to refer emphatically in his classes in religion. That loaf of Italian bread will be placed on the scales of justice and will weigh in Paulo's disfavor and mine.

"Your second mother will surely think up a trip of some kind when the baby is about to be born, since she is so annoyed. If I can be of any help at that time ..."

Second mother. All of her feeling toward Dona Emma is concentrated in that caustic expression. Seldom in our conversations has she failed to use it. And now it came up again, as was to be expected; in her expression I can read unconcealable pleasure.

"Nonsense. Dona Emma has a bad temper, but she would be incapable of abandoning her daughter."

Marcilia concurs with a cautious smile, trying not to displease her mistress. She may not be very bright, but her instinct guides her correctly in understanding human beings and their behavior. She knows about the rivalry that exists between the two old ladies to whom my life is linked, but she pretends not to be aware of it, she avoids taking sides. A goodhearted black woman, an uncomplicated and generous soul, of slow speech, with a look that almost exudes tenderness. Her tall, thin form is associated with the most sensitive part of my past. She cultivates strange superstitions—salt spilled at the table, a spoon that falls crosswise on the floor, an umbrella left open inside the house—almost all of them signs of bad luck. She

34

crosses herself when the barn owls fly out of the church towers at dusk and flutter around Ferreira's grove looking for ripe fruit. If a cuckoo alights in the back yard, uttering its sinister lament, she drives it off with shouts.

"Shoo, you wicked thing! Go take your evil message to the devil's vestry."

An expert on home remedies, on superstitious blessings to cure children's illnesses caused by the evil eye. Her life is a limited one and so her problems are small. The biggest one of them consists in saving up in order to buy an ivory crucifix, with which she wants to be buried. Any other kind, iron or wood, the earth will eat away. An ivory one will last as long as her bones and finally blend with them. I've seen her for years with this fixed idea, putting a few coins aside, only to spend them soon afterward. Why haven't I ever decided to help her, respecting her mystical inclination?

Hands clap at the gate. Slippers shuffle along, unhurriedly. They return after a short pause.

"An order for sweets. The vicar's sister has a birthday tomorrow."

Marcilia seems satisfied. Another inch of the crucifix, and thus, of her salvation, is assured.

My mother is impassive. She ruminates thoughts unfavorable to Dona Emma, seeking to give them form. They could be friends, live under the same roof, run the house in harmony. In their rocking chairs they could talk about old times. They could evoke the young people of their day to show their superiority over the generations they had seen born. They could utter complaints about their children, they could grumble that the world has come to ruin. A great lack of respect, older people are not listened to but are pushed off to one side like useless pieces of furniture. Not even Sylvia and I would be spared. They could thus have an interest in common, confessing to each other that children never do what their parents desire. But no. They prefer to live clinging obstinately to an implacable enmity that will last for all time. They constructed plans that we frustrated, and they won't forgive us. Lauro didn't suit Sylvia, nor did Adelaide suit me. Still Lauro made a good marriage, has a healthy and noisy brood of kids. As for my cousin, she hooked a widower and is producing children to mingle with her stepchildren. All perfectly normal, reasonable. Only my mother and Dona Emma do not see this. They reject the elementary evidence, they poison themselves, they feel unhappy. Now Sylvia's child could appear as an instrument of peace. The discord would come to an end, the animosity would be stilled forever. It was too bad that it had taken so long, allowing the problems to take root. But I can't bring myself to make any optimistic forecasts.

"Camilo seems like a child, he is so pleased. He is sure it will be a boy and he wants it to have his name. As for me, I'm not saying a word one way or another. But I think he ought to have your father's name."

My father's name. I don't know if the boy will be born looking like Mariano. And maybe not like Camilo either. This anticipation is pointless. The child is probably no bigger than a grasshopper and the dispute about the name they are going to give him is already beginning.

The racket of children at the gate announces Julieta's arrival. My mother gets up, her face brightening.

"This one, at least, doesn't forget that her mother is still living."

Julieta approaches, surrounded by her offspring. In her arms is Roberto, dressed in white, cranky, smelling of soap.

"A miracle, you here."

I leave her critical greeting unanswered.

The children come forward, receive their grandmother's blessing. I try to hold Elza back, an agile child with blue eyes and with her hair caught in two tresses, but she runs off into the back yard. Eduardo and Mario follow her, shouting. My mother takes Roberto in her arms, covers him with kisses.

"It's worthwhile living just to have a grandson like this."

Undoubtedly the one that will be born to Sylvia will not have the same significance. He will get no affectionate treatment from either grandmother. Only Sylvia's love and Camilo's. From his father, little less than indifference, or aloofness. To tell the truth, I don't know how I will receive the boy.

Julieta and the old lady begin an animated chat.

Marcilia turns up the fire under the pots, spreads a white tablecloth on the table in the front room. The day, in fact, is coming to an end. The church clock strikes. Five-thirty. I get up, embrace my mother, say good-by to Julieta and Marcilia, I pinch Roberto's rosy cheek. The others are lost in the back yard.

"I won't tell you to stay, because it's a poor people's dinner. You are used to fine delicacies, here we don't have any of that."

Marcilia knows I wouldn't stay because of Julieta, even if it were a banquet. She smiles understandingly, asking me not to say anything, to let the irony pass.

I make my exit, slow steps lead me up the steep street. I never come away satisfied from the visits I make to my mother. Most of the time I find her in a bad humor, complaining of being abandoned, of being forgotten by her children. Impossible to find any comfort in her company, or to give her any. Always a barrier between us, something indefinable that prevents us from really getting close to each other.

A flock of guinea fowl crosses the street in Indian file. All day long they had been clucking away in the fields; now they are returning silently, covered with dirt. Vultures fly close to the rooftops, a blackbird takes leave of the afternoon. From the plaza emerges the form of Aristides in the half shadow that is descending. Thin, his clothing rumpled, his gait ungainly. He catches sight of me and stops, waiting for me to approach.

"I couldn't wait for you any longer. I have a meeting at the Brotherhood after dinner."

He hands me the bunch of keys.

"The certificates have to be signed."

He returns with me to the square, says good-by. I'll talk to Camilo. The man needs a raise. The seat of his pants has been clumsily patched up, the collar of his jacket is frayed. My poor compadre.

I leave the square, walk down the street leading to my house. From a distance the entrance resembles a yellow patch. The sassafras raises its flowery foliage over the gate. The work of Dona Emma, who has extraordinary ability in taking care of plants. The white walls extend from corner to corner, protecting the grove that projects over the red roof. How people envy our lives of peace and plenty! They see Camilo happy, jovial, serene, but they don't know how much a night of arguing with Dona Emma takes out of him. They pass by the office, see me through the window, sitting quietly, signing papers. There's a lucky man, they say. Yes, indeed. They don't know that there's something lacking that prevents me from considering myself a happy man. Just a little thing, a bit less distrust on the part of my mother-in-law, greater understanding on the part of my mother. Little things like that are probably missing in all lives. In mine and Sylvia's it might be that child so tardily begotten.

The house seems to be silent. We never know, Camilo and I, what is waiting for us when we come in from the street.

Sylvia is conversing with Honorata in the dining room. She gets up quickly, comes smiling to meet me, kisses me, runs her fingers over my forehead.

"What do these wrinkles mean?"

"Nothing. Weariness perhaps. I've been thinking all day long. And you, how do you feel?"

"I've never felt so good! I worked all day. Come see what I've made."

She leads me to the end of the table where Honorata is sitting. She holds up a tiny little jacket, of blue wool, with the sleeves not yet finished.

"Wonderful," I murmur listlessly.

I leave her in order to go wash my face, to get ready for dinner.

When I get back to the dining room I find Camilo smiling, puffing on a rolled cigarette.

"Man, what a sad-looking face! You don't look like a man who's going to become a father."

"Were you at my mother's house?"

"Of course. She was the first person I told. Didn't she tell you?"

"Yes, she did."

I remember Aristides, my comadre's request, the patched-up trousers.

"Camilo, I believe that Aristides isn't earning enough. He's having a hard time making ends meet. We ought to raise his salary. He has six children, the oldest one will start school soon."

"So give him a raise. Who told you not to? It's up to you."

"How much?"

"I don't know. Five hundred, perhaps. Raise him five hundred. If it's too much, charge it to my grandson."

He inhaled the smoke, letting it out through his hairy nostrils, smiling contentedly. His grandson was entering into our lives, was already giving orders.

Five hundred. Comadre Augusta would be in seventh heaven, full of gratitude. A tremendous improvement in her family's life. They would eat better, the children would have more clothes. Aristides would have a suit made to order at Deodato's tailor shop, he would buy two or three good shirts at Leitão's. Perhaps that's the only thing lacking in my clerk's life. A material problem that I can solve for him.

Evangelina appears with the platters, makes her way to the table. Dona Emma enters, serious, sulky. On her thin face the two lowest wrinkles seem to enclose her mouth in parentheses. I say good evening to her, she pretends not to hear. We sit down. Sylvia, animated, chatters aimlessly away, addressing her father. She evidently wants to avoid a repetition of the scene at lunch. Dona Emma keeps a scowl on her face, sits rigidly in her chair. Camilo bends his head over his soup plate, answers his daughter's questions as best he can. If Dona Emma doesn't say anything, the dinner will come to an orderly end. Time drags, filled with the conversation of Sylvia and Camilo. When we get to the dessert my mother-in-law raises her eyes toward me.

"Where did you go, since you didn't come home for lunch?"

The tone of her voice presages a storm. Sylvia expresses surprise.

"Why, Mother, didn't I tell you that he had gone to Aristides' house?"

Dona Emma forces a scornful laugh.

"To Aristides' house . . . That was a cleverly arranged excuse. He probably passed by there. He has only just found out that his wife is pregnant and already he's begun to neglect his obligations. You men are all alike."

The blood rushes to my face, my first impulse is to answer with a savage retort. Sylvia's glance intervenes pleadingly, the wave dies down. I leave the insult unanswered. The silence now is painful, oppressive. Dona Emma, on occasions like this, seems disfigured. Her eyelids fall, her cheeks grow pale, her nose get sharper. Only her arteries reveal life. She scarcely opens her lips to speak.

"All right, I see that I am not wanted here. I'll leave so you can feel at ease."

She gets up, goes out stiffly to her room. Sylvia does not try to detain her. She knows it would be useless. Such scenes are an old story, she remembers them from her childhood days. Whenever her father was a little bit late, playing cards at the club, Dona Emma would welcome him with insults and threats. She would search through his coat pockets, looking for proof of clandestine love affairs. She would examine his mail, wouldn't permit him to answer the telephone. In the early days they lived in the same house that the notary's office occupied. I remember Camilo, nattily dressed, close-shaven, his mustache trimmed, not a hair out of place. And, animating that picture of correctness, a mischievous smile, a permanent good humor. His disposition was like that, sunny, communicative, but Dona Emma did not understand it or refused to accept it. In order to put a closer watch over her husband, she had a hole made in the wall that faced on the office, through which she could surprise him receiving or sending secret messages. The way Camilo put up with this at first was admirable. He didn't take his wife's nonsense seriously, he would answer her patiently, playfully, and affectionately. Down deep he was perhaps not completely displeased by all that senseless jealousy that made her suffer. It was the proof of his value as a man, and the sentiment of defense was justified. Later he became annoyed and began to bicker. From this to mutual insults was just a step. Sylvia used to dissolve into tears, she would bite her pillow to keep from screaming.

"There's a limit to everything," Camilo once confessed to me. "I was a faithful husband, pure in body and soul, for five years. I stood up against her suspicions as much as I could. Then I couldn't take it any more. I began to cheat, and thus justified her monstrous obsession. Later on I became excited about playing cards, and even though I'm no real gambler, my biggest thrills came from that."

From the time of my marriage, Dona Emma's distrust has been transferred to me. I had not been her chosen one, I had won out over her godson in Sylvia's affections, and she felt it necessary to prove that "the old lady did not make mistakes," that she knew enough about things to realize that Lauro was the one who was best for her daughter. She did not prove it and she must have suffered on this account. Not a single cloud in my life with Sylvia, not a single major conflict, nothing happened to disturb our intimate harmony. Dona Emma tried to wedge her way in, tried hard to influence her against me. Her weapons failed.

"I am asking you once and for all, Mother: stop harping on that matter. I am not the jealous type and I won't permit your suspicions to poison my life as they poisoned Father's," Sylvia had said to her one night, two years after our marriage.

"You're just a little fool. Well, go ahead and let yourself be deceived, if that's what you want. I won't say another word. But as for

men being no good, well they just aren't any good, and nobody is
going to convince me otherwise."

The dialogue had taken place at the table, after dinner. Sylvia had
burst into tears, Camilo had raised his voice, Dona Emma had left
the room, muttering. It is true that her obsession had diminished from
that time on, revealing itself only once in a while in insinuations such
as that recent one. In time I came to admit that our marriage had
been a mistake. Perhaps Lauro would have provided Sylvia with a
more stable condition, without the ups and downs that she was
obliged to endure with me. She would have complied with her mother's wishes, she might have had a flock of kids to bring up. An irreparable mistake was our failing to have set up our own home and
thus resisted Dona Emma's domination. I didn't have the energy, I
weakened, and it was by a real miracle that our lives weren't spoiled
altogether. Today I feel a weariness with everything, a desire to run
away, to disappear completely. I think of Sylvia, however, and I lose
courage. It saddens me to see her so closely tied to me, so dependent,
so helpless. In her expression at times there is evident a fear that the
last straw will be reached and that I will leave her.

"I don't know what would happen to me if I didn't have you," she
has often said to me, in a kind of warning, in our moments of greatest
identity. "I was always very sad, you are the only one who has brought
happiness to me. Mother ruined Father's life. Such a good person,
with that awful temper."

I know that I would not abandon her under any circumstances,
much less now that she is going to have a child of mine. She may be
right in feeling that the presence of a child in the house will manage
to do away with the atmosphere created by Dona Emma.

We get up from the table, go into the front room. Sylvia puts her
arm around my waist.

"What's the matter? Why are you so pensive?"

"It's nothing. Don't worry about me."

Night has fallen completely, the chirp of the crickets vibrates in the garden. A barn owl twittered on the roof, seconds later in the back yard. Marcilia had probably crossed herself.

Sylvia takes up her needlework again. What a strange and powerful determination animates her face! Her gestures are assured, confident, governed by a conscious force. She has developed a new soul—that's the expression that fits her best. She used to be repressed, now it is as if she were under the domination of some higher inspiration.

Camilo smokes, I leaf through a magazine. Dona Emma has shut herself up in her room, is probably gnawing at her nails. Nobody knows what goes on inside of her. Perhaps she gives in to impulses of the moment, launches her attacks, pretending firmness, and is later overwhelmed with remorse. She knows that these outbursts make Sylvia unhappy and it can't be that she doesn't suffer when she has recovered her reason. I don't know what to think.

Sylvia raises her eyes.

"Aren't you two going to the club? Don't stay home on my account."

Camilo grinds his cigarette butt in the ashtray, stands up eagerly.

"You won't mind remaining alone, daughter?"

"Oh, Father. Such nonsense. This way I'll be able to do my needlework without being disturbed. Have a good time."

She smiles at me, urging me to go.

"We'll come back soon," Camilo says, beaming. "If you can, let your mother know."

We go straight to Domingos' pharmacy, as we always do. Paulo is sitting beside Gonçalo and Mateus, on the bench, under the clock. He gets up, comes to meet me.

"I thought about you today," I tell him by way of greeting.

"In what connection? Some forgotten debt?"

His ruddy face breaks out into a smile. I like the guy, even though he is almost cynical and irresponsible. We were raised together, we grew up, we became men together.

"I thought about the loaf of bread we stole from Humberto's bakery."

A moment's reflection and the episode quickly comes back to him.

"I'll bet that was the tastiest loaf of bread you've ever eaten."

He puts his hand on my shoulder.

"You always were a puritan, you never learned how to value the forbidden. The flavor of life lies in the mystery of it all. And in the matter of love affairs, why that goes without saying."

His laugh, revealing his bright, strong teeth, fills me with envy. His cheeks and forehead flush easily, bestowing on him a frank and communicative nature. His deviations as head of a household, his adventures of all sorts, are well known. Gloria raises his children without protesting, resigned to her husband's ways. I'd like to see him in my position. He would surely tame Dona Emma, he would put an end to her nonsense.

"Doesn't that loaf of bread weigh on your conscience, Paulo?"

"Don't be silly! If little things like that were to weigh on people's minds, no conscience would be able to bear up under the strain. Not at all. And besides, without a bit of guilt to feel contrite about, you can't get into heaven, my boy."

Again that smile of his, again this envy of mine. Paulo possesses a feeling of freedom that he has had since childhood and that conventions have failed to thwart. Nothing prevents him from realizing his desires, he pays no attention to what people may say about him. He plays cards all night long with one of Camilo's partners. He frequently travels to the capital, he is always in motion.

"How are the children?"

"Fine. Gloria is a saint. She keeps those kids in tiptop shape, overflowing with health."

His expression now is serious, grateful. He holds his mate in high esteem, he knows what that means in a man's life. Camilo cannot say the same. He had ended up with a piece of neck meat, whose toughness only God knows. Dona Emma's temper never had adapted itself to his, but had rather become exacerbated by his expansive nature.

Sylvia would have been an ideal wife for me, providing we had lived alone, on our own. Impossible to desire more than what she has given me. The trouble is that what I receive on one side is taken away from me on the other.

I do not tell Paulo that I also am going to have a child. He would come out with a joke, an off-color remark of some kind. I let him move on to join Odilon, who is already on the way to the club.

The conversation on the bench is calm, with no outbursts. Camilo rolls a cigarette, Gonçalo follows the operation with those bloodshot eyes of his. A good man, quiet, useful. He is the tax collector for the Treasury Department, a body feared by the country people. He represents the law, he has an insidious, mighty power, whose influence nobody escapes. Gonçalo became a widower early, with no children, and—who knows—with no further harm. His wife was covered with freckles and was ill-tempered because of the cyst that brought about her death. I remember Dona Alzira, tall, thin, with moles on her face, on her neck, on the fleshy part of her arms. With nothing to do, she spent her time paying visits night and day. In the evening she used to go out for a stroll with her husband after dinner. Gonçalo with red eyes and no eyelashes, Dona Alzira scrawny and wearing too much make-up. People made fun of them.

"There go two of a kind—like a pair of boots."

One of the boots had departed, run down at the heels no doubt; the other one still moves about in God's world. Gonçalo has perhaps become more taciturn, his eyes even redder. He has never given any thought to a new entanglement, or maybe he hasn't met anyone who wanted him. He lives alone with his maid, Ubaldina, who probably takes care of all of his needs.

Domingos comes out of his laboratory with a bottle of liquid that he shakes until it foams. He goes over to the counter, wraps up the bottle, hands it to the wide-eyed little Negro boy.

"It's written on the bottle how to take it."

The boy runs out, Domingos makes an entry in his daybook, beside the cash register. He comes up, leans over the railing.

"Well, Mateus, how's the harvest coming along?"

The planter, caught by surprise, takes his time to answer. He draws in on his rolled cigarette, blows out the smoke, strikes a mental balance of his coffee trees.

"I'm counting on 1,500 arrobas."

A lie. He will gather much more, you can read this clearly in his eyes. He's afraid of the presence of Gonçalo and is hiding the truth. The law is there beside him on the bench, a sickly law, with inflamed eyes and without eyelashes, but with open and alert ears. Better to disparage his crop.

"Two thousand arrobas would be more like it," says the pharmacist, provoking him.

Mateus does not get ruffled, remains impassive, flicks the lighted tip of his cigarette with his thumbnail.

"Your pharmacy is a better business. It's sheltered from the weather. Hail damaged the crops this year."

Another cock-and-bull story. There hasn't been any hail, the rains have been mild. The man wants to bypass the law, deliberately avoids looking into those red eyes. Mateus lies with assurance, but he is contradicted by the expression on his sun-tanned face. A shameless guy, he fritters away his money on common prostitutes, squanders his profits on wild sprees. His family is neglected, his young daughters wear wooden sandals, his sons do not attend school. Dona Palmira has a long-suffering expression that arouses pity. She hoed the weeds, raised the children, made her husband a landowner. After they came to live in the city, her man started to go astray. That is what a passion for skirts leads to. Mateus is slowly being bled, before long he'll be bankrupt. He has two daughters who are terrible flirts. Not even the delivery boys escape. The younger one, a little brunette, with buck-teeth, has already been in my office, leaning over my desk, revealing the furrow between her breasts. I would have applied a kiss there, if Aristides had not been present. The father's example is obvious to everybody. No one can blame these country girls if they go wrong. Dona Palmira deserved a better fate. She could even have had a life of luxury, married her daughters off to professional men, gone to summer resorts. She no longer has any hopes. She knows that the prostitutes over at Sarandi's have taken her husband away from her and will finish him off.

Mateus gets up, touches his wide-brimmed hat as a general salutation. His boots squeak alternately as they move leisurely across the tile floor. His hour of shamelessness must be at hand.

"A fine fellow!" exclaims Domingos, shaking his head. "A hard worker. But he's ruined. He'll end up working for hire again. He has debts everywhere, he's not trustworthy."

"Once a wolf, always a wolf," declares Camilo, thoughtfully, a faraway look in his eyes.

Gonçalo nods his head in agreement, his expression grave, unsympathetic. He is probably less interested, however, in the morality of the case than in the financial decline of a taxpayer who has taken the wrong turn. He has made note of the information in order to assess his taxes for the coming fiscal year.

The church clock strikes eight-thirty. Domingos gets ready to close up, Gonçalo says good-by. A pleasant calmness over the city. A profound and quiet night. The distant stars fail to overcome the dense darkness. In the square, slow-moving groups saunter in different directions along the sandy, tree-lined paths. How often I used to stroll there myself, when I was in my teens, courting Machado's daughters! When we passed each other our glances would cling together with some apprehension, but full of meaning, in a delightful sounding out of each other's intentions. Sometimes it was Amanda, sometimes Jurema, or even Guaraciaba, the oldest, with her big black eyes and long eyelashes. Those days are long past, the girls are all married now, they have given Machado many grandchildren. Sylvia never walked in the park, Dona Emma didn't want her mixing with the common people. She cultivated her daughter's talents at home in order to bestow them on her godson. I would see her sometimes at dances with Lauro, very light-skinned, her hair gathered in a top-knot, a touch of crimson in her cheeks. The whiteness of her skin seduced me, while the hairdo that distinguished her from the other girls of her age I found fascinating. The expression on her face had a mysterious something that intrigued me. She always seemed to be far away, dreaming. I admired her from a distance, with Dona Emma's harsh glance always between us. We exchanged few words until my entrance into the notary's office. My father had spoken to Camilo, he wanted to see me employed before passing away and leaving our family in want. He suspected that he had the symptoms of angina and he was right: only a few years later he was struck down, toppling over on a garden bench. I fitted in well at the office, I began to see Sylvia every day. She would greet me, take an interest in my work, examine my penmanship attentively. She grew up, her sweet features became accentuated, her knot of hair grew thicker, arranged sometimes at the back of her neck, sometimes on the top of her head. Time passed, our relationship became closer. Camilo made discreet mention of a courtship, and his words encouraged me. When Lauro stepped out of the picture some time later by marrying Diana, I rubbed my hands together in relief, I turned somersaults in my room, I contemplated the night as if I owned it. My mother had noted the change silently—my restlessness at home, my indifference to things I had formerly been fond of, the way I avoided my sisters, my hurry to get out of the house. She sensed that some dominating intimate force was pulling me away from there, and that it could only be love. When they told her that Lauro was about to marry some other girl, she gave me up for lost. Sooner or later our lives would separate for-ever. Adelaide was already attached to the widower, the old plan of the family had miscarried. Sylvia and I had become freed, and our contact at the office could only lead to marriage. It did lead to it, but

48

years later, when both of us were already mature and enervated from the wait. I remember even today, in the midst of the lively and curious crowd, three glum faces at the church: my mother, Dona Emma, and Father Bento, who was saddened by my refusal to go to confession. But Sylvia's happiness was enough for me, along with Camilo's imperturbable confidence.

We traveled for a month. Sylvia's initiation into love was passionate. Her white body, that Dona Emma had kept pure for Lauro, had vibrations that left it breathless. We had a perfect period of apprenticeship, of erotic discoveries that moved us to our very souls. When we returned she easily obtained from me a promise of fidelity, in the name of our children. After the first year, everything between us became transformed into habit, even accustoming ourselves to Dona Emma's jealousy.

Camilo had said to me:

"I was really getting worried about you two. Emma has a terrible temper and I didn't think she would be able to contain herself. But everything has turned out well in these first months. As a father, I can see that Sylvia is a happy woman."

The peaceful days have alternated with violent ones, and that is the way we have lived. This seesawing is unsatisfactory to everyone, except Sylvia. For her everything will be perfect now that she is expecting a child. She counted on a lot of them, and at first even admitted the possibility of twins—to save time, she used to say, indifferent to the admonitions of Honorata, "Miss Sylvia, don't eat pieces of fruit that are stuck together. Remember that having the first child is no joke."

But the sterile years succeeded each other until now, when, by dint of prayer, she is going to know the greatest happiness of her experience as a woman. Dr. Leandro will tell me the truth.

Near the club, I see that Domingos and my father-in-law have gone on ahead. I slow down some more, afraid to go in. What will the doctor say? Down deep the hope persists that there may be a mistake. A woman's nature is a complicated set of gears that can easily go out of order. Perhaps Sylvia, suggestible as she is, has created an illusory set of symptoms, deceiving Dr. Leandro. The laboratory tests were positive. But there is always the possibility of a mix-up in material, in test tubes, in labels. I see no room for doubt, however, in Sylvia's statement. "Finally I'm going to be the mother of a child of yours." It's possible that the seeds, after so many years of rehearsal, had mated and had now set a new life in motion.

The marble steps lead me to the lighted rooms. The clicking of the billiard balls, the noise of chips, the hum of voices, a livelier sense of freedom. The bluish, smoke-filled air, so well known to me, does not arouse my interest. Here is where the important men of the city come in search of excitement. Camilo has joined the table of Dr. Orozimbo, the prosecuting attorney, whose excessively dark skin and kinky hair vex him like an itch. He is respected, treats everybody with patient attention, expresses himself gently and eloquently in court. Paulo is at his side, in shirt sleeves, his chips stacked beside his ashtray. Entrenched at the card table, as usual, are Domingos, Josias the superintendent of education, and Colonel Medeiros, who is the mayor and a large landowner. The Colonel is in his declining years and in order to disguise his age dyes his enormous mustache and his closely clipped hair. But his wrinkles betray him and add to his weary expression. A man of little learning and of dubious intentions, he has occupied his perch on the council and as the executive through the support of his rural electorate. In the old days he used to bring his financial reports to me so that I could check their language. "Report of the mayor's *ministration*." When I first explained to him that that was not the correct word I spoke about semantics, I appealed to the dictionary, I displayed erudition, trying to diminish his authority. Colonel Medeiros did not even feel humiliated, nor did he correct the word in his rough drafts of succeeding years. His administration was always his "ministration" to him. And now there he is staring at his cards, fascinated like a bird caught in a viper's mouth.

Next to him, Gabriel of the phone company, excited, is cashing in his profits and depositing them in the inside pocket of his coat. His daughter Sara is the operator, her sugary voice trickles through the wires. Dona Emma bears an old grudge against her. Frequently she calls out to Evangelina and orders her:

"Bring me Sylvia's sprayer. This telephone has a bad odor that I can't stand. It must be the breath of that busybody Sara."

Intent upon their card game are Major Dario, a capitalist, an idle man whose greatest claim to fame is that he has traveled to Europe, and Teodorico the public school principal, who habitually annoys me with his petty concern over matters of language. Acting like a know-it-all, he insists on the proper use of pronouns and the accurate conjugation of verbs, and he never fails to interrupt a person who is talking, to correct him as if he were in a class. A poor pedant who is aging, entangled in the complexities of grammar. In the lounge, a larger group, leafing through magazines and newspapers, smoking, conversing lazily.

Indecisive steps lead me to the billiard room. A sudden feeling of fright stops me short when I catch sight of Dr. Leandro, leaning over the table, ready to take his shot. The doctor is an ace at this game. He scores in the hundreds, few opponents can compete with him. He's playing Fonseca, the dentist. He must have given him a handicap, for they are of unequal ability. The onlookers follow the motions of the doctor, who chalks the tip of his cue before each shot. He is so absorbed that he is unaware of what is going on around him. I sit down in an empty chair next to Matos. Not a particularly pleasant neighbor. The man earns his living by making coffins. His melancholy eyes inspire uneasiness. Quiet, always lost in mysterious thoughts. He is probably wondering when he will have to service Dr. Leandro. He measures his height, his square shoulders, the size of his belly. It will take a lot of wood. Everything first class, cedar lid, silk lining. Gregorio's wife must have gone in a third-class coffin. Wormy pine, rusty nails, no lining. Dr. Leandro will have a big funeral. Father Bento will be at the head of it with his paraphernalia sending out smoke in all directions. Dr. Orozimbo will make a speech, perhaps I may have to write something for Colonel Medeiros to read. Matos makes his calculations, measuring his victim. Dr. Leandro continues to make his caroms, unaware that the undertaker is taking his measurements. His enormous hands hold the cue lightly, strike unerringly. The balls glide along the green quadrilateral, click, settle down in places previously designated. Hairy fingers, on one of which gleams his doctor's ring. Science has conferred upon them the right to enter into hidden places, to examine the very seat of life. Revolting. Sylvia underwent that humiliation. Parts known only to me were seen, invaded, palpated. I feel that I have something in common with Dr. Leandro. I am no longer an exclusive possessor, the rights have been divided. Sylvia showed him her plump legs, her mount covered with fine, light hair. Impossible for the doctor not to have enjoyed himself, prolonging his examination in search of signs of conception. Dona Emma is probably right; they're all no good. What man wouldn't do the same? His long fingers handle the cue, his calculated shot just misses. Fonseca takes his turn. Dr. Leandro comes toward me, straightening up. A muscular, healthy body. Female patients who do not watch out fall into his clutches. A powerful, fearful fellow. He places his right hand on my shoulder. The criminal one, no doubt. He probably didn't even use a glove.

"Everything is fine. If you are all careful there won't be any complications."

A heavy, annoying hand. He withdraws it, goes over to the frame to mark his score. There was no need for that examination. An analysis would have been sufficient.

"How about her age? Doesn't that matter?"

Dr. Leandro comes back, examining his opponent's shot.

"Nonsense. Your wife is still very young. And she has an admirable womb."

I wince. Why talk out loud about such things? Matos moves about on his chair, turns his questioning eyes toward me. He wants the confirmation that he can count on a future client. Sylvia's child is only about the size of a closed fist and that bandit already wants to bury him. He sits up, looks at Fonseca. The billiard table probably represents a catafalque on which he will gradually place all of us. Not even the child has escaped. Admirable womb. I should have answered Dr. Leandro with a good, strong four-letter word. It's admirable all right, but it has an owner. I'd like to expose the scoundrel, chop his hands off, restrict his rights. Sylvia should not have gone alone to see him. An awful risk. An authoritarian class, they give out orders right and left: take your clothes off, lie down over here, tell me where it hurts. Nothing is safe from examination. The hand of science is inquisitive, it does not lose a trick. Everything is an excuse for palpations.

"Have your wife follow my prescriptions to the letter. And once a month bring her to my office."

Dammit, how far will all this go? The man proposes and disposes. Do this, do that. The husband doesn't count, doesn't have to be heard. Sylvia will go, but not alone. Not so fast with that partnership. It's evident that I will lose out in a comparison. Dr. Leandro is much taller, heavier, has a good color. He cuts a fine figure with women. If I had inherited my father's stature, I could match the doctor. My father had a superb build, clothes fitted him to perfection. I didn't grow as much, I remained of average height. Women have simple imaginations, they get impressed by a person's appearance. Sylvia, as a result of seeing Dr. Leandro, will end up by making comparisons, in which I will come out second best. She definitely will not go back to his office alone.

"If you are all careful there won't be any complications." What significance should I attribute to that statement? Some hidden meaning. The child is already interfering in my habits, limiting my freedom. In his name I am being separated from Sylvia.

Paiva gets up from his chair, invites me to a game of chess. I accept, vexed. If I refuse, he will think that I'm afraid to lose. Facing the chessboard, at the back of the room, I realize that I have lost interest in the mute figures with which I have maintained daily contact for years. I have received more pleasure from them than from my association with human beings. They do not talk, they do not envy each other, they do not commit evil deeds. Paiva is one of the most faithful of opponents. He seldom beats me, but insists that he is the stronger and more imaginative player.

"You win by wearing me out. You take too long thinking."

That's the way he denies my superiority. I've beaten the pants off him, but he refuses to be convinced. His ash-gray eyes seem to cringe in their orbits, they avoid looking anyone straight in the face. He especially resents my being in a better social position. Paiva will never be anything more than just a manager at the Power & Light Company, he has a limited future. He will never be able to help his children amount to anything. Fernando and Alipio won't be anything more than lowly workers, his daughters will marry store clerks. If Sylvia gives me a girl, when she is a young lady she will be able to marry into any of the best families. I was not born with a title, I am of humble origin, but the office I occupy confers equalitarian powers upon me. None of Dr. Leandro's daughters will be superior to the daughter of a certified notary public. Neither will Colonel Medeiros', or Major Dario's, who have already traveled first class to Europe. Sylvia's daughter will be wooed by law-abiding young men with college degrees who have careers ahead of them. Dona Emma will try to impose one of Lauro's sons as a husband for her granddaughter. A tyrannical, inconsiderate person. She thinks she's the only one with experience, the only one who knows what's right and what's wrong. Camilo's life could have been different. He would not have aged with that bitterness that grieves Sylvia so much. His wife's jealousy has taken all the joy out of his life. Only cards provide him with pleasure. There he is leaning over the table, his fingers lined up almost sensually. Maybe his grandson will arouse him, will rekindle his joys and enthusiasms. An admirable womb. Dr. Leandro is a man like any other, capable of anything. I don't believe in fairy stories, in old wives' tales. Father Bento's heaven is full of good intentions. The doctor must have moved his hand about voluptuously, unhurriedly. Scoundrel. My indignation leads me to check my opponent in a rash move. There goes one of my knights. Paiva's face breaks into a smile. The manager exults when he beats the notary. His hand trembles as it grasps that hapless piece. His lowered eyes avoid mine, concealing the pleasure that suddenly made them light up. Is Paiva really my friend? In an hour of need, would he stand at my side? Would that same arm that reached out to take my knight be extended in a gesture of support? I don't think so. Paiva would enjoy anything unfortunate that happened to me, but would disguise that sentiment with words. I have lent him small sums which he has repaid by sending one of his sons without any message. He probably thinks it's my obligation to help him out of a tight squeeze. The boyhood pal who rose higher would be duty bound to look after the one who will never be anything more than a needy manager with five kids. It would be a different story with Paulo. I could count on him. He may not be leading an exemplary life, he may be indiscreet, but he is good-natured and tender-hearted. Dona Emma condemns our friendship, she won't forgive Camilo for making him his card partner. My father-in-law also likes him, although he does not approve of or recommend his conduct. The trouble with Paulo is that he does not know how to dissemble; he does anything he feels like doing. There are few persons who do not condemn his behavior, but there isn't anybody who does not admire him and enjoy being in his company. Not even Matos, whose wife has an awful reputation which even involves Paulo's name. Dona Emma declares that she is a loose woman, that she suffers from a uterine furor. The coffinmaker maintains silence, does not get into arguments, does not take matters into his own hands. He waits only for the time when he can assemble his wife's coffin and ship her off to the devil. They haven't had any children, fortunately. I wonder what they'll say about my child. He appears ten years late, and they may be suspicious. They can set their minds at ease, because he'll have his father's features mixed in with those of his mother. Some resemblance to Camilo, perhaps a slight reminder of Dona Emma. Who knows whether some trace of my mother will be reproduced—the classic lines of her nose, for example. Good proof of identification. No one will be able to say that the child is not the son of the notary public.

Camilo approaches.

"It's time to go."

Ten-thirty. Paiva is getting impatient. He has the game won and does not want to lose the pleasure of checkmating.

"Shall we put it off until tomorrow?"

"It's still early," he protests. "There are only a few moves left."

I surrender my king and get up to leave. The manager arranges the chessmen in the box, bursting with pleasure. He is not aware that he owes his victory to Sylvia's child.

Camilo walks along pensively, his hands in his pockets. The night air is light, the mist moistens the stones on the walk.

"Leandro is sure that everything will be all right. It's a problem when you have an only child. You never have any peace of mind, the fear that something will happen to it tortures you throughout your life. You and Sylvia will experience that feeling if you end up with only this one."

The old man is worried about Sylvia. He wants the grandchild, but he does not want to lose his daughter. The trouble is that they think of Sylvia as having a delicate constitution, as if she were a crystal that the slightest jolt would shatter. She is a well-built woman, as hardy as a woodpecker. And she has an admirable womb. Dr. Leandro has gone over her, inch by inch, with extreme care. The whiteness of her skin is the thing that deceives, giving the impression of fragility. The child will have plenty of room to expand in, and to be expelled from, without any complications.

"Didn't he say anything to you?"

"He told me the same thing. He thinks everything will be fine if we are all careful. You shouldn't worry so much."

I can't see his eyes under his hat brim. They are turned downward, submerged in thought. Somber, no doubt, having forgotten the cards that excited them a little while ago. The emotions aroused at the club are transitory, they do not last the night. It would be better not to know such emotions and to go home certain of finding two arms ready to embrace, a sleepy voice calling out in the darkness of the bedroom: "Is that you, dear?" Camilo never knows what is waiting for him. Tonight, especially. Dona Emma must be awake, chewing away at her nails, seething with condemnatory thoughts.

"Life could be so wonderful, if only people didn't have tempers and tried to understand each other calmly. Instead, it's just a tiresome mess that has no solution. If it had been up to me, we would have had half a dozen children. That is what I always wanted. Emma refused. She said that it's easy for us men to make our plans, but that women get the worst of it. Sylvia's birth left her terrified. I never thought that anyone could scream to high heaven like that. She defended herself like a lioness and we ended up with an only daughter. You two won't escape that fate. Not because of you, or Sylvia, but because of *her*, for after all she is the one who orders us about. She will not permit another one after this one."

I had never heard him express his feelings so freely before. There is a bitterness in his voice, which disappears into the silence of the night. This white-haired man has his sorrows, opens his heart in confession. The same sorrow that Gregorio had, the same tone of revolt. Down deep their expressions are the same and can be summed up in the same words: miserable life!

The black mass of the grove looms over the walls. The house is silent, the lights turned out. Perhaps only in the hearts of its dwellers is there no peace.

I grip Camilo's arm, we take the last steps together. Far off, a shooting star streaks across the horizon. Marcilia guarantees that prayers made at such a time will be answered. My thoughts embrace the image of Sylvia, who must be safeguarded from any peril. My supplication at this moment is for her. Camilo is right. All of our concern must be for his daughter; the child is still merely a stranger who is about to come into our lives.

Chapter Two

Six months have passed by, having dripped day by day from the calendar that Aristides hung on the wall. Dr. Leandro called his shot correctly: the admirable womb has grown bigger, the anticipated unfolding has become evident. Sylvia is heavy, she has lost her vivacity, slowed down. But she feels tranquil, confident that the arrival of the child will complete our lives. She does not get upset when I refuse to accompany her on her walks after dinner, pretending weariness or indisposition.

"I know that you are ashamed to go walking with me, dear. Never mind. It must be quite disagreeable to accompany a woman in this condition. I'll go with Evangelina."

A natural attitude, certainly. It's true that I am ashamed to go out with her, big-bellied as she is. Slow steps, a short coat scarcely disguising her shape. Childlike and spiritualized. Our acquaintances stop, stare at the sinful proof, smile, utter banalities. Horrible. Leaning on my arms, Sylvia offers information—it's already stirring its little foot, it's turning somersaults, it's pressing with its tiny hand like this against her side—while I am overcome by a feeling of awkward embarrassment that makes my collar suddenly feel tight. She confesses that she feels astonished, that God may delay but does not fail, and that judging from the pointed shape of her belly it must really be a boy. We went out together at first, now it is Evangelina who accompanies her. The curiosity of our people has no limit, and since my boyhood I have tried to avoid it. A new suit that one wears on the street is the object of comments, of jeers. I remember when Juvenal was a justice of the peace. He was hard of hearing, which hampered him in his work and made him nervous. One day he went to São Paulo and came back with a hearing aid. He practiced using it at home before appearing in public with such a novelty. On the first Sunday he went to mass, people stopped him on the street as if he had turned into some strange new creature. They asked him questions about the way the contraption worked, they examined the amplifier that was inserted in his ear, the wire that descended to his chest. They opened his jacket, tried to unbutton his vest. They wanted to know if the wire went down to his stomach, they asked him to let them try it on. If the man had not protested, they would have ended up stripping him on the street. They never gave him any rest, Juvenal was finally obliged to give up the hearing aid and his job. Sylvia receives almost the same rude treatment, the only thing they don't ask her is when the baby was conceived. It's for this reason that I have given Evangelina the responsibility of accompanying her on her daily walks. I stay later in my office, I find extra work to do in order to avoid that humiliating obligation. Not infrequently the evening finds me wrapped up in speculations that bring me more uneasiness than confidence in the future. I don't know whether Sylvia's prediction will be accurate. Perhaps the child will be a negative element, perhaps he will aggravate the discord in the family.

Dona Emma has softened her initial attitude. She alternates between concern on Sylvia's better days and irritation during her periods of physical depression.

"Just wait, daughter. I have gone through it and I know it's no joke. You two wouldn't listen to me, the experience of the old lady wasn't worth anything."

But she has been sewing for her grandchild, the layette of tiny clothes keeps getting bigger in the wicker basket. She, Sylvia, and Honorata spend hours working with their needles, applying rickrack, embroidering fancy needlework on cambric and linen. This picture raises my spirits, makes Camilo feel excited, like a new man.

"This could have well happened earlier. We would have enjoyed life more," he exclaims, rubbing his hands together.

Knowledge of the past, however, cannot be forgotten, and doubt does not take long to impose itself. His enthusiasm wilts as the variations of light and darkness succeed each other.

The certainty that prevails is that it will really be a boy. The contrary hypothesis has been set aside even by Dr. Leandro.

"Judging from the size, it must be a boy. But, for God's sake, don't even think of having him study medicine. It's not a profession to recommend. One has to participate too much in human sorrows."

I was astonished when Dr. Leandro said that to us. That big, sanguine man has a heart that suffers with his patients, that shares their troubles. The fellow is sentimental, his nature goes out to others, he is not restricted to the emotions of the billiard table. I have already resolved to put Sylvia in his hands at the crucial hour. My mother-in-law keeps talking about Graziela, the daughter of the midwife who helped when Sylvia was born. Not in an ostentatious way, but by insinuations, trying once more to impose her knowledge on us. Sylvia pretends not to hear, for we have agreed that Dr. Leandro is the one who will take care of her. "Don't even think of having him study medicine." Nobody recommends his own profession, nobody wants it for his own children. I don't know what I will do with the boy. Something better than a notary public, certainly. Prosecuting attorney sounds impressive, the title has its importance. But Dr. Orozimbo has also disparaged his occupation, one night at the club when he was half-drunk.

"This business of prosecuting is an inhuman job. How can anyone prosecute, when we're all poor devils?"

Perhaps I'm concocting problems for my son. Sufficient is the one that I am transmitting to him—that of living. He'll take care of the rest. It may be that he will be burdened with a bad temper as an inheritance from his grandmothers. If Sylvia's traits predominate in his make-up, he will be a fortunate fellow. Especially her ability to understand and remain silent. The religious feeling that dominates her will also be useful to the stranger. More moderate than that of Aristides, although equally firm and constant. He will not have to sport those cloaks that members of the brotherhoods wear in religious processions, nor will he become overly fond of ribbons and regalia like my clerk. There he is, leaning over his desk, a string with medals hanging down from his neck, his pockets stuffed with prints and stories of Biblical episodes. A good lamb, humble, peaceful, without any arrogance. The greatest pride he permits himself is in connection with his artistic penmanship that everybody can identify at a distance.

"That's Aristides' work. The man has beautiful handwriting. If he had studied, he would have been an artist."

Aristides is one of the minor glories of the city, his talent is perpetuated on school diplomas. He is aware of it and does not conceal his vanity. Father Bento has probably already told him that it is a venial sin that won't hurt him at all. In this way my devout compadre keeps getting along. The raise solved his financial problems, already allows him to get his hair cut more frequently. His children seem different, they are nicely dressed, clean. Comadre Augusta has been trying to overwhelm me with favors by sewing for my child. My mother has also been sending us articles that she has sewed and which Dona Emma examines closely, looking for defects. She has paid us only one visit, she spoke very little, avoided as much as possible the gaze of my "second mother." Nothing about the house escaped her. She went into the kitchen with Sylvia and me, ran her fingers along the bottoms of the pans, felt the dishcloths. She wanted proof against Honorata, evidence of mismanagement in the pantry. She went out into the back yard, examined the garbage pail.

"Such waste! All that rice thrown away! If you live in such abundance, why don't you keep a pig that you can fatten up?"

Sylvia does not become offended, she limits herself to a smile. She treats her mother-in-law with respect, without getting angry at her for meddling into things that are not her business. In the presence of Dona Emma my mother keeps silent, repressing criticism and censure. Not out of fear, but because she knows that the other one would come out with some rude expression. Thus she avoids giving shape to the veiled conflict. She is probably counting on my mother-in-law's death in order to take her place. What do I know about her most sacred thoughts? She would certainly be glad to move in order to be near her son, to assume the direction of my domestic affairs.

"It's a mistake to leave a house in the hands of servants. They are capable of anything," she has often told me during the course of these ten years.

"Honorata is not a servant," I answer her. "She considers Sylvia almost her own daughter. Besides, she isn't the one who manages the house."

Her gray eyes remain expressionless. Beyond them, there are indecipherable sentiments that stir about without coming to the surface. Only in an incomplete way do they reveal themselves in harsh words, after some silence.

"A married son no longer belongs to his mother. He won't take advice, everything she says is considered to be nagging."

It's not like that with Julieta. She listens to her in the smallest things. She runs to her for help when the children are ill, when she has any personal troubles, when she has any disagreement with Armando. Armando is an easygoing man, he puts up with his mother-in-law's bursts of ill humor without protesting. Especially since he considers that up to a certain point she is justified. He travels a lot on business and permits himself an occasional adventure. But, in general, Julieta can't complain about her husband. He is fond of her, he is affectionate toward their children and is an exemplary provider for his family.

Claudia, however, comes to me with her problems. Less fortunate in her marriage, she has had to go through a great deal. Osvaldo is weak-willed, he settled into an office job in the priest's school and won't go any further. Their five children overburden their budget. They cannot make ends meet. Claudia takes in sewing and in this way manages to increase their income. In the months when she receives few orders, she comes to me and gets the money she needs. "I'll owe it to you, dear brother." Her affectionate treatment of me is my payment in full, her grateful embrace, her tender kiss on my cheek. She is a brunette, with dark eyes, strong teeth, tremulous and nervous hands. She really deserved a better lot, a companion worthy of her lively, creative nature. She is always ahead of her husband in taking any initiative. She is the one who gets their children registered in school, the one who corrects their bad habits. Why destiny linked two such diverse creatures I have never been able to understand. Now she has to accept her fate, no matter what it may cost. Claudia was ambitious for great achievements but got tied down in an insipid marriage. She lives for her children, nothing matters to her except her little flock of youngsters. I am fonder of her children than I am of Julieta's. I feel closer to them, they are the ones I remember when I come back from my rare trips to the capital, my suitcase full of packages.

"Julieta is hurt because you treat Claudia's children better," my mother keeps telling me. "It's not right. They are all your nieces and nephews and have an equal right to your affection."

Undoubtedly I have in my veins the same blood that Julieta and Claudia have. But they are quite different in spirit. Even as a child Julieta was just as she is now, sly, envious, meddlesome. Our quarrels have not been repeated as adults, but the hostility that always existed between us still lasts. If I do not dislike her children, it is true that I prefer Claudia's. No calculation in that sentiment, no attitude. I obey a natural, instinctive impulse. I am for the one who is my friend, the one whose soul merges with mine.

Aristides interrupts my train of thought and my scribbling.

"You ought to sign these papers. They'll be coming for them before long."

I write my signature which makes the documents official, as the clerk applies the blotter to them.

"So, is Dona Sylvia feeling well?"

"She's coming along. The whole business is no joke."

"That's what I say, compadre. We get involved in our children from the first moment. I don't know who suffers more—we or our wives."

He goes back to his desk, starts a new task. Maybe he's right. Our preoccupations begin from the first moment and never disappear, they only become transformed. Sylvia shows no signs of suffering. Her appearance changes from month to month, she gets bigger, her bloated feet sustain her with difficulty. But her expression of beatitude becomes accentuated to a like degree. She protects her child with a strength that I did not believe her capable of. This docile, submissive woman has gained new energy now, knows how to manage herself. She has not permitted me any contact since the morning of her confession.

"We must be careful, dear. Didn't Dr. Leandro warn us? We can't risk losing our child. Let's make this sacrifice."

She wraps her arms around my neck, kisses me, presses her face against mine. I let myself be subdued, my desire disappears. I realize now that it would be imprudent, and also that her swollen body, with its red blotches, no longer attracts me. Consequently, I have been more assiduous in visiting Lia's house. A quick trip to the club until the night gets dark, then off I go to enjoy the caresses of the woman from the North. From the first, the slut began to tease me, screaming and laughing in the dark.

"Lord, what a fast little man! A bantam rooster couldn't be any speedier!"

Dona Emma is annoyed at our arriving home at different hours, Camilo earlier. She sulks, she scowls, her lips tighten. The only thing she does not do is send a spy to follow my tracks. We don't go out every night, but when we do go out we invariably go to the club. Always the same scene there. Dr. Leandro making his calculations, Matos sitting under the scoreboard, Paiva looking for a partner for chess, the games of cards. Camilo no longer has the same enthusiasm, he plays his cards more abruptly and absent-mindedly. Most of his thoughts are on his grandson, who will not be long in arriving. I have taken Paiva on only a few times more, and each time without any success. Sometimes Sylvia's son, sometimes Lia, upsets my thinking, getting between me and the figures on the chessboard. From Camilo, no censure, not even in his expression. The man knows what it's all about, these calls of nature. It's not any betrayal of Sylvia, not any profanation of our love. I think of her when I am with Lia and it's the same as having her in my arms. What harm is there in that? Father Bento would recall the duties of chastity. As if life could be reduced to words or formulas! There are laws that one cannot escape, and Lia is one of them. Sylvia also knows this and does not condemn me.

"Have you been having a good time? Please be careful, dear."

Without grief, without jealousy. She wants a husband in good humor, with his instincts appeased, his accounts up to date. If she were different we'd have scenes of weeping and lamentation. Julieta is like that. She considers herself wretched because Armando, even during normal times, occasionally leaps over the fence. My poor sister! Foolish, cranky, with no understanding of life. I remember that when she was a young girl and our father was alive and well she used to go to Cinira's house to buy little meat pies for dinner. The mulatto woman lived near the cemetery with her children of different fathers. She was a first-rate cook, her clay oven produced delicious things.Their aroma could be smelled from far away and would arouse excitement among the housewives.

"Cinira is preparing some tidbits."

My mother could not resist and would send Julieta to her house.

"That woman is a lost soul but she knows how to cook. Don't start her gossiping, daughter; come back right away."

Julieta would return with her face fiery red.

"You're right, mother. Dona Cinira only wants to talk about nasty things. She said that she can't get along without a man, that that's the best of life."

My mother would explode.

"Don't call her 'Dona.' That shameless hussy doesn't deserve to be called that. Well, you won't set foot there again."

But she did. A few days later the aroma from her oven would reach our house and Julieta would go there to make some more purchases. Claudia used to help in our kitchen and didn't like to go into the street on errands. The woman's licentious conversation was always the same, my sister's protests were repeated. But the meat pies would disappear from the platter as my father praised the talents of the woman who was so expert in preparing tidbits. In time Cinira got fat, resembled a walking oven. She passed her occupation on to her oldest daughter, Deolinda, a mulatto girl with green eyes whom she wanted to see properly married and whom she therefore kept under close watch. But the girl became the object of such a siege that Cinira decided to move far away with her brood, before the girls could go astray. At times we used to talk about her at dinner, thinking about those delicacies of hers, about the youngest daughters who must have been grown up by then. How about Deolinda? Had she married a respectable man? My mother was peremptory.

"Nonsense. Undoubtedly she's installed in a house for loose women. Cinira's blood wasn't good for anything else."

Honorata has been concerned about Evangelina. The colored girl has started getting involved with older boys, she goes out on errands and stays much too long in the street. Advice does no good when the fire begins to burn. She has been going to dances, she's got herself a boy friend.

"Be careful, girl. Men are no good. Don't believe their talk about marriage. The only thing they want is to use that 'wicked thing' of theirs and ruin young girls."

Evangelina bares her teeth in a delighted grin.

"Gustavo is different from the others. He talks seriously, doesn't even put a hand on me."

If she continues to go out, she'll soon get to know the "wicked thing." Dona Emma has also uttered her warnings with fearful threats.

"Don't come to me with any hard-luck stories. If you think that I'm going to admit any illegitimate children into my house you're very much mistaken. I'll send you off at once to the Salvation Army."

Evangelina starts crying, saying that she prefers dying to having to go there.

"Well, then, try to show some good sense."

She won't. Sooner or later the illegitimate child will appear and Dona Emma will wind up admitting it into the house, because that will be the decision of Honorata. Sylvia will also relent, saying that the child will be a companion for hers, that they'll be able to play together. My mother will wait a while and will then make a pronouncement.

"Another burden for my son to bear. That's all you needed, to have to bring up the fruits of sin. If I were the lady of the house, I wouldn't allow such abuse."

She considers me sacrificed, she'd like to see me at her side, with no other love but hers, with no other commands to obey but her wishes. Julieta is the ideal daughter, she does not have Claudia's rebelliousness, she does not continually oppose her as I do. She accepts passively everything she says as if it were from an unimpeachable source, the last word on all questions. What is certain is that I do not recognize any authority in my mother, I do not wish to owe her any blind obedience. If we lived together, we would constantly be uneasy, in a state bordering on animosity. Except if I had married Adelaide, turning over to her the management of the house, accepting her orders and preferences. If Dona Emma should die, she would try to take her place. She gets along well with Camilo and would propose the change to him. She would take Marcilia, one or two pieces of old furniture, her prayer books. She would change the household habits, introducing Sylvia and the servant girls to a system of innuendoes. She would want economy in everything, no waste, the cupboard full of the daily leftovers. She herself would slice the bread that went to the table, she would reserve one beefsteak for each person. Garlic would prevail on all dishes, even on salads. On Fridays, no meat. I can't say whether her government would be better than Dona Emma's. It's pointless to speculate about changes. Especially since my mother-in-law enjoys good health, at the age of sixty shows no signs of weakening. Everything will continue being the same, until the baby is born. Only then will the reform that is being processed gain consistency. The new citizen is coming with definite powers and no one will escape his rule. Four-thirty. Sylvia will soon be going out for a walk with him. In August the evening is announced early in the winds that blow in over the fire-blackened fields. It's necessary to carry the rascal along at a good pace, not let him get too big.

"Don't let that child get fat," Dona Emma never gets tired of warning her. "At least listen to this advice. The pains of childbirth are frightful."

Sylvia does not get intimidated, the threat of suffering does not affect her. Her firmness makes me think that our son is coming at an opportune time. There is truly a void in all our lives, Sylvia with no outlet for her maternal instinct, Camilo with no grandson to fill up his mornings. The heads of lettuce are not sufficient for him, the newspaper ages after being read, the cards do not satisfy him entirely. Dona Emma needs somebody to create disorder in the house and to listen to her untimely scolding. Her nature demands reasons for her to let off steam against everybody around her, to rant and rave all over the place. As for me, I admit to some transformation. I do not feel any excitement, nor even any interest, but a profound anxiety for Sylvia's fate and a slight curiosity about our son.

Aristides leans over the book of records. Before long he will have to enter in it the description of the child. Name, color, parentage. He will take special pains with his writing, maybe he will use Gothic style in tribute to his compadre. It will be stated that Sylvia and I bore fruit, that from our blood a new life was born. Father Bento's registry will record the same thing. Juquinha the sexton writes badly, in tiny scribbles. His successors will tear their hair trying to decipher the identity of my son when the time comes for him to get married. In the notary public's office everything will be clear, the investigation will be made without the shadow of a doubt. I don't know whether I'll get to be a grandfather. I took a long time to become a father, a good part of my existence is completed. In a useless way, no doubt. I have done nothing that will leave any remembrance, no deed that will be recalled in future conversations in Domingos' pharmacy. Only to Sylvia have I linked myself in an enduring way. We have opened ourselves to each other in love, we shall always live in each other's memory if not in that of our own child.

The postmaster passes along the sidewalk. Leisurely steps, his wife on his arm. The two pairs of eyes turn toward the window. Antunes' greeting is the same as always: "Yessir."

Dona Carmela smiles with the air of an accomplice. She has been in our house almost every afternoon, she knows about the preparations that are going on there. She takes liberties that displease Dona Emma, lingering in interminable visits.

"That boring woman!" my mother-in-law says when she sees her turn the corner, after hours on end of idle conversation. "She seems to have no sense of propriety. Can't she see that she's staying too long? We've got a thousand things to do here and she keeps hanging around."

Sylvia observes, "Wasn't she a good friend of yours, Mother?"

"I didn't know that she had this habit of staying so long in people's houses. And she's always famished. She never gets enough, she's always hanging around Honorata in the kitchen. This is no boarding-house for freeloaders. The devil take her!"

The next day there is Dona Carmela back again, in no hurry, eyeing the cupboards in the pantry. She has no sense of propriety. That's what mankind lacks. All visits are made at the wrong times, the telephone always rings when it is least convenient to answer it.

The couple's footsteps sound in perfect cadence along the sidewalk. Dona Carmela's smile was enigmatic. "I know what went on between you two," it seemed to say. "You got together at night, you rolled about on the bed, and this is the result." Everybody does the same thing, that's what the night is for. While on one side of the earth we seek to fill up our day, on the other the yellow-skinned people come into contact with each other and talk the only language that is common to all living beings. Dona Carmela ought not smile. She herself has used that language with Antunes. The proof is right there in their brood of various ages. Antunes maintained a serious attitude, his reproof apparent in his frown. "Yessir." He meant that I took too long, that I should have become a father a long time ago. To whom would I leave the office? I needed an heir to take over my sinecure. Why had I avoided children for such a long time? It wasn't that at all, I would not run about telling everybody in the street that the child was a latecomer through no fault of Sylvia's or mine. He was arriving like a visitor who had been expected for a long time and who was no longer being counted on. We had not closed the door to him, he is the one who had been unable to find it.

Father Bento said to Sylvia, "God has sanctified your union, my daughter. I am sorry only that your husband fails to observe the duties of a good Christian."

I'm probably not one of the worst. I was never given to debauchery, I have no vices, I am not one of the sinners who bring most shame to the society in which I live. Lia is an accident, imposed by circumstances. Maybe I take advantage of them going to her more often than would be natural. A weakness, that's all. Perhaps I'm a bad son. Not because I lack sentiment, but because of my mother's disposition. She won't permit any greater proximity, she continually utters complaints through innuendoes, she seems eternally annoyed. My conscience is heavier in connection with Aristides. I abandoned my clerk, I let him struggle along for several years leading a wretched life. If it hadn't been for comadre Augusta's plea I don't know what would have happened to their children. They would have ended up scrofulous, Aristides himself would have thrown in the sponge, without courage to speak to his compadre about a raise. He has improved this winter, he shaves regularly, has a reasonably good color. I'll make his eldest son his father's successor. He may not have inherited his admirable calligraphy, but he will know the business. He will go to school and study humanities, gain greater competence. Thus Aristides will enjoy a tranquil old age. Now he is ready to leave. The church clock struck five a little while ago. He closes the books, puts them in the closets.

"I think it's time."

I stand up, feeling uneasy. I ought to stay a little while longer, wait until Sylvia goes out with Evangelina. I'll go home. If I have to accompany her, I'll make the sacrifice.

The cool evening is closing in. Sylvia ought to dress warmly. Dr. Leandro does not want any complications. I'll make her put on a coat.

Aristides is already far off. In the square, the black shape of Father Bento. He walks back and forth all day long between his house and the sacristy. The bad Christian goes toward the church in order to walk around it and then head for home. My conscience does not weigh so heavily. If it were not for Aristides I would be a man with no remorse.

Chapter Three

A boy. The forecasts had proved correct: after a hard wait of a day
and a night, Sylvia's child was born. Dr. Leandro had been called in
the morning and had arrived with his satchel. Dona Emma had given
the alarm after breakfast, when she found Sylvia lying down, her face
livid and beaded with sweat. She had come back with a frightened
expression, and at the telephone, while she waited for the connection,
she had muttered harshly, so that we would hear her in the living
room.

"This child is going to be born like an animal in the pasture. You didn't want Graziela, now my daughter may die for lack of attention. The doctor may arrive late."

I ran into the bedroom, my heart in my mouth. Sylvia's pulse was weak but regular, her features serene. I awoke her, dried her face, kissed her eyes. She smiled, took hold of my hand and, in a low voice, murmured, "I think it will be today, dear. I feel such a great weariness! But I know that it will be a boy and I already have a nice name for him."

Dr. Leandro had entered shortly after. He calmed us, assuring us that everything was going well and that the time had really come. He lunched at our house, skillfully brought up subjects other than the one that was worrying us. The tension eased, only to increase in the afternoon. The doctor had begun to frown, kept walking back and forth, his arms folded across his chest. Dona Emma seemed disfigured, she kept gnawing her nails, her wrinkles gradually became more accentuated. She stared at me with rancor, as if she were in the presence of a criminal. Camilo just kept smoking, with his head lowered, without the heart to utter a word. The only imperturbable one was Honorata, who would leave Sylvia's bedroom from time to time to go to her oratory. She was probably fulfilling some silent and urgent vow. The room stifled us, the ceiling became heavier and ever lower, the walls closed in. Sylvia's moans reached us, sometimes weak and regular, sometimes loud and interrupted. We all walked around on tiptoe, as if a loud noise would bring the house down.

When evening fell a cuckoo perched on the tamarind tree. I shuddered. No one appeared to hear it or ascribe any importance to its lament. I thought of Marcilia, I tried to overcome my uneasiness. The bird continued to chirp and there was one instant when its note blended with one of Sylvia's moans. I stood up, got my shotgun from a closet. I put a shell in it and went out toward the back yard. Someone restrained me. Honorata, her features tranquil, almost smiling.

"Don't shoot. The noise would do her more harm than the singing of that poor little bird."

I took the weapon back inside. I stood motionless, ashamed of my weakness. But the lament kept being repeated in the shadows of the orchard, it was as if a lost bird were calling its mate. I approached, threw a stone into the thick foliage. Wings fluttered excitedly off into the distance.

I allowed myself to remain under the trees. It was a relief to escape the anguished faces that moved about in the house, to avoid the uncertain look of the doctor. That vigil seemed connected, not with the expectation of a new being who would emerge into life, but with the drama of a dying person who was losing contact with the world. I started walking about, as the night kept falling. Bats were already passing each other in their low-altitude flights, soon they would be nibbling at the gooseberries and the ripe hog plums. The chickens had gone to roost, the birds had flown back to their nests. Walking slowly, I reached the back wall. If the child should finally be born, they would call out the kitchen door. My legs felt heavy, my hands moist. Why was it taking so long? What would happen to Sylvia? I remembered the cuckoo. I thought of death. I went back almost running.

My mother was in the living room talking to Camilo. She wore a black shawl over her shoulders, her face was lightly powdered. I became annoyed. I could never understand the inclination that sometimes possesses her to put on make-up, even going so far as to apply rouge on her cheeks. It was as if she lowered herself to a vulgar and suspect level, and that bothered me. Dona Emma would go even further: she used lipstick. We would go out to the movies, she and Sylvia ahead, Camilo and I behind. The old man puffing on a straw cigarette, silent, vexed. You could see that his wife's excess annoyed him. Her thin lips, ordinarily almost purple, transformed into red streaks. Preposterous. My mother fooling with face powder, boxes of rouge. Was it reasonable? I felt irritated. Obviously she didn't have to conceal her old age to visit Sylvia under such circumstances. She could have waited at least until the child was born. Then everything would have been pardoned, perhaps even the carmine would have seemed becoming to her, the scarlet on Dona Emma's mouth would have seemed proper. Scarcely greeting her, I went out to the terrace. Dr. Leandro must have been in the bedroom. Dona Emma kept coming and going, her wrinkles accentuated, her fierce glance directed at me. The night was closing in, the crickets were singing in the flower beds in the garden. I lacked the courage to go see Sylvia. The doctor had decided that it was better that way, that we should avoid any unnecessary emotions. The denouement would come at any moment. The child must be huge, to cause so much difficulty. Nobody had thought about eating. The dishes had grown cold on the table that Evangelina had set. I heard my mother say to Camilo, "That's the way these things go. The first one is always the hardest. Especially when one is not so young any more."

Why did she have to remind us that Sylvia was older than the ideal age for such an activity? Better to leave her alone with her pains, her difficulties, for she had more than enough courage to bear them. Her gray eyes turned for a moment away from Camilo and looked at me reprovingly. "If Adelaide were your wife, she would long ago have given you children, without all this commotion." My cousin was as prolific as a rabbit, she had a flock of kids. Her union with Marques had turned out right, their temperaments went well with each other. With me she might have failed. A man with bad seed, like a wild palm. It had been difficult for Sylvia to become impregnated with a child of mine. If she had married Lauro she would be on the verge of becoming a grandmother. She was suffering because of me, tossing about in her bed, worried, in distress. I was afraid of losing her, I felt a lassitude, a loss of energy that made me incapable of any useful action. If I had had to make a choice, all of my wishes would have been for her to be saved.

I went out into the back yard again. The thick blackness made me walk slowly, carefully. I reached out to feel the branches, keeping away from the trunks. In the trees, indefinite noises. Birds do not make love at night, it must have been bats sucking the fruit. I went near the chicken coop, stirred up the fowl, a command by the speckled rooster was answered in one corner by its plucked-neck rival. Fireflies blinked all around, a nighthawk flew over the tamarind tree.

I walked about for I don't know how long waiting for them to call me. I stopped under the locust tree that I had seen grow up, I embraced its trunk in despair. It remained silent, impassive.

I went back in. My mother had left. Claudia had also appeared and had asked for me. Camilo's voice was weak, his eyes sleepy. He was dozing on the sofa and had awakened with a start when I approached. Time seemed to have dilated, the hours unwound with enervating sluggishness. Dr. Leandro perspired profusely, his face red and somber. Dona Emma, disheveled, the hem of her dressing robe dragging on the floor, looked like a ghost. Only Honorata continued calm, efficient. The doctor directed his orders to her. He had quickly realized that he could expect no aid from Dona Emma's senselessness. Honorata kept coming and going, stopping off at her oratory every now and then. Several times she tapped me on the shoulder.

"Don't worry. God is great."

That's what helped me, kept me going. Everybody depended on her serenity, on her confidence. Even Dr. Leandro, who listened to her advice without getting exasperated. Dona Emma, however, irritated him. She would come running into the living room, terror-stricken.

"Doctor, I think she's worse. I couldn't find her pulse."

Doctor Leandro would rush out, a rapid examination would calm him.

"It would be best if you let me worry about her pulse."

At dawn, just when I was thinking of taking Sylvia to the hospital, a louder scream burst out in the bedroom and a baby's wailing was heard. We ran there. Dona Emma barred me and Camilo from entering, while Honorata, leaning over the bed, kept murmuring, as serene as ever, "Thank you, Lord."

We went back to the living room, arm in arm. Camilo was weeping and his smile was that of someone who had seen a vision. I pulled myself together little by little, and only pride prevented me from saying a prayer.

The smell of lavender spread throughout the house, pervading, nauseating. The activity in the bedroom continued. Dona Emma's mask was back on, her wrinkles had returned to the surface of her skin. Her anxious and resentful air had disappeared, only fatigue remained. The morning got brighter and penetrated through the windows, making everything stand out more clearly. Camilo appeared excessively pale to me, his hands shaky and bloodless. Blessed peace came from outside in gusts of cool air. In the bedroom a frequent, monotonous wailing made itself heard through the locked door. Evangelina had prepared breakfast and called us into the kitchen. The fire was burning under the dark trivet, water was bubbling in the kettle. Happy sounds of life. Camilo threw off his drowsiness, rubbed his hands together, slapped me on the back.

"The visitor has arrived. Now we have to find out what sex it is."

Its wailing was continuous, heart-rending. It was protesting, undoubtedly, against some insolence. Why didn't they attend to it? Dr. Leandro was surely busy with Sylvia. The baby would have to wait its turn. The order of preference was clear, the doctor was acting sensibly. But I was afraid that the child might lose its breath and I began to worry. They ought to give it something, make it sleep.

We went out into the back yard, arm in arm. The sun was rising, calling everybody to work. An ant passed beside Camilo's shoes, busy, impatient. A hummingbird cut across the yard. In the distance, a finch was beginning its day.

Honorata called us from the kitchen door. Her smile encouraged us and made us hurry. She embraced us and for the first time in my life I saw her cry.

"Come see the boy we've got."

I tripped over the doorstep, almost fell flat on my face in the kitchen. Dona Emma came to meet us, authoritarian.

"Have you washed your hands?"

We dashed into the bathroom, ran back to the bedroom. I accustomed my eyes to the darkness and before advancing I saw Sylvia's white face, very calm, resting on the pillow. At her side, a bundle of brightly colored clothes. Both were asleep. I approached, kissed Sylvia's forehead. The little face of the baby, contracted and purplish —God forgive me!—made me feel nauseated. Impossible that Sylvia had given birth to that little monster. Only its eyelashes shaped like fans seemed beautiful to me. In silence I embraced Dr. Leandro, who was sitting near the dresser, motionless, affectionate. I went toward Dona Emma, was going to take her hand and kiss it, when the telephone rang. She ran out, closed the door. She came back right away: it was from the doctor's house. An emergency call. When Dr. Leandro left, I noted the weariness in the deep circles under his eyes.

The day came to an end, others went by. Sylvia recovered her strength with Honorata's broth, the child began to look like a human being. His name, chosen by his mother, will be Marco Aurelio. Dona Emma had other names in mind, but she never got to impose them out of consideration for Sylvia's suffering.

"The idea came to me in a dream. I knew it was going to be a boy."

Visitors started coming, little groups stayed for hours. They came to look at the baby as if he were an animal in a circus. They brought him gifts, patted his cheeks, expressed astonishment at his long, black eyelashes.

Now things have returned to normal, according to a new order. The baby is five months old and the house revolves around him. He smiles, waves his arms and legs about like a beetle, is beginning to show signs of distinguishing different people. His mother he knows even at a distance. He extends his little hands toward her when he sees her approach, breaks out into a smile. I am still a stranger to him. I probably have the same meaning for him as a wall or the guardrail on his bed. But a day will come when my status will be recognized.

His features have become composed, the flushed distortion that distressed me so in the first days has disappeared. The features that stand out are the size of his eyelashes and the line of his nose, which resembles Camilo's. It's still too early to look for traits that will identify him with Sylvia and me.

Sylvia says, however, that he is going to be the picture of his father, and in spite of my protests that I want him to look like her, down deep I do not hope for anything else.

Dona Emma has taken my place at Sylvia's side for a few weeks, under the pretext of orienting her and helping her.

"The first nights are terrible. Nobody is made of iron, to bear up under the strain without any help. And the vine can be straightened best when it is young. I must start that child off right. Go sleep in my room."

So I kept Camilo company during the first month. We would converse for hours on end, lying in bed. The old man would enumerate his plans for his grandson, assuring him a wonderful future. My father-in-law is really a new man. He has seldom left the house during the day, and only to go to Domingos' pharmacy. He seems distant from everything, seems to think only about the child. He has never again set foot in the club. Of all of us he is the one who changed most quickly. His gaiety of old has come back, he has regained the vivacity that he used to put into all of his activities. His vegetable garden has had a rebirth, the chicken coop has been remodeled under his supervision.

"The rascal will need fresh eggs and vegetables."

He had a swing with a back on it hung in the mango tree in back of the house.

"I want to be the first to swing my grandson. No one is going to deprive me of that pleasure."

He had said that to us at lunchtime.

"Well, I want you to know that I won't permit any such absurd thing. Do you want to kill the child?" Dona Emma yelled.

"Why so much fuss, Mother?" Sylvia smiled and winked at Camilo. "If he is careful, nothing will happen. Marco Aurelio will enjoy it very much.

There was surprise in everybody's eyes, especially in Sylvia's, for it was as if we had heard somebody talking about a stranger. It was the first time that the child was being referred to as a definite person. Until then the references we made to him were contained in the expressions "that child," "my grandson," "our son," "the baby." The registry had conferred on him the name selected by his mother, but he was still too insignificant a citizen to justify its use. "Marco Aurelio will enjoy it very much." Sylvia was delighted with the spontaneity of her reference to him, and from then on we began to say his name aloud, or in whispers (if he was sleeping), in connection with everything and with nothing. Marco Aurelio took charge of our lives.

Anyone who sees me, through the window, occupied in making these notes, probably imagines that I am in the midst of some tremendous task. There has been no change, however, in the functioning of the office. The machine has not accelerated its movements, everything goes along at the same old oxcart speed. Aristides is curved over the books, his pen continues recording the history of the city.

Marco Aurelio's birth was registered with a gold pen. My compadre the clerk embellished the letters with admirable patience. It was the first homage that the child received. That page has fallen behind, succeeded by many others during these five months. A string of children born after my son, with a predominance of rural offspring.

The law of multiplication keeps being observed with the aid of the night.

The baptism was commemorated with a banquet. Dona Emma and Honorata stuffed a turkey and roasted a suckling pig brought from the farm by Sabino. From my seat all I could hear was the cracklings in Father Bento's mouth as he ate with a hearty appetite. The vicar was in excellent spirits: Dr. Leandro, the godfather, had discreetly slipped him a good-sized paper bill in the sacristy. Dona Carmela's mouth was greasy, she licked her fingers, greedily and hurriedly. My mother wore an expression different from her usual one, and I believe I heard her laugh more than once. Dona Emma carved the turkey with skill, facing Sylvia.

"Pay attention, daughter, and learn. The old lady is not going to be around all your life."

Aristides had a good time talking with Claudia about unimportant, domestic matters. I engaged in a discussion with Sabino about hunting and fishing. It was a peaceful day, with lots of wine and not a single cloud—Dona Emma scurrying about with happy excitement, serving, urging everybody to eat some more. Meanwhile, Marco Aurelio slept in his little bed dreaming about his mama.

To be brief about it, I must say that I feel myself slowly changing. I now live for my son. I have placed his first picture in my wallet. I return home eager to see him and pick him up. I walk through the streets with the assurance of a normal man who has succeeded in continuing himself. Not even Paulo arouses envy in me now.

Chapter Four

I could never have imagined that Marco Aurelio's birth would bring such profound changes into my life. Especially with regard to a matter I am going to reveal with all the propriety I can muster. If anybody had told me in advance about the transformation that occurred, I would have smiled in disbelief. I am a temperate sort of man, averse to adventures and excesses of any kind. What happened was less my doing than the result of a thoughtless decision on Sylvia's part.

In appearance, as I said, everything is for the better in our house. A new happiness, present in all faces, has invaded it. It's apparent even in the foliage of the plants.

Camilo doesn't know where to stop, he is always looking for something new to do.

"Let's get the house painted. These walls have faded, the paint on the doors is peeling off."

No need for painting. The tempera that Ercole put on is strong and weather-resistant.

"Oh, no," Dona Emma breaks in. "As long as I am alive, that dirty Italian thief won't set foot in here again."

She suspects that the last time we had the house touched up the contractor stole a folding stepladder, and since then she has never even wanted to hear his name mentioned. The truth is that Camilo is talking about painting simply to expand his inner feelings of pure joy.

Sylvia spends the days discovering new arrangements for the furniture, she makes sure there are flowers in the vases, she has changed the curtains on the windows. Dona Emma, for her part, ordered through the mail a collection of seeds that she has spread on the flower beds Aleixo turned over. As for me, I got up enough courage to have a suit of English worsted made at Deodato's tailoring shop—a desire that I had had for so many years but for which there hadn't been any good reason before to go to the considerable expense involved. During the fittings, Deodato, his spectacles sliding toward the tip of his nose, his bald head red and perspiring, would say to me, "Nothing like a baby to perk up a family's life. You look like a new man to me, senhor."

Only a little older than I, he had been one of my boyhood companions, yet now he stands on ceremony with me. Maybe he's ashamed of his trade, always with a pair of scissors in his hands—snip, snip, snip—a tape measure round his neck. He went over my measurements carefully, said that although it wasn't necessary he had moistened the navy-blue cloth to guarantee the fit. After the last fitting I walked out as puffed up as a peacock. I went back in from the sidewalk, admonished him to address me, from then on, as one equal to another.

Honorata seems to have frightened old age away, even appears to be rosy-cheeked. She takes charge of the child's soup, with Sylvia's complete acquiescence. Camilo runs out to his garden and comes back triumphantly with the needed vegetables.

Dona Emma observes, "My poor little grandson. To make him eat those awful carrots."

Sylvia gets impatient: "Oh, Mother, he needs vitamins."

"Vitamins, nonsense. In my day we didn't have any of that nauseating stuff, and people brought their children up very nicely. Carrots are for rabbits to eat."

If the child becomes stubborn and rejects the mush, pushing the spoon away with his little hand, she can hardly restrain her joy: "He takes after his grandmother. That's the way, grandson. Don't bend your neck, or they'll put a yoke on it."

Reasonable talk, with no animosity.

The old lady grumbles only about my going out at night, for sometimes I don't get home until dawn. But not everything in a house is what it seems to be on the surface. Doesn't the intimacy of the married couples count, their private and hidden lives? Dona Emma does not know, nor do Camilo and all the rest, to what extreme the arrival of Marco Aurelio has influenced my existence. I have lost Sylvia in an unforeseeable way, I am today a strange sort of widower, alongside a living wife.

I have said that we didn't have the slightest contact during the months of gestation: she did not want to risk losing the child. I agreed without putting up a fuss, although every once in a while, on occasion, I had thought about finding out from Dr. Leandro whether the risk was a real one. I did not get up enough courage to do it, preferring instead to quiet my body's demands with Lia. After the child was born, with her strength regained and leading a normal life, Sylvia's white body that had become rounded and softened, with no bony structure visible, began to seduce me as in our best days. Dona Emma, however, observed:

"Heavens, you're letting yourself get fat. Watch yourself, daughter, if you don't want to lose your husband."

She wouldn't lose him, that plumpness suited me. So I began to lay siege, eager to resume our old habits. Sylvia would kiss me, beguilingly.

"Not yet, dear. I must wear the girdle for a while yet."

The girdle, then, was the barrier during the first months. When she stopped wearing it, I intensified my attack. She would move away from me, under puerile pretexts.

"Not now. The baby might wake up. Let's put it off until another night. Look, he's stirring about."

No movement at all in the crib. But Sylvia would get up, lean over the railing, straighten the covers. In the darkness of the bedroom, I could sense the curves of her body moving about under her transparent nightgown. The blood in my veins became hot. She would come back and from the rhythm of my breathing would guess the state I was in. She herself would be panting, trembling. She would get her dressing gown and whisper to me, "I'm going into the kitchen to get some water. I'm dying of thirst."

She would stay there a long time and when she came back would find me drowsy and defenseless.

One night, in the sixth month, I lost patience and used force:

"After all, now, are you my wife or aren't you? As far as I know, I haven't given up my rights. Let's go to it."

And I tried to undress her.

She burst into tears, pressing her face into the pillow. I got frightened, began to imagine all sorts of crazy things. I shook her by the shoulders.

"What's this nonsense all about?"

Her sobs redoubled, I felt my head spin. I didn't know why, I was convinced that Lauro was the cause of that extravagant reaction. I even reached the point of imagining that the child was not mine.

I made her sit up, I held her face firmly. I don't know what she may have seen in mine, for she suddenly became calm and made a complete confession. She could never again be mine, our nuptials had come to an end with the arrival of Marco Aurelio. She had made a vow to Our Lady, the patroness of safe childbirths, to maintain herself chaste if the child were born perfect and if she were saved.

"Oh my dear, you don't know how awful those hours were. I had one nightmare after another, I would see our son horribly deformed. My God, how I suffered! The only reason I didn't die is that my time hadn't come yet."

From that time on only ideal love would be permitted between us. And what a struggle it had been for her to keep her promise, not give in to my pleas, thwart my natural desires! She had prolonged the use of the girdle for longer than necessary, she had said novenas on top of novenas in order not to break her vow. She was sorry for me, she wanted to be kind, but she was afraid of causing harm to the child.

"I'm deathly afraid that something may happen to him, dear. Imagine if we were punished and he became blind, for example."

Stunned, with a terrible buzzing in my ears, I protested against the folly of a resolution that affected me and that had nevertheless been made without my consent. I argued almost in screams, gesticulating, defending a possession that I perceived was lost and on which my equilibrium seemed to depend. Suddenly I was assaulted by new suspicions: was Father Bento's hand involved in this fraud? Or could the vow have been inspired by Dona Emma to separate me from her daughter? This last hypothesis infuriated me and I shook her again by her shoulders.

"Give me the story straight."

Sylvia kept kissing my hands as she wept and uttered desperate pleas.

"It was for our son that I did it, my angel. Please be calm. Nobody advised me, nobody knows anything about it. It was only for his sake, I swear it. In my agony, I couldn't think of anything else. I was foolish, I could hardly think straight. Don't act like that, for the love of God."

If nobody had interfered, so much the better. My anger abated, I stretched out again on the bed. The thought of liberation, which was struggling to impose itself, was followed by an awareness of the extent of my loss, as my instinct kept raging. The freckles on her bosom excited me, I suddenly turned and began to handle her body with brutality, sinking my nails into her bare arms. I snorted like a boar at stud.

Her weeping became louder and resentful.

"Is that all you see in me? I have a heart, I have feelings, too."

Her body trembled, shaken by sobs, tears came from her grief-stricken eyes. Just then Marco Aurelio stirred about and sighed. Sylvia raised herself halfway and looked at the crib.

"Be careful. Don't wake him up."

The child grew quiet, I looked at him through the curtain, tranquil, so distant from our drama. Sylvia took advantage of the pause to rest her face against mine. She kissed first my eyes, then my mouth. I felt the taste of her tears and a sudden calmness enveloped me. I became ashamed of my weakness, steeled myself so as not to weep with her. How beautiful and pure Sylvia seemed, how despicable I felt myself to be! I caressed her hair, I wiped away with my fingers the laggard tears that were dropping down her cheeks, I kissed her with tenderness. She became animated, rested her elbows on my chest, looked straight into my eyes.

"This will not affect our love, will it, my darling? See how beautiful our little son is! Isn't he worth our sacrifice?"

I agreed, although some last pockets of resistance were still throbbing inside of me. He was worth it, he was an incomparable child. But would it not be possible to alter the promise, to give it some more useful direction? Father Bento would be able to find some honorable and purposeful way out. Maybe he would agree to receive a monthly sum to purchase bread for the poor.

"Don't even think that. I made the promise in the name of Our Lady, it was an understanding between the two of us. Nobody can undo it. She was the one who saved me."

She became pensive and, not quite with sadness, but rather with assurance in her new resolution, observed, "We shall never travel together again, my dear. Now you will belong only to other women."

That was the way we used to refer to our acts of love. Travels that took us far away, in an absence from our own selves, in total fusion, our mouths pressed tightly together, almost bleeding.

"Don't you think of me any more as your husband, do you no longer feel any desire?"

She smiled with wonderful serenity.

"I think of you only as the one love of my life. And as the father of my son, who is the most beautiful child in the world."

The sincerity of that confession diminished my scorned male pride, and I tried to insist.

"Don't you feel anything, anything at all?"

She shook her head, smiling.

"I've become accustomed to it. During pregnancy a woman feels a kind of disgust about sinning. And now, with our little son, I don't have the time to think about it."

Now in command of herself and seeing that I had surrendered, she skillfully changed the subject. I continued to feel stunned, but was now conscious of the fact that we had come to represent two perfectly distinct bodies, synthesized as much as possible in the child with long lashes who slept beside our bed. I had the sensation that a wedge had been introduced between us, that a breach had been made in our intimacy.

I spent a sleepless night, lost in confused thoughts. My muscles ached, a heavy, harrowing weariness weighed me down, pressing me into the mattress. Sylvia had fallen asleep, fitting her legs between mine and with her hands snuggled up on my chest to keep herself warm. I felt tormented by the contact of her breasts and her belly, as if I were close to committing incest.

The day that followed, and many others, entire weeks, were sad ones. I could not resign myself to the new situation, I considered Sylvia's resolution thoughtless. I insisted a few times more that she should reconsider the unnatural transformation imposed on our lives, but she would not give one inch. I spoke to her about the possibility of other children, of her old dream of a large family.

"I see no change at all," she would answer smiling. "We love each other just as much, and even more through Marco Aurelio. As for the idea of more children, compadre Leandro warned me to avoid them. I am getting a little too old, dear."

She would kiss me and go take care of the child.

Aristides found me taciturn, morose. He insisted on asking me how things were at home, relating my apathy to possible domestic problems.

"Everything all right there, compadre? Is your heir still in good health? Does Dona Sylvia still have milk?"

I gave him precise but brief details, without enthusiasm. The clerk seemed suspicious, resumed his work. How could I tell him that my sickness was one of mutilation, that a part of my own being had been detached by an illogical act? How could I confess to him that I no longer felt myself to be the same, that my conjugal function was now purely contemplative? Neither to him, or to anybody, would I have the courage to reveal what was happening to me. My mother would surely find it a good reason to censure Sylvia and would never forgive her. It wasn't a matter I could discuss even with Claudia. Paulo would answer that I was a lucky dog, that I ought to grab my certificate of freedom and enjoy life. No advantage in telling anybody, it would be better to keep to myself the secret of my amputation.

While I was thus depressed, the widow of the railroad station agent came to my office to see about some papers. She believed she had a right to a pension and she needed assistance. She came more often than necessary, dark-haired, mysterious in her cheap mourning clothes. Aristides became uneasy.

"Compadre, be careful. A widow without virtue is an open door to sin."

I limited myself to smiles, flattered by the woman's interest. I took care of the matter for her, I wrote letters, had her sign petitions. Between the transmittal of one paper and the arrival of another she came in often to find out if there was any new development. Discreet, restrained, her small daughter holding on to her skirt. One afternoon she asked me, during a moment when Aristides was distracted, to bring the railroad company's final answer to her house. I was startled, I sounded her eyes. Beautiful and deep. In her smile, a vague promise. She gave me the address of the place she had been living in since the death of her husband, I answered her with an affirmative sign. I went there one night, the official envelope in my hand like a pass permitting me to wander about after hours in suspicious places. She lived near the reservoir, in a little house of wattle and daub. She received me in a light-colored dress and seemed considerably younger and more attractive to me. We studied the company's answer, pausing to discuss insignificant points. Our hands touched each other in chance contacts, at times our shoulders, and even our knees. She then told me about her married life, her disagreements with her husband who had been old and sickly, their financial troubles. Not because he earned so little, but because he used to gamble in the lottery and had little of his salary left by the end of the month. I saw that she was about to burst into tears, I took her hand, offered to help. She leaned her leg against mine, I lost my composure, planted two kisses between her breasts. She began to pant, got up to put her daughter, who was sleeping on the cane sofa, to bed. She came back with a robe over her naked body, pulled me into her bedroom, put out the light.

The affair has shocked Aristides, he seems as jumpy as a hedgehog. He has reduced himself specifically to being one cog of the organization. At first he tried to dissuade me by pointing out the harm it could cause and the impropriety.

"A man with two houses loses public respect, compadre. It was a sad day when that woman set foot in here."

Nonsense, I do not see how I can be harmed. Emiliana is different from Lia, she's not depraved, she feels uncomfortable when she takes money from me.

"If it were not for my daughter, I wouldn't accept anything."

Her dark face becomes tinged with red, her round eyes look down. Younger than Sylvia, her flesh firm and sensitive, they are about equal in size. What draws them close together in my sensory field is their way of making love. I do not know whether I think of her or of Sylvia in my new travels. Perhaps I fuse them into one single passenger.

I have won for myself, not only the accusation of Aristides, but also the ire of Father Bento. His Sunday sermons constantly and intentionally make mention of the sixth commandment. Sylvia has been dragging me to Mass.

"We must be grateful to God for what we have received."

I assure her that I am thankful, that I do not forget it for a single day.

"That's not enough, dear. Why not visit the Lord's house?"

We sit down on one of the last benches, she kneels, her rosary and missal in her hands. I pause to examine her pure profile, the movements of her lips in prayer. I feel that I am irreverent, distant from her soul which is almost saintly. The vicar ascends to the pulpit and soon his authoritarian words reverberate through the crowded nave. He repeats himself like Nicola's hurdy-gurdy, his poor language lacking convincing images. "One must flee from temptation in order to reach the summit of the mountain." Don't worry, Father Bento. I am not a man for summits, I do not intend to go that far. The notary will remain on the mountain slopes, he doesn't have enough wind for great altitudes.

The fact is that I will not give Emiliana up, nor do I fear for my salvation. I have lost Sylvia, whom I would have preferred, with her varicose veins, to the station agent's widow. I'll let matters stand and time run its course. I feel I have become warped by cynicism. The new conditions of my life do not exclude melancholy, but I shall not go back. I enjoy the flowery perfume of Emiliana's body.

Chapter Five

The weaning was easier for the son than for the mother. Next month Marco Aurelio will be one year old and Dr. Leandro ordered that he be taken off the breast. Dona Carmela was present and offered to sleep with the child. Dona Emma left the room so as not to insult her. It was difficult to get Sylvia's breasts to return to their normal size. They remained swollen for several days and the pain distressed her.

"The milk will have to be pumped out," the doctor had ordered.

Claudia heard about it and came to our house. My sister did what Dona Carmela was incapable of doing. She offered to suck out the excess milk that Sylvia had. Sylvia protested, vexed. But so great was her suffering and so pure was Claudia's expression that she ended up by consenting. Three times, in two days, she sucked her breasts.

"What sweet milk, Sylvia," she kept saying, clicking her tongue. "It's no wonder that Marco Aurelio is so plump."

A wonderful woman. She would leave Sylvia's room smiling, happy over the good she was doing. I embraced her, overcome with emotion, speechless, full of respect. It was necessary to have the courage of a saint to do that. I would feel nauseated, and I think that even Dona Emma, Sylvia's own mother, would be incapable of such unselfishness.

Sylvia felt relieved, her bust returned to its former shape. The milking left her thinner, with a rejuvenated expression.

"Notice how maternity has agreed with her," Dr. Leandro said to me a few days ago, stopping by here in my office. "You have a brand-new wife."

Brand-new, but lost. Sylvia will not give in; nothing will make her betray her promise. Dr. Leandro does not know to what extreme she had been led for the sake of her son. Perhaps only Father Bento has any knowledge of it. It's even possible that he has suggested that I participate in the vow. Sylvia had granted me exemption, had given me freedom of action. I went to Emiliana with no problems of conscience. Father Bento's malediction does not disturb me; I won't even accept my mother's condemnation.

"My son, your behavior brings shame on your father's memory."

Mariano would have done the same thing, if not worse. When I was only a boy I heard about my father's backsliding. Paulo did not spare me, whenever he saw him go into the back door of the Fortunato widow's house.

"There goes your old man, out to have a wild time. He's got good taste. Dona Aurea is really stacked."

I wouldn't dishonor him with my attachment to Emiliana. Everything happened in a natural, reasonable way. Sylvia does not even ask me for any accounting of my actions outside of the house. She did not allow our beds to be separated, she kisses me, she sleeps embracing me. Frequently she spends a long time smoothing my eyebrows, silent, pensive. Then she sighs and murmurs, "How dearly one has to pay to have a child!"

I agree that the price was high, yet it was worth it. Marco Aurelio has turned out to be a healthy and almost beautiful little boy. If it were not for his slight squint, not permanent, but visible when he fixes his sight on something close by, his face would be perfect. He is beginning to walk, his grandmother on one side, Honorata on the other. His wobbly little legs, made of pink pastry, move timidly in his first steps.

"Come, baby, here's a penny! Come, baby, here's a penny!"

The voices alternate in the deceitful offer—one gentle, weary, the other harsh and authoritarian. Camilo contemplates the picture, contented.

"Notice how the human being is hoodwinked from the time he begins to walk. They make a proposal to the poor little thing that they won't keep."

He laughs with wheezing sounds in his chest that now and then turn into fits of coughing. Sylvia becomes alarmed.

"I don't like to see Marco Aurelio hanging on to Father so much. I'm worried about that cough. We ought to ask the doctor if there's any danger."

The days pass by, the consultation is not made. Camilo is completely divorced from anything that does not pertain to his grandson. There is no attraction outside of the house, nothing that interests him enough to separate him from the child. I have not attained that state of rapture, but I do love my son. When I take him in my

arms, feeling the weight of his body, receiving his smile punctuated by little white teeth, an almost mystical joy envelops me. I am part of that nascent life; I am one of his creators, I think to myself in amazement. A feeling of plenitude then dominates me and leads me to kiss my son's hair with adoration.

His growth is rapid, comparable only to that of a cornstalk.

"He's going to be taller than you, dear. Maybe he'll be as tall as your father was."

Dona Emma protests.

"Don't exaggerate. The boy does not have to grow so much. I hope that he's not going to be a policeman or a doorman at a hotel."

He may be nothing more than a notary, like his father. He won't need to be a big, handsome fellow.

He hasn't given us much trouble. His young life is regulated in a definite schedule, he cries very little, he falls asleep as soon as they put him to bed. His eyelashes close like the leaves of a poppy. Sylvia is right. He cost us a heavy price, but he is a precious possession.

He goes out in the afternoon in a buggy pushed by Sylvia. They go to the square, return through the garden, his lively little eyes staring at the flowers. Our acquaintances stop, pat the boy's cheek, ask stupid questions. Sylvia flushes, is on the point of protesting. The abuses were greater when Evangelina was present. They would take his chubby little hand, kiss it, even lift him out of the carriage. The child would become frightened and begin to cry. He is free now of the worst abuses: Evangelina has gone away. It took a while, but her illegitimate child showed signs of life. Dona Emma raged: "Go on back to your parents' house and get into all the trouble you want to there. I kept warning you, now you can suffer the consequences."

Evangelina broke into sobs. She was crazy about Marco Aurelio, had been helping us raise him from the very first. Sylvia tried to ease the situation, backed up by Honorata.

"The poor girl, Mother. It would be cruel to abandon her in that condition. Maybe she'll have a boy, and that would be nice, for he could play with Marco Aurelio."

No use. Dona Emma would not give in.

"I won't permit that shameless girl to stay another day in this house. Either she goes or I go."

No satisfactory settlement was possible. Evangelina bundled up her things and, bawling, said good-by to the child. I hired Timoteo to take her to her mother's house in his car. It's a good three leagues to Sabino's farm. On foot the poor mulatto girl would have brought the proof of her sin into the world before its time.

Sylvia has arranged for a new nursemaid. The daughter of Dona Carlota, the seamstress, is coming to watch over Marco Aurelio. A somewhat giddy teenager who dropped out of primary school. She plays with urchins in the street, spins tops, shoots slingshots. She'll have to clean her nails before touching Dona Emma's grandson.

Ernesto appears at the window, interrupts my line of thought.

"Try your luck, boss. The monkey is due to win."*

And he holds a stack of lottery tickets toward me. I shake my head, the man persists. I see in Aristides' eyes a desire to take a chance, to make a pile that will liberate him from the office. He debates with himself, feeling that gambling is a weakness, but that it would be his only chance to make a fortune. And what if the monkey does not win? It might be a hoax on the part of the ticket seller, maybe the monkey isn't even overdue. The clerk stepped forward, retreated, caught my eye, became embarrassed, went back to his desk. Ernesto has smelled a customer, asked for permission to come in.

"We're busy. Nobody here buys tickets."

He drew his arm back, twisted the tips of his mustache, shrugged his shoulders.

"If you don't want to win, that's O.K. with me. But the monkey is going to win. One of these days he's sure going to win."

* This refers to a gambling game widely played in Brazil in which the numbers correspond to animals.

Scoundrel. He made a fool of the station agent with his eternal false tip about the animal that was due to win; now he wants to trap Aristides. If my compadre should weaken once, he would be lost. Ernesto continues on his way, his powerful voice proclaiming his deceiving merchandise.

Dona Barbosinha and her daughter come in. The old lady, grouchy, scarcely greets me; the daughter, lively, with protruding teeth. They've come to order the marriage banns, for the daughter's wedding has been arranged. I remember Dona Barbosinha in the catechism classes.

"Are you a Christian?"

The class, in dissonant chorus: "Yes, by the grace of God."

She has become old, she's completing her stay in this world. She's counting on marrying off her last daughter before delivering her soul over to the Creator. She is certain that mine will be lost, because of Emiliana. Her efforts in teaching sacred history were wasted. She spent her youth in showing us the straight and narrow road, but her pupils have gone astray. Paulo was a complete lunatic, as everybody knew. Armando, more discreet, was also going wrong. The notary public, so placid and accustomed to the domestic life, had lost his stirrups after reaching maturity. The little pictures of saints that she had distributed with dedications written on them, the medals that she had offered as prizes for effort and good behavior, had all been misused. Her hair had turned white not only under the burden of her years; there were other factors, and one of them was Sylvia's husband who used to behave himself so well but had suddenly turned out just like the others.

They discussed the documents with Aristides, then said good-by, the old lady without looking at me, Anesia with the same smile that she had when she entered. What does the opinion of the school-teacher matter to me? From the time of the catechism to the present the earth had made many a turn. She ought to know that we all have our own problems in this life, that we act in this way or that way for motives we cannot confess. We all have our own reasons; Dona Barbosinha must agree that we all have our own reasons.

"Don't we all have our own reasons, Aristides?"

The clerk turns around, surprised.

"What?"

"Nothing. I was thinking about Anesia's wedding."

He casts a wondering glance, as always, at my notes. I make them at intervals, at the whim of my reminiscences. He sees me with a pencil in my hand, sometimes filling pages upon pages at a stretch, sometimes sitting quietly, thinking. The pile of papers is getting bigger in the bottom drawer of my desk.

Aristides does not know the nature of these records made alongside the official books and no longer feels sufficient intimacy to risk an inquiry. Here he is approaching, upset.

"Compadre, the writ for Mateus is due for tomorrow. We should get started on it."

As a matter of fact, Colonel Medeiros will take over the mortgage on the Boa Vista farm. He will pay practically nothing, but Mateus is in debt up to his ears and even so will have to sweat it out. The whores at Madame Sarandi's did their job well. The man ruined himself in their clutches. Aristides has been worrying about the fate of our office ever since I began to associate with Emiliana. Nothing to be concerned about. No danger. With Lia, there might have been. Now it is different. The station agent's widow is not a calculating woman, what she needs is to be loved with frenzy. My compadre can rest easy. From Emiliana no ill will come that will affect him. Besides, I am not the same as Mateus. Mine is not a case of passion but of second nuptials.

Part 2 MARCORÉ

NC.

Chapter Six

Doralice has caught on quickly to the way Sylvia wants our boy watched. Lively, vivacious, talkative, she has a patient and affectionate disposition. In the very first days she abbreviated Marco Aurelio's name. Coming in from the back yard, after lunch, Dona Emma said to Sylvia in a fit of exasperation, "That uppity girl has already given my grandson a nickname. You'd better talk to her before I do."

Sylvia got up from the rocking chair and went to see what was going on, a slight wrinkle in her forehead. The nursemaid was telling stories to the child as they sat under the shade of the trees.

"Once upon a time, Marcoré, there was a kitten . . ."

She approached.

"What did you call my son?"

"Oh, Dona Sylvia. Please excuse me, but I shortened his name. It was too long. To me his name is Marcoré."

Sylvia smiled and mentally examined the corruption of the name. Marcoré. It wasn't bad, it even sounded like an affectionate diminutive.

"It's not a nickname, Mother," she had come back saying. "It's an abbreviation that's really very nice."

I also approved of it, thus vexing Dona Emma even more. Camilo felt the same way, and in a few days Marcoré was transformed into a name that became almost sacred for us. Just pronouncing it seemed to fill the house with a pure luminosity, giving it warmth and meaning. Dona Emma herself, in her hours of insomnia, probably uses no other name for her grandson when she evokes him in her thoughts.

My son has no equal. No one has a smile like his, an expression that radiates the happiness of a person who is the master of the world. There is no doubt that he is the master of the one that we live in. Everything revolves around him, there is no other reason for our actions.

Before long, in November, I'll be forty-three years old. I feel a sensation of maturity as if fatherhood had sharpened my visual ability. I actually do see better the pattern of things, I feel my perception of their mystery has broadened. I am experiencing, in short, the emotions of a man who has become multiplied and endowed with a new dimension, the ineffable existence of which he did not know about before.

What is undeniable is that Marcoré's arrival shook the very roots, good and bad, of my being. It led me to practices I didn't think myself capable of and which served to increase my knowledge of my-self. First, driven to Lia by circumstances of debatable merit, I broke the vow of fidelity I had made to Sylvia. It had not been difficult for me to maintain for ten years the status of a faithful husband, nor was I ashamed of it. Even in my trips to the state capital I had re-sisted the easy, transitory solicitations that came my way. I ended up by making my resistance a habit and adjusted myself to the pat-tern. What passed for virtue, then, was really no more than the re-sult of that adaptation. When the arrival of our son became a reality, I was surprised to see that my moral nature capitulated easily when my instinctive nature began to snarl. I convinced myself that in the matter of eroticism it is the basement that rules and I went to Lia recommended by Paulo. But not a trace of her hired love remained with me. It was of Sylvia that I thought when I threw myself on her, in an almost perfect transmigration. I would leave her, therefore, with my instinct pacified and my heart light, with no feeling of guilt. I can see today that I showed weakness, and that saddens me. I could have maintained continence until Sylvia's confession. At that time I would be free to act in accordance with my own desires. Emiliana would appear at the right moment, it would only be necessary to hold out my hand and seize the appropriate solution. I am divided today between two women. If I have transferred to Emiliana my physical life, I maintain my emotional reserves intact for Sylvia. If it were not for the hair shirt that she had imposed on herself, I would always be at her side. I love her in the same old way and I complete that love with Emiliana. I never imagined that I would know such a dissocia-tive experience. And there is no jealousy between the two of them, only a veiled absence of harmony because of their incomplete pos-session of me. They had known each other by sight in earlier days, when we would sometimes go past the station on our afterdinner walks. We used to see her then leaning out the window of their red-brick house, her glance lost along the tracks that fled until they fused in the distance in an embrace. Sylvia wondered: "What do you suppose that woman is thinking about, always in the same position, staring at the same spot?"

We would converse with the agent, who greeted us courteously by tapping the visor of his cap, smiling, and bowing.

"When will this illustrious couple bestow some scions on us?"

The illustrious couple would smile at his pedantry and reply evasively. The agent, changing the subject, would enumerate the passengers who arrived and departed. We had taken over from him for use in our house an expression of affection that Sylvia applied. He had spoken to us once about an important person whom he had met in another station he had worked in and with whom he had become friendly. They exchanged letters and gifts, talked to each other over the telephone from time to time.

"You understand," the agent concluded proudly, "our hearts touch..."

Sylvia introduced the expression into our house. When relatives of Dona Emma came from São Paulo for a visit that never lasted less than two weeks (pious old ladies with whom my mother-in-law corresponded as if they were sweethearts), she would purposely inquire during lunch, "Mother, is it true that your 'touching hearts' have written that they will arrive next week?"

Dona Emma would get peeved, finishing her meal in silence. Then she would say, sighing, "That's right, daughter. When you get old you will appreciate friendships like these."

The "touching hearts" would arrive and fall into her arms. Those were days when the constraint the rest of us were under was compensated for by the truce from Dona Emma's temper that we enjoyed.

Now the agent was wandering in other places, where perhaps there were stations where silent trains took on shadowy passengers. He left me Emiliana and I should be grateful to him. He should also be thankful to me. I've taken care of the small debts he left behind, I've given his widow a decent little house which is in no way inferior to the agent's house, I provide for the kitchen with the greatest regularity. A good arrangement all around, no doubt about it. Emiliana has no reason to complain. She stays cooped up at home, doesn't show herself to anybody, which pleases me very much. I don't want other men laying eyes on her, lusting after her dark body. Let the man who was born to be a cuckold leave his door unlocked. Sylvia, absorbed with our son, pretends to ignore the strange situation we are living, but from time to time she inquires, sadly, when I stay out longer than usual, "Do you really like her so much? How easily you've managed to divorce yourself from me!"

I didn't divorce myself, I protest. She was the one who had brought the situation about and, if she wanted to go back on her promise, I would give Emiliana up. The remembrance of her vow left her disarmed, much to my relief. There was no longer any sincerity in my words and a more detailed interrogation would have ended up by throwing me into confusion. Emiliana had become so much a part of my life that I could no longer do without her. If Sylvia decided to return to normalcy, I am sure that I would hold on to both of them, alternating them, mixing them into one single passion. Emiliana is discreet, asks me no embarrassing questions, makes no complaints. Only when I leave her, in the dead of night, do I notice her expression become clouded. Then I see her get up and go into her daughter's bedroom and lie down beside her in the double bed. It may be that she dreams of Sylvia's death so that she can possess me completely.

Dona Emma treats me like a stranger, permitting me nothing beyond formal greetings. At meals, we do not exchange any words directly, even though we participate in the general conversation. I find the situation advantageous, for the risk of conflict is now less. I don't know what she thinks of the life I am leading with Emiliana, nor do her opinions matter to me any more. The one who stands out, above everything and everybody, is Marcoré. The image of my little son, his tears that cause me so much anxiety, his musical little voice, his bright laughter that suddenly bursts out in the shade of the orchard, are always present in my thoughts. I feel as if Marcoré were not a work of mine but my own creator. I can no longer accomplish anything that does not involve his name. I transfer to him whatever good comes to me; if I weaken I fear the evil that may touch him. I contemplate for a moment, in front of me on my desk, his latest picture next to Sylvia's. The frames may be no bigger than envelopes but they contain everything that's most important in my life. This child's smile arouses indefinable emotions in me. If I look at him for any length of time I almost reach the point of bursting into tears. My sentiment is made up of happiness, fear, anxiety, melancholy. I would like a different situation for my son, a grandmother and a father who got along better together, a home without shouting and discord. I'd like to see him playing with his toys all day long, never to hear him cry of frustration caused by adults, to sleep at his side. Everything falls into second place when compared to this little child whose legs haven't even become strong enough yet to walk. Even Sylvia, at his side, with her tranquil glance, her gentle features, the line of her mouth expressing simplicity and purity, loses significance, drops into a lower category. Not infrequently I am tormented by the desire to take flight and seek freedom. To hand over the office to Aristides, to gay good-by to Sylvia and Camilo in a brief letter, to take Marcoré with me to the ends of the earth. Perhaps I would take Honorata along to take care of his most immediate needs. She would be just like nobody, she would not be any bother, would lend her services in an invisible way. Her silence would blend with that of our retreat, she herself would be happy. The portraits, side by side, seem to be unconcerned with my senseless plans. Aristides moves about the room, scrutinizes the cabinets, leafs through the books. He is unaware of the extent of the change that has taken place in his compadre. He sees me with my suit brushed, my countenance the same as always, my gestures deliberate, and imagines I have no problems. A lost sheep—that's what he considers me. A man with two houses and thus with two faces. He is no doubt sorry he made me his compadre. He attributes the duplicity in my life to my lack of religion. In the beginning he tried to save me, distressed, uneasy, with tears in his eyes, his voice trembling.

"Compadre, remember that the commandment gives us the right to only one woman, in a union sealed by the sacrament."

Aristides' anguish moved me and sometimes I almost took it seriously. Not, of course, with any intention of heeding his advice but with the thought of revealing to him the secret of my relationship with Sylvia, my status as a carnal widower. Even so he would probably not have understood. I remained silent and continued on my way. There he is right now, obstinately mute. He and Dona Emma make a pair, although for different reasons, in their hostility toward me. My mother-in-law considers her daughter a victim of my character and condemns me; Aristides attributes the dissolute life I lead to my estrangement from God and will not forgive me. It seems a long time ago that he applauded me when I discussed literature with Teodorico. He used to be overcome with an admiration that I found flattering and that I sought to encourage at every opportunity. But when I took up with Emiliana I toppled from the heights and now I am worthless in my compadre's opinion. I feel that if he could he would leave his job for another, one in which sin would not be so shamelessly conspicuous. His conscience undoubtedly pricks him when called to account by Father Bento in confession. Have nothing to do with that lost soul, is what the pastor no doubt demands. The clerk continues carrying out his duties as a good Christian pertinaciously. And also his job. Perhaps his penmanship is declining, is not executed with his former skill. Yet he continues to apply himself conscientiously, the documents come out legible, with no erasures. To be frank, I am glad that my relations with my compadre have become restricted. Anything that does not concern or pertain to my son represents a dispersion in my life. Marcoré is my mainspring, the plummet that sounds the depths of time for me. The rest is subsidiary, has no powers of destruction. My existence is circumscribed by the figure of this boy in the portrait, I know that I belong to him and to no one else. I even feel more and more distant from my mother. My old habits, to which I used to consider myself a slave, have been forgotten. Paiva has never again had me as a partner, I no longer dispute the reading of the newspaper with Camilo, the September fishing trips on Sabino's farm have not been repeated. I have given up the movies, the friendly meetings in the pharmacy and on the benches in the garden. Maestro Militão's band concerts are invariably repeated, the parish festivals follow one upon the other, circuses are set up in the Market Square. No inclination any more for the emotions of former days. In confrontation with Marcoré everything else has become reduced, has crumbled away, has lost its importance. The office and Emiliana form the bridge over which I pass through the world. A silent, tranquil, aloof citizen, whose inner life no one knows. Impossible to cry out that Sylvia and I have become divorced, that I live her in Emiliana, that nothing matters but my son. My notes reproduce scraps of my story and descend into the drawer, under the intrigued glance of my clerk.

The secret of my relationship with Sylvia will remain undisclosed.

Chapter Seven

Another year. Three little candles were lit on Marcoré's cake. He blew at them but not very accurately. Doralice, wearing a white apron that her mother had embroidered, helped him put them out. Under Dona Emma's wrathful gaze Dona Carmela devastated the table of sweets that had been set up outside in the arbor. Marcoré laughed happily, showed his collection of toys to his guests, ran about, took tumbles that frightened me. Honorata, however, was missing, and we all thought of her. It was Marcoré's second contact with death. The first had occurred shortly before, in a strange way. Dona Emma had brought him a tame black-throated cardinal from Lauro's farm. The little bird hopped about the house all day long, climbed up on the furniture, darted under the beds, never stopped moving about. Marcoré kept running after it, feeding it. He prepared a little bed for it in a shoe box and made it sleep under his own bed. When he awoke, his first concern was for his restless companion.

"Oh, Mommy, I dreamed my birdie flew 'way."

Sylvia protested, "This ungrateful little boy doesn't dream about his Mommy any more, all he thinks about now are little birds."

Marcoré would hug and kiss her, then receive my blessing and hurry barefoot downstairs to examine the cardboard box.

One afternoon he ran up to Sylvia, his eyes wide with fright.

"Mommy, he feels hard and won't stop sleeping."

Sylvia explained that it had died from eating too much.

"What does 'die' mean?"

The question remained suspended on his half-open mouth and in his perplexed look.

"It means that he can't fly any more, or sing, or eat. He can't open his little eyes any more."

Doralice buried it in the garden and planted a rosebush beside it that Marcoré watered faithfully for a few days. Then he forgot about his companion and never spoke about him again.

The second contact was when he saw Honorata stretched out in the coffin, motionless, livid, emaciated.

"Mommy, can't Nata open her eyes any more?"

Sylvia started crying even harder than she had been, and Marcoré, half-frightened and half-afraid that he had said something wrong, began to sob also. Gangrene had put an end to that life which was part of our own, had immobilized the arms that we most needed during our difficult hours.

Dr. Leandro had been worried.

"If it's gaseous, the patient will have to be hospitalized."

He explained that there was a risk of contagion, that treatment at home was not advisable. Dona Emma began to rant when the doctor left.

"That poor thing will not leave here all alone. I'll go to the hospital with her and I don't care if the gangrene attacks me, too. Only I know how much my poor sick friend means to me."

Of course, she meant a great deal, but there was Marcoré, who meant everything to us and whom we had to guard against all perils, immediate and remote. We acted selfishly, Sylvia and I, and refused to yield. Unless, I said, Marcoré went to stay at my mother's house. Dona Emma retorted that there was no need to bother a person who already had problems of her own. She didn't care to permit any long contact of her grandson with his other grandmother, for she didn't want any rival in the child's affection. Sylvia went back and forth, discussing the matter with me, with her mother, with Camilo. I was on the point of committing the folly of suggesting Emiliana's house, where Marcoré would have someone to play with. I held back in time, but Sylvia perceived my intention and looked at me, offended.

In the end there was no need for either one to leave the house. The progress of the sickness did not confirm Dr. Leandro's pessimism and our old friend was able to deliver her soul to God in her own room. The sickness she suffered from was senility, nothing more than that. Her right foot gave way, her legs no longer articulated. No moan was heard, no complaint. She knew the end had come and she said good-by to all of us. I went to see her, ill at ease. I wasn't sure what judgment I would find in that last glance and I was afraid that it would accompany me for the rest of my life. Neither pardon, nor censure. It was tender, understanding. She took my hand, slapped it smartly, in the mute language she had always used. She wept only when Marcoré came in. He was the one it grieved her to leave, the squint-eyed

grandson who had brought her so much happiness. Father Bento had arrived in the morning, for the extreme unction.

"Come, my daughter, confess your sins."

Dona Emma became indignant.

"She can't talk and she hasn't done anything bad to confess."

She died in the afternoon without a sigh. The black-throated cardinal must have departed in the same silent way, humbly.

Aristides had helped us take her to the cemetery. Matos had prepared an elegant coffin for her, by order of Dona Emma.

"She is going to be buried like a white woman."

We walked slowly, on that same afternoon, along Otherworld Street, the light load alternating between my hands and those of my clerk, Sylvia, Dona Carmela, Armando, Claudia, and a few others. Camilo had stayed at home with his grandson. The shovel of Zé the gravedigger filled the grave with the red earth. The sun was descending, the shadows were gently insinuating themselves between the varied shapes of the gravestones. On all of them, the same inscription: *to eternal rest*. Is there an eternal rest? I have my doubts that Honorata will find it. Her thoughts will continue to be directed toward Marcoré and Evangelina's son. She will not stay far away from her children and it will distress her that she will never be able to intervene in their favor again.

Honorata was absent from Marcoré's party. She would have made cupcakes, coconut candies, meringues. But it was the same as if she were present. The adults spoke about her and the impression we had was that her shadow was moving about everywhere, making sure that nothing was being overlooked.

What is true is that Marcoré is three years old. He talks with ease, he walks firmly, he won't stand still for a single moment. A mischievous child, he continually torments Elisa the cook, a stout, neat blond woman who came to work for us six months ago. He goes into his grandmother's sewing room and spills her bobbins and spools on the floor.

"Get out of here, you rascal! That child is full of the devil."

He rolls on the floor with laughter at Dona Emma's anger. His eyes are lively, still a bit crossed. His ability to reason develops day by day, while his imagination becomes more active, like a toy being perfected. He picks fights with Doralice, scratches her face, bites her arms. The maid pays him back in the same coin, he runs crying to Sylvia.

"Mommy, I don't like Dalice any more. She beat me."

A few minutes later they are having a good time together again in the back yard.

I have replaced his picture with a more recent one. Dressed just in shorts, he seems perfect to me, possessing an ideal beauty. The last image I have of him every day comes to my mind, kneeling beside his bed, repeating the words that his mother dictates: "Child Jesus, lie with me, protect my little body, and guard my little soul from all danger, amen." May his fragile little body, his carefree smile, his little head swarming with fantasies, be truly well protected. Sylvia, in the picture next to his, retains her former appearance, smiling, healthy, happy. But in reality she has undergone changes. To me she seems taciturn, she has grown thin and has been complaining of a shortness of breath. Dr. Leandro prescribed sedatives. I don't know to what extent continence may be influencing her health. When I see her feeling especially downcast, I am overcome with remorse. I make her sit down on my lap, cuddle up in my arms. She quiets down for a long while, then, without looking at me, says in a weak voice:

"I have been having palpitations at night. If I suddenly died, would you marry *that other woman?*"

I scold her, caress her, make her change the subject. Nevertheless, the idea takes root and torments me. If Sylvia were missing, what would happen to our lives? Particularly to Marcoré, who can't remain far from his mother even when he is sleeping? I tremble and hold her closer to me. The protective gesture does her good, her voice takes on an ardent tone.

"Our little son is really wonderful, isn't he, dear?"

I agree, kissing her hair. White strands stand out in her carefully arranged topknot, from which emanates a vague perfume. Her light skin is still fresh, the down at the nape of her neck is still soft and endearing. Yet there is no further appeal, only subjective feelings remain now. With Emiliana, in the same situation, it is different. We can remain composed only a short time. Our blood starts to speed up, our breathing quickens, the invitation to a more intimate contact erupts. I no longer know to which one I can attribute the greater portion of my love. Emiliana and Sylvia have become fused, it is impossible to individualize them. I would not be satisfied to live with only one of them, it would not be enough.

Her voice takes the subject up again in the same tone as before.

"Do you promise not to have any children with *her?*"

Marcoré's arrival on the terrace is providential.

"Mommy, I found a little *flyer-fly*."

He comes in looking for a little box in which to imprison the firefly. Covered with dirt, his fingernails black, his hair tousled. From the depths of the back yard Doralice calls him to make new discoveries.

"Sometimes I'm afraid that that girl teaches him nasty things."

Sylvia recalls the episode of the other afternoon. We were sitting on the front porch with Camilo and Dona Carmela. Dona Emma was moving about among the flower beds, watering the plants with the garden hose. There wasn't the slightest breeze, the air lay tense and stifling. Sylvia breathed hard in her chair, Camilo seemed exhausted. There was no subject that could enliven our conversation. We had talked about the rigor of the summer, about the drought that was threatening to continue and that would bring about a rise in the cost of living. Camilo had declared that in forty years there had not been a season like that. Dona Camela had nodded confirmation and added, "It must be punishment. Humanity is full of sin."

Dona Emma, who avoids expansiveness in my presence, had limited herself to a noncommittal grunt. The matter had died out, the air seemed to have become heavier. That was when Marcoré appeared, just out of the bath, all in navy-blue. He went up to Sylvia.

"Mommy, do you have a 'peenie'?"

It was as if Dona Emma's garden hose had suddenly squirted us full force. Sylvia sat up at once in her chair, her face turning red. Dona Carmela cleared her throat, scandalized, while my mother-in-law stared in astonishment. Only Camilo did not move.

"Who taught you to say that, my child?"

His round little eyes displayed seriousness, his eyebrows arched.

"Nobody."

Sylvia embraced him, trembling.

"Don't ever say that again, my darling."

But his questioning glance persisted.

"Do you?"

"No, my son. Such a question! Don't ever ask it again."

"Then how do you make 'pee-pee'?"

Camilo's guffaw ended in a fit of coughing. Dona Carmela became a fiery red and went inside, pretending thirst. Dona Emma disconnected the hose and walked away, fuming.

"It's no wonder. In this house the bad examples come from above."

I flushed with anger, a rude retort came to my lips. But the child's expression, compounded of fear and wonder, stopped me. They were seeing evil in a question that was natural and logical, and they were trying to blame me for it. Stupid old ladies, let them go to the devil. I calmed Sylvia, who had feared the worst from my protest, and I sent Marcoré to ride his tricycle on the sidewalk. The incident ended there. Only my mother-in-law's insult remained, latent. Dona Carmela had said good-by without looking at me, offended. She probably felt that her honor had been compromised.

"Stupid creature," Camilo had said. "She left here horrified, as if the child were depraved."

Sylvia had become calm and now seemed to smile at the episode.

"Children say the strangest things!"

Camilo rolled a cigarette.

"That woman will undoubtedly claim that Marcoré ought to confess his sins to the vicar. I've never seen anything more asinine."

Sylvia egged him on.

"Which woman are you talking about?"

The old man struck a match brusquely.

"Perhaps both."

Sylvia feels supported at such times, it is like a reprisal against Dona Emma, taken by involving her father's comments. It's impossible to hide the conflict between the two women over the slightest matters concerning Marcoré. The measles, for example, ran its course amid disagreements, one of the women keeping him covered with blankets, the other one leaving him merely between two sheets. Nor did they agree on the time for him to take his medicine.

"In the old days it was different, measles was treated with elderberry tea and you watched out for drafts. Today they put the child right in the middle of a draft and they fill him up with spoonful after spoonful of medicines with complicated names."

"That's enough, Mother. Times have changed."

It is Sylvia's custom, even today, to sing him to sleep.

"Absurd," the old lady protests. "The child is old enough to go to sleep by himself. He doesn't need lullabies."

"I don't mind doing it. To me he will always be a little baby."

He goes to bed at nightfall—with the chickens, Honorata used to say. Then Sylvia's voice, lulling him to sleep, reaches us on the terrace.

> *Over this deep, deep river,*
> *Oh, my Lord,*
> *Who will be able to cross,*
> *Oh, my Lord?*
> *Sad is the one whose love remains,*
> *Oh, my Lord,*
> *On the other side of this river.*

The melody contains a sadness that lulls me also. Even Camilo becomes pensive, silent in his hammock. He must feel that that deep river runs between all of us and is a dividing line that no one can cross. Her voice yesterday seemed tired, uneven, at times hoarse. Sylvia is slowly losing her strength. She has difficulty breathing at night, the shortest walk leaves her exhausted. It's impossible that she should follow the path taken by Honorata. Too early yet. Marcoré is a little child, he needs to hear his mother's voice in order to go to sleep, he needs to hold her hand tightly over his heart. If Sylvia dies, what will happen to my son?

Chapter Eight

My mother appears in my office with Marcilia. They sit down, tired, taking a while to catch their breaths, the latter more than the former. Aristides hurries over to the water jug and fills two glasses.

"Old age is an incurable illness, Aristides. Fortunately you are a long way from it."

"Not at all, Dona Antonieta. Appearances are deceiving. I've been feeling quite ill lately."

Marcilia imitates a smile for me.

"Your son is beautiful."

Her voice is emitted with an effort from her sunken chest. Marcilia looks like an old rag. My mother's hair has become whiter during these four years, but her body is still erect, well governed. Aristides has really aged, doesn't seem much younger than the old ladies. Father Bento is also reaching the end of his road, the steps that lead him to the moribund have been losing their agility. A branch of the monkeypot tree in the square dried up and was sawed off. Everything is slowly perishing, crumbling. Only Marcoré sparkles more each day, justifying Marcilia's expression.

I take him to my mother's house every Sunday. Marcilia welcomes him with coconut candy, his grandmother gives him cake. Marcoré doesn't stay long in the parlor that has been prettied up for his visit. He scoots off into the back yard, disappears among the trees. When Julieta's children are present, there's a commotion. The cousins fight over the ripe fruit like tanagers, they quarrel, they batter each other. Although he is younger, Marcoré does not labor under any handicap. One day Roberto began screaming under the myrtle. We ran out, imagining a disaster such as a fall from the tree. It was nothing. Marcoré had bounced a stone off Roberto's head and some blood had spurted out. Julieta was furious.

"Good! That's what you get, my son, for playing with children who have no upbringing."

I felt like swearing at her, but held back because of the presence of the children. The only thing that came out was the childhood nickname that she hated: "You dry old cat!"

Marcilia had also rushed up and had taken Marcoré's side. My mother arrived a bit later and took Roberto into her arms, livid, trembling. She cast a fearful glance at my son and thundered, "What have you done, boy? Are you turning out to be bloodthirsty?"

Julieta felt fortified, blustered about, called her children together.

"We're leaving. And I want you to know, Mother, that I won't set foot here again when you have such crude visitors."

It was spite that raged in her. She saw Marcoré radiating health, as lively as a minnow, beautiful, with hair of burnt gold, and she chafed with envy. Roberto was turning out to be very small, a delicate, sickly child they mollycoddled. Marcoré was already going to Dona Maria Rosa's nursery school, where he painted with water colors. At the school party at the end of the year he had even been the soloist with the gourd rattle. Julieta could not forgive her nephew's progress, his liveliness, so she talked about bad upbringing.

The two old ladies, side by side, sitting under the schedule of marriage banns on the wall. That's the way they've been going through life, each one supporting the other. Marcilia will likely depart first, to decorate heaven with stars. A drudgery for the poor thing, who is already so tired of the chores of this world.

"I came to ask you to recommend Marcilia to Dr. Leandro. We're going to his office."

I call the number and converse with the doctor, then I send for Timoteo's car to take them.

"You didn't have to do that, my son. We walk along slowly, supporting ourselves against the walls. You'll have this added expense. We already are such a burden to you."

Marcilia can't take her eyes off Marcoré's picture. I never remembered to give her one. This one, the latest, is faithful from every standpoint. He's all there inside the frame, barefoot, beside his barrel hoop. In one of his hands, the stick to guide it with. I take the picture out and hand it to the black woman.

"Keep it, as a remembrance."

Her trembling hands take it to her breast, over her heart. I never knew a grandmother, only Marcilia who was worth all grandmothers put together. Marcoré is probably fonder of her than he is of my mother, feels closer to her, likes to hear her stories. At his request, Honorata, who also knew it with minor variations, would tell him a story that fascinated him: the cleaning of the world. The picture Marcilia now has in her hands represents a great deal to her. It's as if it were a son of hers, of her own blood. Honorata felt the same way. For her, the child's desires had to be satisfied, no matter what. If she were still alive, Marcoré would have had his puppy. A few months ago he kept talking to Sylvia about it for days.

"I'd like so much to have a puppy, Mommy."

Sylvia would answer vaguely, "We'll see. I'll talk to your father."

I promised to get him a purebred. Marcoré clapped his hands.

"I'm going to call him Jewel. Dalice picked the name."

Dona Emma, who until my intervention had said nothing, warned Sylvia, "I want you to know that I do not approve of the idea. If any animal like that should enter this house, I'll leave through the same door. I haven't been going to the trouble of taking care of my plants just to have one of those pests trample over them all day long."

Marcoré began to cry.

"Please, Grandma. I'd like so much to have a puppy to play with."

She didn't allow it. She must have tortured herself in seclusion in her sewing room, biting her nails, arguing irresolutely with herself. To refuse her grandson anything cost her years of her life, but on the other hand it pleased her to show greater power than her wayward son-in-law. With Honorata alive, it would have been different. Marcoré would now be running through the back yard with his Jewel. My mother is also against dogs, I could never have one when I was a boy. I would go to play with Paulo's police dog, we'd hunt cavies in the marshes of his father's farm. Her gray eyes are turned toward Aristides, without a shadow of remorse for the dog I never had.

Timoteo pulls up at the curb. Marcilia gets up groaning and goes out holding on to my mother's arm. Aristides and I accompany them. I ask them to let me know what the doctor says and tell Timoteo to take them home from the doctor's office. The car starts up, headed toward the square. There goes Marcilia, with little faith in Dr. Leandro's science. In the rectangle of the back window the white-haired head sways beside the one that is still dark, vigorous, resolute. Always together in life, one of them is now leaning and may fall forever. I am unable to say which one of them I shall remember longer, which one I shall miss more. They drive off, only the white shape is visible, they disappear around the curve.

Poor Marcilia. It won't be long before she leaves to join Honorata. Wherever they may be they will take care of getting a puppy for Marcoré and will watch over Sylvia's and Camilo's health. Above all they will invent a huge broom to clean the world with.

The clerk enters at the same time. Bent over, his shoulders dotted with dandruff. My compadre is deteriorating, the muscles of his neck stand out under his flaccid skin. He is waiting for me to invite him to bring in his oldest son and initiate him into his job. When Bernardo is older and more experienced, Aristides will be able to withdraw and take his rest. His eternal repose, on which he is also counting and with greater certainty, would come later. He needs treatment for his kidneys, should stand up straighter and fill out his thin body. Marcilia expresses sympathy for him in our conversations:

"Poor man. Trouble with urine is no joke. Has he tried breakstone tea yet?"

Life is on Marcoré's side. He is full of joy, the exuberance of this young plant makes itself felt from a distance. His bright voice is as pure as the song of his pet goldfinch. When he was younger I used to feel exalted above all other human beings when, seeing me come home, he would shout, waving a little arm, "Dad-dee, Dad-dee!"

The high-pitched tone would vibrate in the tranquillity of the afternoon and envelop me in a wave of happiness. I'd take his sweet-smelling little body in my arms and hold him tightly to my breast. He seemed so dependent, so fragile, that I'd feel like crying.

"Dad-dee, we go walk?"

Seeing me look at Sylvia, hesitating, he'd pull me by the hand.

"Tum, Dad-dee, we go!"

We'd go as far as the bridge over the river, where he amused himself by throwing pebbles into the water.

His language has evolved, his mind develops day by day. When he calls me now it is with the correct pronunciation. He is the creator of a word that I have searched for in vain in the dictionaries. Aristides is a witness. He came here to the office one afternoon, riding his tricycle, Doralice at his side. In his hand he held a brightly colored paper whirligig that Camilo had made for him. He got off, called me outside, pulled a piece of string out of his pocket.

"Daddy, would you *instring* my whirligig on the handlebar?"

Gasping with pride, I looked at Aristides. The blondish little head that was following the movements of my hands was creating words, possessed his own resources of expression. That evening I went to the club, looking for Teodorico. I wanted to bowl him over with the news by flaunting Marcoré's neologism in the face of his philology. The wretch listened to me in silence and continued reading his newspaper.

"I don't see anything original in it. *Instring*. So what?

I walked out of the club, indignant. That second-rate linguist had no sensitivity, was unable to appreciate an innovation that sprang from a child.

The following day I sounded out Aristides' reaction. What had he thought of the word that Marcoré had invented?

"I didn't pay any attention."

Another blow. My son couldn't even count on the admiration of my clerk. It didn't matter. Marcoré was growing, dominating, different from everything that had already existed on the face of the earth. Life escaped from everyone else in order to become concentrated in my son. I myself lived only in him, nothing mattered for me other than his image and his look.

I had said this very thing to Faustino, one afternoon when I met him in the church square, resting in the shade of the monkeypot tree, his axe on the bench. He looked at me with his good eye; the other one, blighted, could only see inward. He smiled at the rapture I displayed as a father and finally said, "I know what you mean. But remember that only owls boast about their offspring."

There was no paternal boasting in my enthusiasm, just the expression of truth. The woodcutter had limited vision, that's why he saw exaggeration in my words.

My eyes turn toward the empty frame. Sylvia on the other side, watchful. I must fill it, so I won't feel alone.

Chapter Nine

Six months away from Marcoré, I've become thin, have spent many sleepless nights, feel exhausted. I've acted harshly toward Aristides, have been impatient with my mother and mistreated Emiliana. Alone with Elisa in the big, silent house, I felt my nerves become taut. I kept walking back and forth, rummaged among my son's toys, spent hours sitting in front of his little bed. He had caught the whooping cough and had gone to Sabino's farm with his mother and grand-parents to recover. Dr. Leandro had told us that Sylvia and Camilo also needed a change of air to strengthen their blood. My father-in-law really had become as moody as a raven, was depressed, spiritless. He was nearing seventy and gave the impression that he was not going to live much longer.

"All of my family passed away before reaching sixty," he would say to us on his better days. "I don't know if I'll last much longer."

His hands tremble, his legs are not as firm as they used to be. His straw-colored mustache perches above a wilted mouth, wrinkles en-circle his eyes, his hair is thinning out on the top of his head. My good old father-in-law is coming to the end of his days. Sylvia, for her part, has been aging with frightening rapidity. Her body has become blotched, her varicose veins have become enlarged, her breathing has become more labored. Of her past charms, only her topknot remains inviolable. All others are extinguished, finished for-ever. I have been going to see her on weekends, she kisses me with emotion and I find her as affectionate as ever. Her color returns, her movements become more vivacious, her eyes brighter. But she does not delude herself nor does she try to conceal her physical deterior-ation from me. Dr. Leandro had warned me, "My comadre has been declining considerably. We have to watch out for those coronaries."

Sylvia knew this, her labored breathing during hot nights de-pressed and worried her. She would fan herself, go to the window, take in deep gulps of air.

We went for walks along the paths near the house. Marcoré would run off ahead of us until stopped by fits of coughing that almost choked him. I became terrified.

"He's going to lose consciousness."

"Keep calm, dear. That's the way these things are."

And, certain that the crisis was only temporary, she would wipe his mouth, slap him on the back, blow against his cheeks. The child would recover and dash away again.

"I have a premonition that I won't live to see our son graduate from school. Don't you think he has a talent for engineering?"

We'd reach the vicinity of the water mill and listen to the slow, monotonous pounding amid the cascading of the water. Marcoré sent little paper boats spinning into the current.

He really did have the makings of an engineer. He would amuse himself for hours on end with games that had to be assembled, he talked a great deal about bridges, showed an interest in mechanics.

I was afraid that Sylvia would pass away suddenly. It would not be fair for her to die so soon: she had made such a great sacrifice that she deserved to see our son grow up. To see him choose a profession, study, graduate, distinguish himself in his work. Later on, to give her a good daughter-in-law and lots of grandchildren to fill her old age. The trouble was that her old age was arriving ahead of time, an implacable water mill was grinding my poor companion down.

Sitting under the mimosa tree, I felt her snuggle up closer to me as she sighed, "A weariness I can't explain is cutting my life short. You will have to take care of his education all by yourself."

I was moved by the tone of farewell in her words, the dejected accent of one who sees the day come to an end before the task has been completed. I embraced her tightly and said to her in a tremulous voice:

"Don't talk like that. God won't allow it to happen."

I saw her smile and turn her playful eyes toward me.

"Only at times like this do you remember that there is a God . . ."

It was true. Whenever I had a premonition that some serious threat was menacing Sylvia or Marcoré, I would weaken in my pride and appeal to that mysterious entity that really seems to be everywhere, even in the very essence of fear. I have never conceived of it as controlling my mind, because I lack religious feeling, but I do respect it and fear it if it attempts to reach me through my wife and my son.

"When I think I might lose you two . . ."

A lump in my throat prevented me from continuing, she turned her eyes toward me again, serious now.

"Do you really love us so much? Sometimes I have my doubts."

I took her back, and as we walked the pounding of the water mill became more muffled, until it died away completely. On the veranda we found Camilo settled in his rocking chair. He was another one who was being ground up and who would soon be reduced to trash. We sat down near him and amused ourselves watching Marcoré playing with the children of the tenant farmers. Dona Emma was in the kitchen, preparing calf's-foot jelly or quince jelly for the convalescence of her grandson. Sabino and Aurora must have been busy with their late afternoon chores. The cattle lowed as they were driven into the corral. Cowbirds sang in the floss-silk tree, near the granary, flocks of doves passed over the patio to dive into the shadows of the orchard. The sadness produced by the late afternoon did not touch the children but afflicted us with a vague uneasiness. I saw my father-in-law wrapped in his shawl, his arms like two sticks of wood crossed over his flat chest, Sylvia very pale, with deep circles under her eyes, her mouth half-open, and I melancholically concluded that they were the ones who caused our feeling of depression rather than the night that seemed to descend out of the forest. They were withdrawing from life, losing their vibration, their presence only brought despondency. The good hours were spent with Marcoré. I put myself on his level and went fishing in the river when we weren't ambushing bumblebees in the passionflower plant, catching them in the red blooms and listening to their desperate buzzing. We climbed the lower trees to spy on the nests or lost ourselves in the fields searching for fruits and berries. We walked softly and spoke in whispers, making a delightful mystery out of everything. His lively little eyes opened wide when he saw dense shadows, his little hand reached for an imaginary pistol in his belt.

"Careful, Daddy! I think there's a wolf behind that mango tree."

Our activities on the farm were a reproduction of those we carried on at home. I taught him how to fly a kite, shoot marbles, fire a sling-shot. Dona Emma did nothing but grumble.

"He'll turn out to be a perfect little tramp."

The truth is that I feel revived in my son through childhood experiences that I supposed dead, and it is as if I were playing with a part of myself that had become detached and animated with a soul of its own.

Now they are coming back, by the end of the week the house will again be filled with the shouts of Marcoré returning from school. He already knows how to read, there is no printed page he comes across that he does not try to spell out, he is always concerned about the correct pronunciation of words. He no longer cries out to the maid: "Dalice, the bell is *dinging*."

Nor does he come in from the back yard any more whimpering and complaining about the red ant: "The *itta* ant *bited* my *itta* finger."

I miss the little child that Marcoré used to be, mutilating words in his own ingenious way, transforming Honorata's cake roll into *croll*. Today he is ashamed of that, his mind is acquiring an exact vision of things, with a propensity toward freedom. The tight lines are being cut, and little by little he is allowing himself to be drawn into the middle of the current.

The knowledge that my son is gradually acquiring about the world is further developed at school with his companions. He knows some hair-raising cuss words which, however, he does not repeat at home. One afternoon Doralice went up to Sylvia, her face red.

"Senhora, you must teach Marcoré some manners. He's been trying to look under my skirt."

Sylvia burst into tears, not because of the gravity of his crime but because she recognized that she was gradually losing her son as he grew older and became initiated into the secrets of life.

Marcoré is changing, his hair has darkened somewhat, a few freckles have appeared on his cheeks and have increased rather than lessened his charming good looks. Julieta's children respect him, are afraid to do any swaggering in his presence. Roberto has held a grudge against him since the stone-throwing incident. He is friendlier with Claudia's children, often runs off to his aunt's house and does not come back until after dinner. My sister is fond of him and treats him with an affection that moves me.

"We drank the same milk," she said to him one day. "I think that's why I like you so much."

Claudia is well preserved, age has not made much impression on her appearance. If only Sylvia had her health, her energy, her ability to assume control. Julieta, although younger, has become worn out, faded, her breasts have shrunken. Armando feasts far from home, there's a whole legion of women in his experience. My mother is still as sturdy as a fence post. Her hair resists the brush strokes of time, turning white slowly. The expression on her face has become perhaps harder since Marcilia's death. She lives alone, with her jasmine shrub. The thrush disappeared long ago from her property. It left no children, the guava tree has never again heard its song.

And what effect has time had on me? Strictly speaking, no substantial change. I believe I still present a reasonably decent appearance. Only my suit measurements in Deodato's book have altered, having become larger. I've retained my strength, Emiliana has not worn me out. I have safeguarded myself, to be sure, during these last two years, by leaving her, sometimes, after having had no more contact with her than futile kisses that she herself initiated. At first she used to protest when she saw me pick up my hat to go out. She would almost burst into tears, would say that I wasn't the same man any more and that I must have found another woman. I calmly argued with her the first few nights when I left early, later I became firmer and convinced her that there was no other woman. Sylvia brightened up when she saw me come home early and we would converse until late at night.

Time has left deeper marks on the city. Colonel Medeiros had to give up his position as mayor because of illness. Jonas, the owner of the creamery, has taken his place. The colonel didn't entrust his last reports to me, Laurindo's paper published them with somebody else's corrections. Perhaps the editor himself put them in order, sending his bill to the municipal treasury for payment. The colonel no longer goes out of his house. He is as listless and depressed as Camilo.

A new doctor has arrived in town. Dr. Camargo, who just recently received his degree and is single. The daughters of Major Dario are undoubtedly having some fancy new dresses made. Dr. Leandro has been talking about moving to São Paulo: it's difficult to provide a good education for children in this provincial environment. Sylvia, who is dependent upon our compadre's prescriptions, is worried about his leaving. I calm her down by pointing out that I've heard him talk about that project for years. The federal tax collector is also new, he has come twice to my office to introduce himself and get oriented. Matos the coffinmaker is as taciturn as ever, always measuring with his eyes every person around him. Paulo has moved far away with his family, having gone to seek his fortune elsewhere. Trains have run night and day along the tracks, back and forth. The seasons have succeeded each other, people complained when the drought was at its worst, cursed when the rains lasted too long. The books in the office have become thicker, marriage banns have been posted and later replaced by others. There have been births, there have been deaths. Aristides' handwriting, only a shadow of what it used to be, records the facts, my signature makes them official. The waters keep flowing past, the water mill grinds away ceaselessly, crushing those who are going downhill. Marcoré is far in the distance, hasn't reached even halfway up the slope yet. He may go higher than his father, may get to see the summit of the mountain. Father Bento wants to make him an altar boy after his first communion, to draw him closer to his flock. He spoke to Dona Emma about it in the sacristy a little before the whooping cough arrived, he sent a message to Sylvia. The boy's father stays out of religious plots. A day will come when I will enter into possession of my son. I am counting on the water mill for that.

Now I am awaiting his return. The hours drag by, there are still three days to go. After leaving the office I'll spend some time at the club, some more at Emiliana's house, I'll make some visits. I'll stroll through the smoke-filled rooms, will hear an indistinct buzzing, vague and meaningless laughter. From a distance Paiva will send me a silent invitation to play a game of chess. I'll have no desire to play, the figures that move about on the chessboard and used to communicate with me have become transformed into mere pieces of wood. I'll see Dr. Leandro bending over the billiard table, taking pride in his playing. I probably won't know how to explain how it is that marbles grew so big, or why one of them is painted red, much less why they are propelled by a cue rather than by a thumb cocked against the middle finger. The balls became inflated and pursue each other on the green velvet. I'll stop for a moment at the card game, will see Gabriel's eyes nervously follow the showdown of the cards. A stupid thing, for a man to get excited over pieces of cardboard. I'll leave there without understanding anything at all about the actions of the men of my town. With Marcoré far away, what meaning can the world have for me?

Elisa also misses him.

"Without the child this house is sadder than the bottom of a well. I can't wait for him to come back."

A good person, sensible, soft-spoken. She does her work with a cheerful look on her face, has never uttered a word of complaint about anything. She goes to church every morning for six o'clock mass, acts as a custodian in religious processions. Dona Emma no doubt thinks the worst about our relationship. She considers me a libertine, a man who would not even respect his own house. At night she won't let Doralice out of her sight, fearing that her son-in-law will take advantage of the young girl. Aristides has the same opinion of me, perhaps would not even leave my goddaughter alone with me. All because of Emiliana, admirable Emiliana who represents for me the aspect of Sylvia that is dead. But nothing really moves me other than my son. Father Bento's judgments, my mother-in-law's rancor and distrust, Aristides' indignation, none of this affects me. I think about Marcoré and I rise above such base matters. I am as faithful to Emiliana as I used to be to Sylvia. They are different parts of the same person, made complete by my love. The gossip that arose in connection with the affair ceased a long time ago. This town of mine normally leads a plodding sort of existence, without any exciting incidents or emotions. It takes occurrences such as the one I became involved in to shake it out of its torpor. Novelties of this kind arouse malicious talk in some, condemnation by almost everyone. The participants are viewed with reservation, like rare animals. At the club it was malice that predominated.

"We missed a good thing. That rogue has the devil's own luck. I wonder what the agent's widow can have seen in him."

Whenever I went there the comments would start up anew, my standing would rise in the conversation groups that formed all around me. They did not know that there wasn't any spirit of adventure in the affair but merely a normal arrangement of life. What they saw in it was animality, unchecked instinct. At the pharmacy the old men would stare at me with envious curiosity, would look at me as if at a reproduction of their past. They all had their own tales to tell, episodes they could identify in each other's stories, and there I was present to revive them. Even Camilo revealed the same feeling. Our relations with each other had not changed at all, and I recall his only comment on the matter, not intentional but formulated during the course of a conversation: "There are things in the lives of all men that are extremely intimate and that others do not know about. In general, women deteriorate after childbirth, and this leads us to look for adventure away from home."

He was in this way offering his justification for my behavior, but I made no reply. I couldn't tell him that I did not know whether or not

Sylvia had deteriorated in the matter of making love, that there was a different reason for my journey to Emiliana, with a stop at Lia on the way. That was one of the intimate, unrevealed things. Propriety prevented me from speaking to my father-in-law and confiding in him. In religious circles the criticism was ferocious. Dona Carmela had stayed away from our house for a long time and stirred up hatred against me. The brotherhoods were horrified and beat their breasts. Father Bento kept clamoring away, poking his finger into the air, like the point of a knife. If he could, he would have condemned to the Inquisition the notary public who had changed from a model husband into a libertine, who had set up a house for his mistress in full view of a respectable community. That nonsense did not bother me, and I let time take care of defining my relations with Emiliana. I was very well acquainted with my accusers, I knew their weaknesses. Those Jesuits did not fool me. Night offered a sanctuary for rascality, and few escaped its invitation. I even had my doubts about Father Bento himself. I had never borne false witness against him in front of anyone, even in the form of jest or insinuation. Not once had I cited his name in my moments of greatest intimacy with Sylvia, when we would discuss the habits of our acquaintances, imagining what they might be doing at that hour. Humanity grappled with itself at night, what it wanted to do was love. Father Bento had the mulatto girl Cecilia as a cook, and I don't know if he would have been strong enough, as a young man, to resist temptation. Juquinha the sexton used to tell me, laughing, that the vicar would put saltpeter on his food to calm his blood. Maybe the salts were not enough and he had to relieve his humors. Cecilia lived there, right at hand, timid, servile, humble, wholesome. Who would blame him if he should make use of her during the worst moments of his struggle? We are all weak, pusillanimous. I can't answer for anybody else in this world, and neither will I accept maledictions and excommunications from anyone. Time and my indifference have caused the wave to subside. Dona Carmela has come back, more voracious than ever, her prejudice

against me has waned. Father Bento's still remains; it dates back to the time when he discovered that I was reading forbidden authors, and it became aggravated when I took a mistress. New reasons for malicious talk have appeared, my own case has fallen into oblivion, it has been incorporated into the normal routine. Only Aristides' distress bothers me. My compadre leads an upright, sincere life, but he has ideas and concepts that are limited by blinders that are more religious than moral. With my comadre it was as if nothing at all had happened, she continued to bestow her friendship on me and avail herself of my aid during their periods of need. My mother has confessed to me that she regretted living so long and having to witness conduct that tarnished my father's memory.

"If you persist in the error of your ways, I shall be obliged to shut the door of my house to you."

Her eyes blazed, her nostrils quivered. However, what was most latent in her was not my father's memory but another one. It grieved her to remember her thwarted plan that involved Adelaide, and she seemed to be vexed with Emiliana, not because of our deceased Mariano, but as if she were the cause of my betrayal of the daughter-in-law that I did not provide for her.

I paid little or no attention to her words and kept letting the days pass by. I rejoiced at her words, in fact, as I did at everything that gave me a feeling of freedom. I did not try to go back to see her, I waited for her to send for me. It wasn't long before she handed Aristides, in the street, a note addressed to me. She wanted to know what had happened to the son who had forgotten that his mother was still living, who did not go to see her any more. That "any more" referred to one month, if that much, and sounded like one of her sorrowful sighs. She had unlocked her door and had received me without any allusion to the reason for my having stayed away. And while Marcilia, who hobbled around but was happy and pleased with the outcome of the matter, stationed herself at the stove watching the water boiling for coffee, I remember that her voice had vibrated in the kitchen, addressing the Negro woman more than me.

"I know very well that one mother can take care of a hundred children, and that a hundred children cannot take care of one mother."

Never again, from that time on, had she made any mention of Emiliana. But in Dona Emma, although mute, reprobation was a living, permanent thing. She would mutter an answer to my greetings between her teeth, would keep her eyes averted and always pretended to be in a hurry in my presence. I knew that this was her nature and that I would have to put up with it until the end. She would spare me her neurotic outbursts only to discharge them without purpose on Elisa or Doralice, who were also already accustomed to the old lady's temper. On such occasions Sylvia would come out of the bedroom, alarmed.

"For Heaven's sake, Mother, don't scream like that. It's bad for the child. I don't want him to grow up nervous and cranky."

"That's the way things are these days," my mother-in-law would yell. "Children ordering their parents about. I can no longer even give orders in my own house. And I want your lordships to know that this house is mine. I'm the one who set it all up when your father and I got married, and those weren't easy times. It's mine, mine, mine!"

And she would beat her breast, in a gesture of exclusive possession. We lordships would exchange glances and could only smile. It wasn't worth the trouble to take her provocations seriously, or to create any unpleasantness that might harm our son's future. Her fit of anger would subside with our withdrawal to our room. A few hours later it would be as if nothing had happened. But Emiliana remained stuck in her throat, that was obvious. She also could see that I was determined not to give Emiliana up, not to give in to threats and innuendoes, and she did not dare to make any frontal attacks. Time has reduced the size of the fishbone, and Dona Emma has softened like all the rest.

Now they are about to come back home. Marcoré will return as thin as a piece of string; the whooping cough has been hard on my boy. Dr. Leandro will give him tonics, and before long he'll be tormenting Julieta with his lordly airs. I'll greet him with a new kite. The September wind is good for kite-flying, and Marcoré will be able to send it word that he has recovered and has come back home. And, above all, that his father is once again a happy man.

Chapter Ten

A cold and windy winter. My stiffened fingers find it difficult to write.
The somber weather, associated with memories that are equally somber, constrains my will and my movements. But I must register the fact
that I lost a part of my life at the beginning of the year: Camilo died
of uremia. He had returned from the farm full of life, would go out
into the back yard in the morning, go walking around the block, leaning on his cane. He had even given up smoking, at Sabino's advice.

"Brother, why don't you give up that nasty habit? You look like a
walking chimney, puffing away at those straw cigarettes night and
day."

He had given it up and had felt better.

"Sabino was right. Smoking was making me sick. Let's see if I can't hold out for a few more years. I'd certainly like to see that boy grow up. He came along late, you two were asleep at the switch."

His cavernous laugh resounded again through the house, a forced laughter that left him gasping. He spent hours dozing on his hammock or listening to Doralice read the newspapers to him. He would call Marcoré to come close, would ask him what mischief he'd been up to. The boy would make up stories, trying to amuse him. Sylvia would pace up and down nearby, without the courage to interfere. When Marcoré walked away, she'd go up to him.

"Better wash your hands, my son. Grandpa is sick."

Marcoré would wash them in the washstand in the bathroom, pensive.

"Does Grandpa Milo have a sickness that's catching?"

"No, darling. But he's always coughing."

She was afraid that her father had tuberculosis and might transmit it to the boy. She recalled Honorata's words: "Always be careful, senhora. An old person's cough can fool you. It doesn't always come from old age."

Besides, there had been cases of illness in Camilo's family. They said that when he was young he had lost two sisters to galloping consumption and that he himself had been a sickly child. But Dr. Leandro attributed his bronchitis to smoking, which he had given up only in the last few months. Nevertheless Sylvia tried to protect her son, didn't want to expose him to any danger, even if imaginary. Sometimes she would feel remorse and say to me, "I feel sorry for Father, but that wheezing of his worries me. I want our son to be healthy."

I'd calm her down, telling her that Dr. Leandro would be incapable of making any error of such proportions in his diagnosis.

"I hope you are right. The intimacy of those two worries me so! The only thing they don't do is eat off the same plate."

His friends would come to see him, inquiring about his health.

"I'm getting along all right, just waiting for the end to come. One of these days it will arrive. I didn't expect to live so long. I come from a short-winded family. Sabino will be the only one left to carry on the strain."

He seemed resigned, the idea of death upset him only because it would separate him from his grandson.

"After all, you only die once. What good does it do to be afraid? The worst of it is that the ones you love remain here and you're sure to miss them bitterly when you're on the other side."

The final crisis came when it was least expected. Dr. Leandro had examined him and had called in his colleagues Aleixo and Camargo. Their verdict after the conference was that Camilo could not escape. Dona Emma was not happy to see Dr. Aleixo there.

"That fellow ought to choose between medicine and politics. I don't want him giving us any of his opinions about Camilo's health."

But the doctors' prediction proved correct and my father-in-law lasted only a few hours. Marcoré cried out desperately, clinging to his mother.

"Don't let them take Grandpa away!"

He took his departure in a slow procession in which the whole town joined. Businesses closed their doors, work at the city hall was suspended. Everyone came to say good-by to a man who never raised his voice to anyone, who would get up from his chair to shake hands with the poor and the humble who came to ask him for favors. It was said of Camilo that he brought to his work the peace that he experienced in his family life and that that was what made him such an imperturbable man. A lucky dog who had married a good all-around woman, an excellent companion. Those poor blind souls did not realize that that wrinkled emaciated body had been a prison of almost constant torment concealed under the civility with which he had always treated everybody.

I can see in front of me the plaque given to him as a tribute by his friends, a long time ago. The bronze has blackened but remains intact. The words at the bottom are the most visible: "On the occasion of his retirement as a notary public." I remember his tears when Teodorico had made the speech at the city hall, describing him in flowery terms. A thanksgiving Mass was said, and Dona Emma and Honorata had served a luncheon to his most intimate friends on a table set up under the tamarind tree. It was one of the greatest days in Camilo's life. I'll have Aristides polish the plaque, so that the homage will be renewed.

Sylvia was overwhelmed with grief at her father's death, deep circles underlined her eyes, bruised from weeping.

"I never realized how fond I was of Father. What a fine, happy, and tranquil man, and how good he was to all of us!"

Marcoré went about despondently for several days, sobbing in the corners, smoothing the hammock in which his grandfather had spent most of his time. The lace trimming had become frayed, the handles had yellowed, the hooks had rusted. Dona Emma called Elisa one afternoon: "Fold this up carefully and put it away in my basket. It makes me feel that my old companion is still sleeping in it and won't wake up. I can't bear that memory any more."

Her face seems to have darkened, marked by fatigue and sleeplessness. And perhaps by a feeling of guilt in relation to the deceased. No one can decipher what goes through that contradictory mind, for it keeps oscillating between a state close to infantilism and a kind of hallucination that makes her feared by others. She must be aware that her volatile temper brings unhappiness to those around her, but she has never modified her conduct even in the presence of her grandson. For many days after Camilo's death she locked herself in her room, and only for the boy would she open the door. She spent the time in prayer and in the voluntary penance of fasting. She knew that her husband had passed away dissatisfied with the companionship she had given him; now she engaged in small sacrifices for the salvation of his soul. She eulogized him to the skies, placing him above all men who previously existed.

"There was nobody like him," she would say. "He was incapable of deception, of disrespect. I only hope my grandson follows his example."

A dark cloud passed over Sylvia's face.

"That he was the best goes without saying. What I could never understand was the reason for your jealousy, since he was such a good man. We certainly could have been happier and lived in perfect harmony. Father cannot have died contented with the little that we gave him."

The pendulum impelled Dona Emma into the dark corners, while her nostrils quivered and her expression darkened.

"I always was an undesirable in this house, always the one who caused unhappiness. But your father was free to act as he saw fit, he could have obtained a legal separation and kept company with other women. A person is not a clog."

It is impossible to talk in harmonious terms with a person dominated by impulsiveness and suspicion.

"It's not that, Mother. You always twist the meaning of words, you get insulted over the slightest thing. We all have our own faults, what we never learned was how to tolerate one another."

Dona Emma's breathing quickened, her impatience made her crack her knuckles.

"So I'm completely useless. I can't even understand what people tell me. I am the one who should have died and not Camilo. He loved life, while I have always hated it, ever since I lost my mother. She was the only person who ever understood me."

Marcoré stood there, distressed and perplexed. He saw his mother, so fragile in her black dress, turn paler, her almost transparent hands tremble. He looked at his grandmother's face and read in it unconcealed bitterness. In me, a muffled sense of revolt that was gathering force and threatened to explode. He could not understand why persons that he loved so much spoke in that tone, accusing each other, tormenting each other, almost hating each other. Heavenly Father, what was going on that should cause these three people, to whom his little life was bound so closely, to be at the point of coming to blows? All because Grandpa Milo was not there any more with his air of tranquillity to impose respect on all, make them all listen to reason. Sylvia went up to him, kissed his hair.

"Don't look so sad, my son. Grandma is very nervous and tired."

And, turning to Dona Emma: "Let's at least spare this child, Mother."

Her steps faltered, I rushed to help her, took her into the bedroom. Dona Emma called the boy over to her.

"The only one who understands me in this house is my grandson. He is the only one who knows that the grouchy old lady doesn't wish anybody any harm."

We miss Camilo, the insecurity in which we always lived has increased since his death. Sylvia has no strength to fight with, she just manages to keep going with the drops that Dr. Leandro prescribes for her. The doctor has repeated insistently: "You must not get excited, comadre. Your heart needs peace and rest."

He takes her pulse, consults his watch, uses the stethoscope.

"If you avoid excitement, you'll get to bring up your grandchildren."

Sylvia smiles and shakes her head skeptically.

"I know you are just being kind to me. I won't even see my son go to high school. I will soon be taking the road my father took."

Marcoré is in the third grade, he always receives high marks on his report card. He is studious, locks himself up in his room and remains there hour after hour poring over his books. He discusses geography with Doralice, does sums for Elisa, reads aloud for his grandmother to hear. Sylvia feels proud.

"This boy will go a long way. When it's time for him to study engineering, we'll have to move away from here."

Forgetting that she is ill, she boldly and animatedly faces the problem of her son's future.

"We'll go to São Paulo," responds Dona Emma, busy with her sewing. "Maybe we'll find a house near Dr. Leandro."

The doctor is going to move by the end of the year. He's leaving us in order to find better resources of education for his children. Sylvia shudders: she is reminded of her condition. The yellowness in her cheeks is accentuated again.

"It would be so good if we could go with him! My treatment wouldn't be interrupted, I wouldn't have to have another doctor examine me."

She trusts her compadre, wants to remain under his care. No one else would merit the same confidence.

"The problem is the office," Dona Emma intervenes. "We can't leave it alone with Aristides."

Her greatest desire would be to move far away with her daughter and grandson, leaving her son-in-law chained to his official record books, delivered definitively over to Emiliana. But she knows that I wouldn't part from Marcoré for anything in this world.

"The office is our least problem. We'd have Aristides made a notary public and leave him in charge. Couldn't we, dear?"

I tried cautiously to dissuade her, showing her that it was still too early to think about the matter. When Marcoré became old enough for college we could then give some thought to moving.

"Until then . . ."

Sylvia sighed, sank back into her apathy. We had mentioned age, and the certainty of a premature end came back to distress her. No one would have said, before Marcoré arrived or during his first years, that that most perfect constitution would weaken to such an extent that it would wither away like a decaying tree. Dr. Leandro's scientific knowledge cannot explain the ruinous transformation. He talks about coronaries, about imbalance, without knowing what agents are producing the loss of equilibrium. The pregnancy seemed to have consolidated her health, had even rejuvenated her, made her more attractive. She had not told the doctor about the sacrifice she had imposed upon herself. So many times had she vacillated about confessing it to him!

"I don't have the courage to speak to him about it," she used to say. "Let's suppose that it is the reason for my illness. On no account would I go back on my word. I don't want anything to happen to Marcoré because of me."

So Dr. Leandro does not know the extremes to which Sylvia has been led through love of her son. He believes merely that the critical age came early and that that has disorganized her circulatory system. Or else that the insufficiency is congenital and that her tardy maternity has revealed it. The conjectures that Dr. Leandro makes in the conferences with his colleagues, dividing responsibilities, do Sylvia no good at all. Her snow-white body, which had aroused so many emotions in me, no longer functions properly, seems unable to be put back in order. Her deep mourning weakens it even more. I insisted that she should not wear the black dress that Dona Emma had made: all it did was make her more depressed.

"I can't, dear. I must wear it until the anniversary Mass. What wouldn't they say about me if I didn't wear mourning for my father?"

I tried to show her that she was ill and therefore excused from the hateful convention. No one was going to censure her for such a small matter and, if they did censure her, what difference would it make?

"It may be that everyone would understand and accept it, except for one person: the one who made the dress."

She smiled with an effort, and sought to change the subject. I came back with a powerful argument: Marcoré. It would do harm to our son to see her dressed in all that black which made her look so thin and pale. The boy would become upset, his health would be injured. Dona Emma, who was the one who went out of the house most often, would keep up the good name of the family, wrapped in her black scarf. Sylvia would not give in, delaring that, on the contrary, I ought to wear a tie suitable to the situation. I did as she wished, and now everyone who passes along the street to the square can see me through the window, wearing mourning for my father-in-law. But the old tie I'm wearing around my neck has little to do with my feelings about Camilo's death. His memory is worth more than a yard of crepe, and I miss him more than I can say. Considering everything, I never thought about my own father with the same tenderness and sense of loss. Nor with as much respect. They are the two deceased persons who stand out in my memory, but Camilo with greater stature and significance.

I thought of composing a few sentences for Laurindo's paper, describing the best aspects of Camilo's nature as a human being. I spent two or three days in concentration, trying to put my ideas and reminiscences in order. I could not write half a dozen phrases, however, without the figure of Teodorico insinuating itself between them and raising the problems of syntax. I was afraid of committing solecisms that would be picked out like lice by the professor and crushed in my presence between his thumbnails. Indeed, the subscribers to Laurindo's paper might be less likely to look for the moral traits of the dead man than for my grammatical errors. I convinced myself that my meager reputation as a notary would be at stake, and, seizing this pretext, I tightened the knot on my tie and crushed the sheet of paper. Camilo's memory rested in peace.

Today, when I return home, I do so with the insecurity of one who enters a house that lacks a ridgepole. As if the walls were threatening to topple and the roof were going to fall in. The main beam of our dwelling is missing, we no longer have any guaranty of stability.

At Sylvia's request, I have shortened my visits to Emiliana: she feels nervous knowing that there is no man in the house. Camilo was old and halting, but his cough, at least, commanded respect. Marcoré had good intentions, but he also needed protection, perhaps more than all the others. Sylvia's fears are imaginary, we've never had any cases of robbery, not even of fruit or stock. Nevertheless, I took to coming back early. Emiliana at times tires me, she is too demanding, never stops complaining. It's preferable to put up with Sylvia's complaints, which are always gentle and related to the state of her health. I try to overcome my sleepiness, in order to entertain her, and we talk until late at night. I tell her what's new at the office, what is going on at the town hall, the malicious rumors that circulate at the club. She appears quiet and pensive, and during a pause asks irrelevantly, "Do you like my mother?"

I am flabbergasted, unprepared, taken by surprise.

"Now why should you ask that question?"

"I keep thinking, dear. If I should die suddenly, how will things be at home? Mother is impulsive, but she has a good heart. Try to get along with her, promise?"

I make a vague gesture, of dubious meaning.

"Don't think about that, you're going to be all right."

I recalled the fluctuations of Dona Emma's temper. Untimely screams, threatening heaven and earth; at other times transformed into a child. I recalled her on an occasion years ago, teaching Marcoré to clap his hands at the winged ants that flew about among the trees.

> *Ant, ant, fall, fall*
> *For the sake of your father's soul.*

Another time, seated with her grandson on the edge of a flower bed, she kept making him repeat an affectionate verse.

> *A tight embrace,*
> *A deep sigh,*
> *An endless love.*

She could have always been like that, but it was the fits of fury and anger that predominated, the screams and insults, the threats to leave and never return. Age has defined her psychology more clearly: determination is portrayed in the line of her pallid lips, a vigilant distrust is evident in her eyes that are marked by networks of tiny wrinkles. The deepest ones, which descend the length of her cheeks, reveal a terrifying rigidity. Her movements are still rapid, her voice has lost none of its imperious accent. Alongside of Sylvia, their ages seem reversed. Dona Emma rules the house without the slightest interference on our part. She decides on matters involving the kitchen, she deals with the tradesmen, regulates Marcoré's schedule, polices Doralice's love affairs. The position of authority suits her temperament, and it is preferable that things be this way so that order will be maintained. Sylvia arranges things so that my association with her mother is restricted to mealtimes. We miss Camilo. Death shattered our alliance, left me out in the open. I have proceeded with caution, to avoid dangerous situations. Not for Sylvia's sake, really, for she is already far removed from my inner world, but for Marcoré, in whom I live more than I do in myself. For the sake of my son I keep acting with prudence, avoiding Dona Emma's thunderstorms.

Camilo's plaque emerges from the shadows of the afternoon. It's necessary to polish the letters on it, to call my father-in-law to keep me company. Aristides left a long while ago, the cold wind is announcing nightfall. The thought of withdrawal that dominates me exists solely with Marcoré's interests in mind.

Chapter Eleven

Dr. Leandro has moved away with his family. The council unanimously passed a declaration of regret over his departure (an irreparable loss for the city), drawn up by Teodorico. The club gave an elegant formal dance in his honor, people came from miles away to attend. The station wasn't big enough to hold all the friends that came to see him off. Dr. Leandro had tears in his eyes, while Dona Regina sobbed like a fountain. Only their children were happy, proud at exchanging their small-town citizenship for that of the state capital. Dr. Leandro would have to give up his billiards, the easygoing talk at the bench in the pharmacy, renounce the popularity that won him a lifelong seat on the municipal council. His country patients would never again fatten up a suckling pig especially for "our good Doctor," no one would travel miles and miles with a pole full of chickens, a half-dozen bricks of raw brown sugar, cheese and curds, to offer them to him with a timid and humble smile. He knew he was trading the good name he possessed for a position of anonymity, and that exchange troubled him deeply. To give up the familiarity he enjoyed with his people, whose personal problems he perhaps knew better than did Father Bento, to lose the right of entering into all houses with the intimacy of an obstetrician and compadre. This was hard for a man of his temperament. Dona Regina, so charitable and unassuming, was enduring on her part the terrible threat that she would not be able to go visiting or receive visitors. They had warned her: "That custom doesn't exist there."

Her astonishment was almost childlike.

"Good heavens! How can people get along without going visiting?"

So they had left for their adventure in the immense and noisy world. Sylvia felt abandoned and that night complained of palpitations. Dr. Leandro's recommendations didn't help at all.

"I am leaving you in the hands of Dr. Camargo. I guarantee that he is a better doctor than I am."

That wasn't the point, their prescriptions might be the same, the difference lay in their images. His enormous figure, his sanguine face, his sincere look, his friendly words, infused more confidence than all the remedies in the world. Dr. Camargo is tiny, a half pint, he has a sickly and long-suffering air about him.

Sylvia wept at her last visit.

"He may be very good, but he can't compare with you. This is the last time I'll ever see you. You will soon receive news of my death."

Dr. Leandro's voice trembled.

"Don't talk nonsense, comadre. I will still have all of you some day as neighbors in São Paulo. And I am thinking about making Marcoré my son-in-law. If he decides to study medicine, he can be my successor. My son Lucio is going to study law."

The suggestion had pleased Sylvia. To be Dr. Leandro's neighbor in the capital, to guide Marcoré into a career in medicine, to see him marry one of the doctor's daughters—that's the dream that lived in her imagination for several days. She selected her daughter-in-law, prepared the wedding dinner, imagined a flock of grandchildren. Renata was the one she chose. A little brunette with wide eyes and black hair, she would contrast nicely with Marcoré. She was studying piano, enjoyed household tasks. That was the one who would make her a good daughter-in-law, and if God gave her life and health, she would try to arrange that marriage. She had moments of euphoria, would embrace me closely, her eyes lit up like a child's.

"Oh my dear, if only that should happen! I'd be the happiest woman in the world."

But her depression would soon return, and her awareness of her condition would bring an air of unhappiness back to her face.

Dr. Camargo has been coming to see her, but he spends most of the time talking to Dona Emma, sitting at the table in the breakfast nook. The old woman bakes corn bread for the doctor, strains the coffee for him herself, surrounds him with special attentions. Dr. Camargo won her over by telling her that she reminds him of the mother he lost many years ago, for they both had the same manner of speaking.

"That's just what I've been telling you, doctor. There's no one like a mother. I can see you are a goodhearted man."

The doctor is very pleasant, but his face is darkened by a shadow that suggests intimate problems. As far as anyone can tell, he isn't planning to get married: Major Dario's daughters have wasted their hip-swinging. He lives in the hotel, plays cards at the club, goes fishing on Saturdays. He has inherited a good part of Dr. Leandro's clientele, is called from afar, operates at Charity Hospital, presides over meetings. He has become friendly with me, comes by the office every so often and remains a long while, sometimes silent, sometimes leafing through the books absent-mindedly, as if he were only looking for company.

Besides Sylvia, his greatest concern is for Colonel Medeiros, who is getting weaker every day. I went to see him one afternoon recently in his sickroom. His eyes, sunken in their orbits, stared at me, his bony hand made a sign to me. I drew near, sat down at the side of his bed. A wisp of a voice came out.

"Camilo tricked me, he went first. I will soon be on my way, too. If you want to send a message to him, tell me while there's time."

He smiled, Dona Clarinha approached and scolded him.

"Keep still, you're not allowed to talk. Be patient, nothing is impossible for God to do."

The room smelled of stagnant urine, Dona Clarinha went to open the shutter that faced the back yard. In the rectangle stood a cherry tree dotted with red. I immediately thought: oh, if Marcoré were here! He'd climb the tree and have himself a treat. The woman undoubtedly guessed my thought, she went over and closed one side, cutting off my vision.

"It's very windy on this side."

The old lady is a real skinflint. She keeps everything carefully measured in the kitchen, the leftovers go into the cupboard, stay there for days and days. She makes manioc meal dressing with meat that's a week old, she won't throw away even one wormy bean. Camilo told me all about her, he knew all of her eccentricities.

"How is your son?" she suddenly asked me.

In a flash I became reconciled with her and proceeded to go into minute detail.

"If he takes after his grandfather, he'll turn out fine."

My aversion returned, I scowled at her. Contemptible old lady. She is prejudiced against me because of Emiliana, does not recognize in me any good qualities that I can transmit to my son. Why take after the grandfather and not the father? I am not unworthy of Camilo, nor do I judge myself inferior to this person or that. Each one has his own good and bad characteristics. Colonel Medeiros, who was lying there, wasting away, was he any better than I? He had had plenty of women, it was rumored that on his farms there were countless laborers who were children of his, whites, mulattoes, high yellows. The old man wasn't particular, he grabbed the first woman who crossed his path. With Thomas' Tita hadn't he had two boys and two girls that he had sent to study in São Paulo? These were consummated and accepted facts. Father Bento frequented his house, ate at his table, conceded him long-term indulgences. But with me it was a different story, I was a sinner and unrepentant. Dona Clarinha could go straight to hell. Marcilia used to detest her for her meanness, would call down curses on her. She would knock on her door with a tray of candies and tidbits. The woman would pick them up one at a time, weigh them in her hand, put them back in place. The crumbs remaining on her fingers she would raise to her mouth. She discussed prices, haggled, abused the black woman by claiming she was out to rob her. Marcilia would go away, trembling.

"That old turkey puts her dirty hands on my sweets and doesn't buy a thing. She'll see where all that stinginess gets her. When she dies, she'll have to remain hanging in the air like St. Peter's mother."

Aleixo the gardener had already told me one day, "I don't like to talk badly about anyone. May God keep me from that. But Dona Clarinha is very miserly. When I work there she rations things out to me little by little."

She barred the cherry tree from my sight, diminished me to magnify Camilo. Marcilia's prediction was correct. In Father Bento's heaven there could be no room for that old hag, and in hell they wouldn't want her. She would remain like a soul in torment, wandering around in space in search of her cupboards full of leftovers.

"Wife, how about getting some coffee?"

The wisp of a voice still ruled. The pair of slippers went off to the kitchen to give orders.

Colonel Medeiros kept wheezing, the heat brought perspiration to the roots of his hair. He no longer dyed it, now the color that was natural for his age was taking over.

"They say that the little doctor is causing trouble at the town hall."

I defended Dr. Aleixo, energetically declared him to be innocent. But the dim eyes did not entirely believe me. Down deep the doubt persisted.

"Well, they say he is bleeding the sewer budget."

I protested, raised my voice, gesticulated. Accidentally I struck the urinal under the bed with my heel. I got up feeling nauseated and looked at the cuff of my trousers. It was dry. Breathing with relief, I redoubled my efforts. Dr. Aleixo was a good man, the Colonel should pay no attention to slander. I walked over to the window, cast a glance at the cherry tree, a new burst of anger inflamed me with an idea.

"These people of ours aren't worth a cherry, Colonel. All they know is how to defame others."

Dona Clarinha is the one who wasn't worth anything, but I generalized the insult in order to let off steam. The somnolent eyes blinked behind their arches seeking mine. They seemed to say: "You've probably done your share, too." Humanity was the same in all hearts, it tended to see evil everywhere. I recalled the words I had heard old Faustino utter once: "The heart of man is a road that only God knows." Colonel Medeiros was on his last legs, about to kick the bucket, and yet he was using up his strength to slander Dr. Aleixo. The most he had done, in years and years of administration, had been to plant trees and flowers in Market Square, rebuild the bandstand, construct roads that served his own convenience. He forgot he used city employees for his personal benefit and that he borrowed building material from the municipal storehouse that was never accounted for. Hell, the law begins at home. Now the office of the executive was in the hands of a young man who had a college education and spoke English like a foreigner, and they were starting a campaign against him because he was trying to improve the water supply, pave the streets in the neighborhoods, construct sewers. The Colonel was annoyed, was gathering up what strength he had left to lambaste Jonas' successor.

"He's a good man. I'll answer for him."

I lowered my voice when I saw that Dona Clarinha was entering with the tray of coffee. It tasted stale and bitter to me, I asked for more sugar. She served it to me herself, cautiously.

"Did you stir it well?"

The Colonel, resting against his pillows, drank his coffee in gulps sucked from the saucer. There were folds of skin on his neck, his ribs showed. Recalling Camilo, I sighed, seized by a deep longing for my father-in-law. Everything comes to an end in this world, reduced to a state of wretchedness like that, for one reason or another. Sylvia was like an old rag, even though she was still young. Dona Emma took pride in her strength, but it would waste away some day. Gabriel of the telephone company imagined that a whistle was a bagpipe and he had remarried at the age of seventy, against the will of his children. The result: he dragged himself about winded and drooping. As for Dona Clarinha, did she think she was going to last forever?

"As I said, Colonel, I'll answer for him."

We were alone again, he was still resting against his pillows. His malicious little eyes suddenly lit up and seemed to inquire: "And who will answer for you?"

"Nonsense, a sewer is a luxury, it's for large cities only. Here we have plenty of land. Just open a pit and that's all that's necessary. I don't see any need to spend all that money. Let them stop all that tomfoolery, because they'll never convince me."

He had said this in one breath and ended up gasping. To catch his breath again, he stretched himself out at full length.

"But, Colonel, a civilized city that has any notion about hygiene cannot do without that service."

The old man ran his handkerchief over his perspiring forehead, blew his nose, wiped his mouth. I could see I was wasting my breath talking about hygiene to a man as sloppy as he. Again I thought of Camilo: he also used to use his handkerchief indiscriminately for small emergency cleaning. And he didn't hesitate to lend it to Marcoré for the same purpose, if Sylvia didn't happen to be present.

Soon the Colonel regained his breath.

"And how about those jackasses, the councilmen, who won't put up with a veto by the mayor? We miss Leandro already."

I left there, saddened. The old man was ending his days eaten up by spite, Dona Clarinha hadn't retreated an inch in her stinginess. Death was lurking at their door but they acted as if it were just an ordinary visitor. They owned three farms that produced coffee and cattle, several houses that they rented, lent money out at interest. Their sons-in-law were getting restless, their eyes on the legacy. If they thought about the Colonel, it was to wonder how much he was going to leave them, whether he had made a will, whether he had any debts. Dona Clarinha would take care of their hunger.

Aristides and Bernardo are leaning over the books, the clerk is instructing his son. I took him in two weeks ago at the request of my comadre Augusta, for Aristides wouldn't have had the courage to ask. Partly because of his make-up, partly because of the uncomfortable relationship that had existed between us ever since Emiliana entered my life. My comadre brought the boy to my house, declaring that she was leaving him in my care. He has pimples on his face, an insecure voice, thick lips like his mother's. I examined some things he had written, school compositions, letters asking for imaginary jobs. He composes better than Aristides and his handwriting is acceptable. There he is practicing, learning how to handle the machinery of this office. Aristides is proudly transmitting his knowledge to his son, makes him admire the father who used to write like an artist. Polite, diligent, quick to learn, I'll benefit by having him take Aristides' place. At least, I'll have a change in scenery. My compadre is worn out, he is going to retire to his repose, the old part will be replaced by a new one. His long-suffering air has begun to annoy me. He is

no doubt quite ill, needs medical treatment. But he would keep working until he fell out of his chair, without opening his mouth. He
wouldn't ask for a leave of absence, wouldn't mention his son's name
to replace him. All of his capacity for pleading is used up at the
brotherhood. For the poor of St. Vincent he spends Sundays knocking on doors, travels to farms, writes letters to big shots in other
cities. When it comes to doing something for his own family, words
fail him, he clams up. If it weren't for comadre Augusta, Bernardo
would not be getting initiated into this job. My goddaughter has become quite a young lady and comes to see me occasionally. She sings
in the church choir, takes part in the fiestas at the parochial hall. If
we didn't have Doralice, she could be at our house taking care of
Marcoré. Dona Emma would not like it, for Susana is the affectionate
type, is fond of kissing. She even kisses me on the cheek, hugs me, puts
her face close to mine to talk to me. Without any ulterior motives,
without the sensualism of Mateus' daughters. Those country girls
had gone back to the farm, were at the Boa Vista farm, hoeing coffee.
Barefoot, their sturdy legs sunburned, their gluttonous eyes ogling
every man who might pass by. They were married, but it was impossible to tame the restless blood that Mateus had transmitted to
them. The old man had calmed down with age, was working like a
dog again in order to pay off the mortgage. He was hoping to do it
before the Colonel's death, he didn't want any trouble with heirs.

The world I know lives its petty life, it resembles Sabino's corral.
The cattle move about on the pastures in different groups, they eat,
work, bellow, make love. The calves run around, leap over the thick-
ets. The old oxen are taken away, headed for the cleaver. Aristides
will take off his yoke, will also slowly approach his end. Everything
is as in a corral, from the mooing and bellowing to the wiles and bad
habits. There's a difference only in the odors. Colonel Medeiros' bedroom had an evil smell. I prefer the odor of a cow barn. We live with
mooing and bellowing all around us. My mother on one side, Julieta
on another, Emiliana, Sylvia. All of them with their sorrows, their

woes. The Colonel bellows weakly, Dona Emma stridently. Father Bento attends to his herd, fails to calm it down. Sometimes I consider that the act I committed with Sylvia which resulted in Marcoré's existence, was a criminal one. Why inflict on another person something about whose value we have doubts, something that we have already experienced without being convinced that it was worthwhile? Marcoré was becoming aware of reality, was beginning to understand that it has its harshness, its hidden side. He lived with three persons who were his most important connection with the world, but he could see the dissension that existed among them, see them treating each other with excessive formality, his father and his grandmother silent in each other's presence, his mother stretched out on a chair, always weary. Why was it they treated each other as strangers, so harshly and stiffly, without any affection? The expression on his little face clouds over at the table, he lowers his eyelashes in sorrow. The noise of the tableware is disturbing, even irritating. The one he understands best is Doralice, with her there is nothing but joy. They lose themselves in the back yard, argue, play hopscotch. He is fond of school, walks out of the house with his briefcase, a happy look on his face, freed from prison. Poor Marcoré! So early has his disenchantment begun, still just a boy and already he has shadows in his expression. Sylvia observes this in despair.

"If I had guessed that our son was going to be a melancholy sort of child, I would have prevented his coming. Poor little thing. He isn't to blame for anything—his grandmother's temper, my wretched health. I feel so weak, dear, that I don't even have enough strength left to love him."

Marcoré, meanwhile, adores her, is afraid of losing her and of being unable to go on living. So many times, when I've come home late, I've found him lying beside her, his face tranquil, calm. Sylvia makes a sign to me with her hand, urging silence, as when he was small, and indicating that I should go into the other room to sleep, in Marcoré's bed. I go there, lie down on the kapok mattress that Dona Emma had made. I enjoy the freshness of the pillowcase, the soft pillow seems to retain the perfume of his hair. I sleep better there, without Sylvia's interruptions. She asks me to count the drops, asks me what time it is, goes over to the window to breathe. In Marcoré's room it is different, everything is wholesome, happy, expansive. The pictures hanging on the walls represent hunting scenes cut out of magazines and framed in cardboard by his grandmother—an alert dog, a hunter aiming at a bird that has taken flight. There is also a movie cowboy, in full regalia, his hand on the holster on his belt. All childlike, of an admirable purity. Over the head of his bed, a crucifix that his godmother gave him. He still says his prayers at its feet, when he goes to bed and when he gets up; he must pray above all for health for his mother. Sylvia does not feel strong enough to love him, she has given me that duty. I don't want any other, I'll renounce everything in order to enslave myself to Marcoré. Nothing means anything to me except my son, his happiness, his joy in living.

Chapter Twelve

I have no feeling of guilt for yesterday's incident, which I hasten to record because it may bring a new condition into our lives. Sylvia regretted the outcome of an ambiguous situation that had been prolonged for many years and that had become more tense with Camilo's death, but she has not accused me of acting badly. She wept the whole day, locked up in her room, didn't eat, didn't touch her medicines.

"What's the good of continuing treatment, if my whole life is going to be a martyrdom like this? Mother could have learned from Honorata how to be moderate, not to say things without thinking. Her temper ruined Father's life, and ours, and now is poisoning Marcoré's."

It happened that the boy had gone out to play in the square with his friends, and Dona Emma, who was passing by on her way back from the post office, had grabbed him by the ear.

"No grandson of mine is going to spend his time loafing on the streets. Go home this instant, you wicked boy! Learning things from those little sneak thieves who signal to each other by whistling!"

I heard him crying in the back yard, went to find out what the trouble was. It was ten o'clock in the morning, the islands of shadows were beginning to form under the trees. I found him sitting on a root of the tamarind tree, sobbing softly. My voice tremulous, I asked him what had caused those tears. Marcoré didn't want to utter any complaint against his grandmother, said that it wasn't anything. I imagined that he had been beaten in a fight with some of the kids and that it was humiliation that prevented him from confessing. I was going to insist, when Doralice, who always comes to his defense, came up to tell me the truth. His flaming ear, where he was holding his hand, enraged me. I lifted him up violently, pushed him toward the back gate.

"Run off and play, and stop your whining. A big boy like you crying like a baby. I thought it was something serious. I'm the one who decides what you can do. There's still a man around this house to give orders."

I was yelling, afraid to be heard in the kitchen and wanting to be at the same time.

Marcoré went out, timid, with listless steps, uncertain. He had a frightened look, his taste for playing games had cooled. I went in and heard the uproar Dona Emma was making in the sewing room. She was stamping her feet, kicking the chairs, slamming the closet doors, screaming that she wasn't used to being deprived of authority.

"Well, make up your mind to get used to it," I answered in a low voice, more to myself.

Sylvia had come in, distressed, I explained to her what was going on, perhaps exaggerating the details. She tried to remedy the situation, but it made matters worse.

"What nonsense is this, Mother? It's most unpleasant. People will think this is a madhouse."

Her distorted features, glimpsed through the open door, caused a strange impression. It was an animal standing there, possessed, uncontrolled.

"Everyone turns against me. I could never count on anyone in my life. Even my own daughter thinks I'm crazy."

She had begun to cry, as her anger broke out again. Mine also was boiling, and Sylvia feared a scene that would lead to a rupture of our relations. Elisa had moved away from the stove and slipped cautiously outside, avoiding having to take sides. Doralice in her turn had followed after Marcoré.

"That treacherous girl had to go and stir up trouble against me, but she'll pay for it. An ulcer will eat her tongue away. I can't set a hand on my grandson without having everybody jump all over me. This is too much. I'm like trash in my own house."

She eased up on slamming the doors but kept stamping her feet violently.

Sylvia was also weeping.

"You always enjoyed making a scene for the slightest reason, just to see me unhappy. It would have been better if we had lived apart."

I needed air, felt my hands perspiring. That outburst of Sylvia's gave me strength, a courage that I had never had. I awaited the old woman's answer in order to attack, to lay all the cards on the table.

"Don't let that worry you," I heard her cry out in a suddenly serious tone. "I won't stay here another minute, I'm not going to put up with this hell."

I walked toward the kitchen and retaliated: "You've stayed here until now because you wanted to. Nobody asked you to stay."

Sylvia came toward me tottering, I reached out to support her before she could fall to the floor. Her legs went limp, her arms hung loosely, her head fell back. I carried her into our bedroom and remembered our wedding night, vague and distant. I set her on the bed, grabbed a bottle of perfume from her vanity and put it to her nose. I was afraid that she was dead, and for a moment I desired it, so that the other one would die of remorse. It took her a few seconds to recover her senses, while my anxiety increased. She saw me kneeling beside the bed, glanced around the walls, tried to understand. Dona Emma's screams brought her back to complete consciousness. She pulled me by the hand, made me sit down beside her.

"This had to happen some day. What is surprising is that it took so long. I'm only worried about Marcoré. He is still too young to witness scenes like this. He could have been spared this, the poor child."

There was a strange noise outside now. I got up to look out the window. With a hatchet in her hand, Dona Emma was destroying her plants, her ferns, the orchids hanging from the branches of the imperial acacia.

"I'm going away from here and I don't want to leave anything to remind you that I ever lived in this house."

The hatchet blows sang out on the flower pots, reducing them to fragments. The dicksonia ferns were torn to pieces, bits of foliage flew off in all directions. She went to the front of the house and trampled upon the beds of violets, cut the tea rose bush off at its roots, laid waste the clumps of caladium. She was like an unchained Fury and I began to think that she had really lost her mind.

Sylvia got up with my help and walked slowly over to lean out the window.

"Don't be a child, Mother. Why all this hatred, this desire to destroy?"

"Do you think it's a small thing for me to be thrown out of my own house? I'm being driven away like a mad dog, but I won't leave one sign of my existence."

"Good Lord, what nonsense! Nobody has thrown you out of the house. Just think for a moment what consequences this will bring to Marcoré's life."

"I'm the only one who is supposed to think about consequences. Nobody thinks about me, nobody respects my age. I won't stay here another day."

It was true, neither of us paid any attention to her age. Bordering on seventy, she did not look like an old woman because she had an intense, indomitable vitality, yet she did not receive the respectful treatment that was due any human being in her condition. We were always disposed against her, we took too seriously her slightest fits of anger. I recall the mornings when she got up late, depressed, with deep circles under her puffy eyelids.

"What's the matter, Mother? Are you ill?" Sylvia would inquire.

"No. I hardly slept last night."

"It was something you ate."

"No. I began to think about life, one idea coming after another, and my eyes stayed wide open. I didn't doze off until morning."

"Thinking about life? Nonsense. If there is anyone who doesn't have any problems it's you."

The old lady stirred her coffee and sighed.

"That's right, daughter. I don't have any problems. But each person knows about himself, and I don't know whether we know enough."

That was the way it was, we did not even admit that she could have any problems.

I analyzed more deeply our behavior toward her and began to feel pity for her inconsistent nature, her changing moods. My decision to carry on our violent quarrel began to weaken. After all, the corrective she had applied to the child had been bland and perhaps timely.

I saw her throw the hatchet on a flower bed, climb the steps to the front door, disappear into her room. She kept muttering inside, while she dragged out suitcases, opened and closed drawers noisily. She was preparing to move out.

Sylvia was sitting quietly in the rocking chair, her head leaning back, her hands resting on her lap. I looked at her from the terrace, through the open door, and my intention to seek peace became stronger. A strange and harsh old age was stamped on her young face. Her skin was still smooth, without wrinkles or blotches, while only a few white strands stood out in her combed-back hair. But the fatigue in her eyes doubled the number of her years, her defeated and tormented expression marked the end of an existence. I felt a sudden calm. I went in and sat down beside her. I took her slight and trembling hand, kissed it, held it between mine. She turned to look at me, smiled.

"We could have been so happy!"

"We are happy," I protested. "Don't we have Marcoré?"

She straightened her head, her expression continued thoughtful but not absent.

"In spite of my illness, we could have been very happy. Mother's temper ruined everything."

"All this will pass. Soon everything will be forgotten, the flower beds will be restored, new plants will be seeded."

"I know that, dear. Everything will go on in the same way, as always. Ever since I was a child, when I heard her quarrel with Father because of the jealousy she felt, she has been threatening to move out and never come back again. It finally becomes tiresome and annoying."

Her distress, her air of suffering, the passiveness that was natural in her and that her illness accentuated, awakened a new impulse in me: to prove to her that I was capable of acting with decency and nobility. I tried to gather courage to go up to Dona Emma and ask her forgiveness, without going into long explanations. I would set aside my pride and make this sacrifice for Sylvia. Not even Marcoré at that moment played any part in my intention. What I would do would be only for the sake of that wonderful woman who had first come into my life with her sweetness, her gentleness, her love. It was the mother of my son who sat there, wasted away in body and spirit. I ought to save her from any new sorrows, with a tiny act of renunciation and humility. I would gain strength from her confidence, she would talk to Marcoré about my action, the child would think highly of me. I stood up with no further hesitation, took her head between my hands and whispered my intention to her. I felt her quiver as her eyes brightened, causing her fatigue and inertia to disappear.

"I always had faith in you, my angel. I can see that everything isn't lost. Go right now, she'll melt completely. Mother has a temper, but she's goodhearted."

I bent down again to kiss her when the door to the room opened. Without changing my position, supporting myself on the arms of the chair, I glimpsed Dona Emma standing in the doorway, observing the scene. Her appearance was different, although her obstinate expression persisted.

"You can talk about me all you like. I have already made my preparations. Now you two will be able to live as you always wanted to."

Sylvia had gotten to her feet.

"Don't be hasty, Mother. We were just now going to ask for your forgiveness."

"It's too late now. There can be no forgiveness for the harm you have done me. I have been driven out of this house and I won't set foot here again, even to see my grandson dead."

She went out into the kitchen, calling for Elisa. She tried to control her voice, her steps, her gestures, in order to disguise her emotion.

Sylvia had come back to her chair, sobbing.

"How is it possible to come to an understanding with a person who is so distrustful? It would have been better if she had left long ago, or if I had died at childbirth."

She spoke convulsively, angrily.

"Father was an extremely unhappy man. He never fooled me with that carefree air he put on. I saw him weep many times when he was alone in his room. I was only a young girl, but I remember it very well. Even as a daughter I haven't been happy. That fiendish temper that hurts everybody!"

Her sobs redoubled as she gnawed at her wrists, half-crazed. I got angry, trying to call her back to reason. Dona Emma, on her way back to her room, stopped at our door.

"Tears won't do any good any more either. They can only be tears of satisfaction over my leaving."

I raised my hand to Sylvia's mouth, prevented her from retorting. It wasn't long before my mother-in-law went out, accompanied by Elisa, whose eyes were red.

I suddenly lost control of my own actions, as if I were caught in a whirlpool. Everything began to whirl around me, without my being able to do anything about it. A heavy weariness forced me to sit down, someone said that it was time to act. "Ask for forgiveness and everything will be all right." A distant and fuzzy voice to which I paid no attention. Could it have come from Sylvia or from within me?

I saw her breathing heavily at my side, I got up with an effort, went into the kitchen to get a glass of water from the jug. I drank slowly, with each swallow my internal order gradually recovered, objects seemed to resume their normal places. I filled it again, carried it in to her.

The bedroom door opened once more, several packages were transported by Elisa to the front terrace. Sylvia's weeping was now serene, nourished by the sight of that baggage that represented all of her past. An existence of almost half a century was enclosed in the hampers with their silver-plated clasps, in the bundles tied with silk thread, in the baskets and handbags. The best of her dreams, her childhood, her joys, her tribulations, her hours of dejection which perhaps had prevailed above all the others, the mistakes, the good words and the bad—it was an entire life parading past in the strong arms that strained and moved in front of us. A melancholy vision of fragments that had long been buried and were now being taken to another dwelling, like the ashes of the dead.

Sylvia's expression cleared up. I dried her eyes and made her blow her nose in my handkerchief. The sound of Timoteo's car approached and died beside the gate. Where would Dona Emma go?

"A strange thing: Mother is leaving our house and I don't feel anything, either happiness or sorrow. Perhaps it's because I'm certain that she'll return soon. Maybe even today, who knows?"

She couldn't believe that she had left forever, it was as if an old threat were being acted out in a dream, tenuous, improbable. How could she accept a definitive separation, unless it were through death? Camilo had gone away forever, but he had been carried off by an incurable sickness. Marcilia had died of old age, as had Honorata. They would have preferred to continue living with us, even if it meant living in rags and almost blind. Now Dona Emma was also leaving, but of her own free will. Our lives were being truncated for no sensible reason, and this stunned us.

We remained silent for a few minutes, waiting for Elisa to reappear. Dona Emma had gone around the house, in order to avoid being seen. Timoteo started the motor, the car drove off toward the square. Elisa seemed to take an eternity to return to the living room. Her face was troubled, upset. Her red cheeks held traces of tears.

"Did my mother say where she was going?"

Elisa nodded, with her eyes lowered.

"She's going to Lauro's farm. She'll spend a while there, later she'll come back and rent a house to live in."

She wasn't going very far away, would soon be back among us, as if she had just gone out for a walk.

"Please excuse me for interfering, Dona Sylvia. But what has been going on in this house has been a lot of confusion. People should talk to each other calmly, to understand each other properly. The one who is going to suffer from this is the child, who has always been very much attached to his grandmother."

I lost my temper, yelled at her, "Well, he'll just have to get unattached. His father is still alive and capable of bringing him up."

Sylvia begged me to calm down. I fell silent, panting.

"You lost patience, senhor, every time anyone talks about your son. Nobody wishes him any harm, he's always in our thoughts here. But you really should excuse Dona Emma's peevishness. She's not young any more, her nerves are upset."

Sylvia intervened again.

"All right, Elisa, let's change the subject. What happened, happened. You can attend to your duties now."

She went into the kitchen, haughtily, her behind squeezed into her tight skirt. It was Dona Emma who made her dresses for her. They examined samples of cloth, discussed prices, selected patterns. They would spend hours and hours talking in the sewing room, between meals. That's what the trouble was. Elisa had really been bought, she had become Dona Emma's accomplice. Dona Emma sewed for her, had ensnared her. Sylvia had made the same discovery.

"You know, dear, if Mother does not return we'll lose Elisa. Better ask Claudia to see about getting another cook for us."

Elisa would leave, another one would come. The essential thing is for Marcoré to remain. He was the only one who couldn't go away without throwing our lives completely off course.

The morning was almost over, Sylvia had gone into the bedroom to rest. Marcoré had stayed away in the streets for an extremely long time. I got frightened, wondering if he could have gone away with his grandmother. I walked about the back yard, removed the debris caused by Dona Emma's hatchet, ran my eyes into all the corners with a new and strong feeling of ownership. Then I went back inside and tried to read, but the words became jumbled up, made no sense. I started to turn on the radio, drew back in time, remembering that

Sylvia might be sleeping. The house was silent, as if there were a wake for a corpse. In reality, Dona Emma seemed dead to us, perhaps never again would her screams be heard there, nor those outbursts of temper that used to intimidate us. The walls retained the echoes, as did our memories. Dona Emma had suddenly become extinguished, she was nothing more than a distant image.

Marcoré came in, flushed, long after the noon hour had struck. He had been playing in the square, did not yet know what had happened. Timoteo had passed by there, but he had not seen that the person in the car was his Grandma Nena. I sent him to the bedroom to talk with Sylvia. Mother and son did not appear for lunch, nor did I insist on calling them. Doralice served me, her countenance gay, relieved. Here was somebody who was on my side, who loved my son as much as his grandmother did, who appreciated a boss who was incapable of disrespectful acts. Cute, with a nicely shaped body, her lips red and full, her breasts taut in her light blouse. I had seen her grow up, gradually become a woman, without ever being goaded toward her by a single evil desire. Elisa could say the same thing. During the many months we had spent alone together in the house, when they had taken Marcoré to Sabino's farm, not once had it occurred to me to take advantage of her to relieve my boredom. On the evenings that I did not spend with Emiliana, when I stayed up late reading, she would bring cinnamon tea and cookies on a tray to my bedroom, would sit down on a chair and start talking about the ones who were away. Not that she is a bad-looking woman: except for the wart bordering on her left eye, she possesses convincing attractions. But I wouldn't be the one to practice that despicable act in the bed in which I slept with Sylvia, where Marcoré had been born of our love. Elisa couldn't make me weaken, even Emiliana couldn't, if she should happen to come in the middle of the night looking for companionship. I thought about these things while having lunch, trying to build up my self-esteem, to exonerate myself, find reasons for my behavior toward Dona Emma.

Marcoré spent the day in the bedroom with Sylvia, crying, inconsolable over his grandmother's departure. He refused to eat, did not go to school, paid no attention to Doralice's invitations to play in the back yard. Sylvia attempted to console him, saying that it was actually a good thing, that soon his grandmother would come back and that the arguments and quarrels would be ended forever.

In the afternoon Marcoré came to the office, near closing time. Grief-stricken, pale, he seemed almost shrunken in his duck outfit. He greeted Aristides and Bernardo, embraced me silently. I felt my heart swell. At last I was going to enter into exclusive possession of that which was mine, of the greatest boon I had in life. Marcoré would now become more dependent on his father, with his mother ill and his grandmother absent. I felt that egoism was dominating me, but I found the sensation good and did not repress it.

"Don't worry about what happened, son. It will all be ironed out in time."

Aristides had found out what had occurred. No doubt it was the only topic of conversation in the whole town. The good-for-nothing son-in-law had kicked his mother-in-law out of the house, was killing his legitimate wife with the grief he caused her. Timoteo had surely been charged with the task of spreading the news. Father Bento would not go that far, he was prevented by canon law. He had been called in to counsel Sylvia, had heard the whole story from her. They had thought at the sacristy that it was a matter of death and they began preparing for the viaticum.

"Dona Sylvia is dying."

The vicar, however, had taken the trouble to telephone first and Sylvia herself had answered, requesting a simple confession. He had gone there, had calmed her uneasy soul, had sat down at the table to have the lunch Elisa had prepared. He had spoken to Marcoré, had given counsel to his altar boy. But he wouldn't be the one to divulge the disarrangement that had come into our lives. Timoteo is the one who had trumpeted it about, unable to keep his mouth shut about the news when he returned from the farm. He must have gone to Conrado's billiard hall, taken a swig, and spread the news: "A big flare-up over at the notary public's house."

Aristides was getting ready to leave, embarrassed, without knowing what to say. Bernardo was in less of a hurry and seemed unconcerned. He didn't have enough experience yet to grasp the meaning of such a situation. Aristides understood its gravity and the consequences it might bring with respect to Sylvia's health, the influence it might have in Marcoré's upbringing.

They both said good-by, I soon left with my son. On the way it occurred to me that there was still enough light for a session of target-shooting with the Winchester. He brightened up at the idea, made me quicken my pace. In this way I drew him out of his sadness and managed to get him to smile.

In the evening the phone rang, it was Lauro with news about the old woman. She had arrived safely but was in a vile temper and kept talking about ending her days all alone even if it were in the infirmary of Charity Hospital. Sylvia hung up, pensive.

"I'm afraid that Mother will never come back to live with us." And sighing: "May it be as God wills."

This is what happened yesterday. I am now waiting for Marcoré to come home from school for another session of shooting.

My conscience does not weigh heavily on me, I feel as if my heart were bursting with happiness.

Chapter Thirteen

Five months have passed by since Dona Emma moved out. She spent some time on Lauro's farm, traveled, wrote to Marcoré, spoke to Sylvia over the phone. She is coming back and has told Elisa to rent the pitched-roof house that is attached to Adelino's bakery; she had heard that it was vacant and that the rent was reasonable. Her accomplice had taken the necessary steps, has had the little house whitewashed, the floor waxed, the grass in the back yard cut. She is going to leave our service and go to live with the old woman.

This would have been a golden age if it hadn't been for my mother's meddling in our affairs. She had begun to visit our house every day, she gave out orders, changed the arrangement of the furniture. She yelled at Doralice as if she were an employee of hers, criticized Elisa over wastefulness in the kitchen. There was no let-up in her rude and annoying vigilance; she was always on the move from one end of the house to the other, seeking to impose her authority. Marcoré became aloof and resentful over that interference with his liberty. He used to enjoy visiting his "other" grandmother in her house in the suburb, spending hour after hour deep in the orchard, poking around among birds' nests or shooting with his sling-shot at hornets' nests. But he wasn't at all happy to have her right there beside him acting like a jailer. The grandmother who had moved away used to scream over the slightest thing, used to quarrel and threaten, but she did have her good moments, sometimes was as nice and gentle as the pullet that came up to eat cracked corn out of his hands. Grandma Nieta was different, she never smiled, always looked cross, spoke seriously and with deliberation. What my mother aspired to was to replace the one who had moved away. To take her place, to occupy the sewing room with her own things, to assume the management of the house. I could see in Sylvia's expression the fear that I might invite her to live with us. I smiled at her, ran my hand through her hair.

"What are you smiling at, dear?"

"At your fear that I will ask my mother to stay here with us."

A blush enlivened her pale face for a moment.

"Nobody can hide anything from you. But don't you think I'm right?"

"Yes, just as you've always been in everything. You can stop worrying, I won't invite her. Marcoré is also worried. Tell him that it won't happen."

It pained me to talk like that about my own mother, to refuse to have her stay with us, to demonstrate that I could be fond of her only at a distance. But there was sufficient reason for this in the attempts she had always made to interfere in my life, in her prejudice against Sylvia, in her rivalry with Dona Emma, who was always the object of unjust remarks and innuendoes. I could not admit her into our midst, it would be to run the risk of new conflicts. She also has a temper, takes offense easily, is always susceptible to the most idiotic suspicions. She still feels strong, walks with firm step, ages very slowly. Her hair has taken on an ivory tone that imprints a greater coldness on her impassive face. She could have been a great help to us if her disposition had been different. She could have taken care of Sylvia, replaced Dona Emma in Marcoré's affections. But it wasn't wise to try it: even the boy could see the result.

After two months, or a little less, she began to space her visits until she broke them off completely. Later she sent me a note via Alcina, Evangelina's aunt, who had come from Sabino's farm to live with her. It said that she wasn't going to come to our house as frequently as before, that the one who rides on a horse's hindquarters does not control the reins, that the place for undesirables is in their own corner. She would remain there at our service (she underlined the word) for our hours of need, since a mother is always the last one to be sought, even though she is the only one who is faithful. It was in these tones that she gave vent to her feelings, in that slanting handwriting of hers which was so familiar to me and which time had not deprived of its firmness. I showed it to Sylvia, who read it slowly and commented, distressed, "The same case as my mother's. Except that one expresses her sentiments while the other one represses them."

That was indeed true. The same authoritarian and domineering temperament in both of them, the same difficulty in dealing with each one. They must have suffered, each in her own way, for while one used more words than she should, the other shut herself into a deliberate muteness, expressing herself by means of dry monosyllables, never looking anyone straight in the eye. It was bad with Dona Emma, it would be worse with my mother. It would be senseless to attempt to substitute the latter for the former. The problems would be the same, not so much in form as in substance.

Sylvia has always hit the nail on the head.

"There's no question but that our mothers suffer from persecution complexes. They get insulted over the slightest thing, yet they consider that they have the right to say anything they want to to us. They complain about being abandoned, they constantly blame their children for imaginary faults. Down deep they must feel extremely unhappy."

One of them had suddenly left, the other had tried to take her place. My mother's calculations had gone wrong, had brought her a new disappointment. Dona Emma is announcing that she is now going to be back in a house of her own, where only her voice of command will be heard, where no other person's desires will clash with hers. Elisa has made arrangements for her reception. Her ally's abode is undoubtedly shining, the windows all washed, the floor polished, the walls without a single flyspeck. Elisa can go, we already have someone to take her place in the kitchen. What we have to do is keep an eye on Marcoré, set up a schedule for his visits to his grandmother. He could easily be duped by her, for my enemy has the means of attracting the boy. She knows how to bake a biscuit like nobody else, she makes delicious cheese custard. I have been worrying about it, sometimes I wonder if it would not have been preferable to maintain the previous situation. I believe I may have acted hastily in provoking my mother-in-law's departure. All because she had brought the boy in from the street by his ear. All things considered, there wasn't any reason to fly off the handle. The old woman had made a fuss over nothing, it would have been better to let things take their course. Everything would have quieted down, as on so many other occasions. Now it would be necessary to keep him at home as much as possible. Maybe it would be a good idea to have Lazaro the carpenter make a two-wheeled trap for Marcoré to go riding in in the mornings and after school. We'd get a pony from the farm, Chico would make the reins and the breastband of different colors, the spokes of the wheels would be painted blue. My boy would go riding through the streets, clicking his tongue at the horse, sounding his horn at the street corners. He would drive through Cathedral Square like a rich man's son, a gang of kids running after him pleading for a ride. In my day hadn't I myself often begged bicycle rides? There is the risk, though, that Marcoré might find the contraption made to order for him to use for visiting his grandmother. It would be better to think it over some more, sound him out cautiously. He appeared excited over the news about her return, even though she is going to live a distance away from us. He has forgotten that she made him suffer also on the day she left by including him in her fury. The old woman had taken scissors and had cut up the crazy quilt that she had made for him herself. It had grieved him to see the colored pieces spread out on his bed. He kept picking them up tenderly, while his sobs increased.

"Why did Grandma do this?"

He no longer remembers the episode, or perhaps he is planning to ask her to replace the torn quilt. I shall try to be forceful, I'll defend my rights: either the quilt or the trap.

I interrupt the composing of my notes in order to attend to the young servant who has arrived from Colonel Medeiros' house with a notice of bereavement. The ex-mayor has finally passed on. That contradictory soul is on its way to give an accounting of its "ministration" on earth, which, if it wasn't brilliant as a man or as a citizen, nevertheless did inspire envy. Whoever does record it will admonish him disdainfully, "My dear Colonel Medeiros, please watch your tongue. The correct word is 'administration.'"

Father Bento had a busy time during the last week, although his sciatica kept bothering him. He spent his days perched on his buggy, riding up and down, his bay horse going at its gentle gait, taking snoozes under the warm April sun. Its master also drowsed on the driver's seat, but they would arrive safe and sound at the dying man's house. The Colonel's death pangs lasted a long time: just when they would give him up for dead he would astound his family by thrashing about on the bed. His sons-in-law seemed impatient with this resistance which delayed them from dividing up his lands. For her part, Dona Clarinha was upset because she was obliged to serve coffee day and night to the always numerous visitors. There would be a shortage in the new crop, there might not be even one sack left over to send to Father Bento. But a man who had been cantankerous all his life would not be likely to abandon his obstinacy in the face of death. Only two days ago I saw him stretched out under his bed covers, breathing heavily through his half-open mouth, his eyes dull and distant. The room stank, I felt nauseated and withdrew into the parlor where people were talking in whispers, but without restraint. They talked about everything except the sick man. It was as if he didn't exist any more, as if he had dissolved into the past. Those last convulsions no longer participated in our world. Gardelim, the automobile dealer, was proudly enumerating the advantages of the new models as if he himself were the manufacturer. The cylinders, the gears, the brakes. When Dr. Aleixo came in, Fonseca the dentist called him over to our corner.

"Come over here, doctor. We're getting into a subject that will interest you."

Dr. Aleixo sat down, listened attentively to Gardelim's explanation, spoke about replacing the municipal truck and getting a street sprinkler. Aguiar, the chairman of the council, just kept shaking his head importantly: "We'll see about that later on. Who knows whether our colleagues will understand the necessity . . ." Fonseca jumped up from his chair as if he were wielding a pair of forceps. He defends the mayor's policies and tears into the municipal council. What colleagues? A troop with ears two feet long. Were they already planning to pigeonhole the project? Aguiar reddened, but swallowed the insult which was meant for him also. He got up and went into the sick man's room. Fonseca resumed his attack: "A council presided over by an ass like that, who doesn't know how to put two sentences together! Unfortunate town! That's why we're not progressing." And he lambasted the majority, probably because they had denied him the chairmanship of the board. When Fonseca's indignation was at its height, Dona Gabriela Tristão and her daughters came in, strutting like peacocks as always. They nodded distant greetings to all sides of the room. Fonseca, excited, gesticulating as if he were in a courtroom, answered in a loud voice, "Good evening, Dona Cabritela."

At the other end of the room by now, the woman turned around for a moment, scowling.

"Excuse me, Dona Gabriela."

The correction sounded comical and we couldn't disguise our laughter. Dona Gabriela is full of airs, inordinately arrogant. The nickname we have given her—"little kid goat"—is the one that Fonseca thoughtlessly let slip out. Everybody enjoyed the mistake, including Garcia, who was sitting a short distance from our group. He half-opened his wolflike mouth and his shifty eyes came to life. He always remains aloof like that, unhappy with his split lip, angry at the world. He is definitely not one to engage in idle talk, he doesn't believe in wasting words.

As Dona Clarinha appeared with a tray of coffee, we reminded ourselves about the sick man, recomposed our expressions, fell silent. We were going too far. Colonel Medeiros was taking leave of his pleasant little provincial life and it was necessary to respect this moment. He didn't know much about the workings of syntax either, and yet he had made a fortune, had governed the town, was leaving behind him a name that everybody knew. He was going away against his will, had no desire to part from the piece of earth that belonged to him. This hour called for composure and respect.

Fonseca was embarrassed over the incident, or must have been worried about the danger of losing a wealthy patient. Dr. Aleixo got up every once in a while to go in and take the dying man's pulse. It seemed to me that I was reliving episodes out of my past, when years before the same Dr. Aleixo would disappear into Camilo's room and stay there for a long time, making endless examinations. The only thing that was not repeated was the anxiety with which I awaited his return to the parlor. Of course, Camilo was a part of my inner life, whereas I can't say that I felt any more than a bit of sympathy for Colonel Medeiros. Dr. Aleixo came and went, frowning. Sometimes he would stop to meditate and then would say out loud, if he didn't see any member of the family nearby, "Amazing resistance. I've never seen anything like it. It's his arteries that are feeding his heart."

Fonseca, in order to relieve his embarrassment, asked him for explanations and the doctor proceeded to deliver a lecture on physiology. I tried to strike up a conversation with Aguiar, who had returned from the bedroom with that scowling air of his that no one takes seriously. But the chairman was uncommunicative and wouldn't open his mouth. Near an Austrian sideboard, Juca the shoemaker was telling his troubles in detail to Costinha, who was nodding his head sleepily.

"It all began with a little fever that seemed like nothing but I ended up spending a fortune on medicine and almost lost my daughter."

He added, with an unhappy air, "My life has been as hard as a curbstone, Costa."

Under a print of the Holy Family, Dr. Miranda was listening to Pedreira discourse on stamps. The collector spoke unhurriedly, and the deputy seemed to be listening to his stories with interest.

A little beyond, Renato the schoolteacher kept looking with his hard eyes at the different groups, suspicious that someone might be saying something nasty about him. He held his cane, made out of a bull's pizzle, across his legs, in silent warning. A weapon feared by all, for it can cut as deeply as a steel wire. I cautiously removed my glance from his, affecting naturalness and friendliness. I believe I managed to smile at him. The fact is that the teacher isn't at all slow about demanding satisfaction.

The whole town, in short, was there, big shots and little ones. They came in treading gently, speaking in whispers, with a great show of gravity and contrition. They asked after the sick man, sat down and changed the subject, raising their voices. There were conversations going on throughout the house, in the dining room, in the kitchen, in the bedrooms, on the veranda in front. Dona Clarinha's tray visited each one of the little cliques. I observed to myself that that behavior was reproduced exactly at public demonstrations. I sought for an example and, although I'm not sure why, the procession of the Deceased Lord occurred to me. Perhaps because I had heard the name of Father Bento in a snatch of dialogue.

It must have been about eleven o'clock when one of the Colonel's daughters passed by us, her eyes red with weeping. I remembered Sylvia being equally agitated on the day when Camilo was buried. And I began to think about how human affairs resemble each other, how life repeats itself in all experiences. The same sure things, in good and in evil. Maria Candida's grief-stricken eyes distressed me, a deep sadness touched me. She was one person who was suffering over the old man's departure without thinking about the property he would leave. Her tears were not false, like those of the rest of the family. She loved her father and was full of grief to see him breathing his last. Could Sylvia's despair have been any different when Camilo left his house in a coffin? It was exactly the same, and yet men lived disunited, simulating a solidarity resembling the husk of a gourd. If you drove a nail into it you would find it all hollow inside. There were Aguiar and Fonseca, two old friends and compadres, separated by politics. Why didn't people understand each other, why didn't they control their passions? Everything would come to an end, everything would come to naught. I suddenly found myself sentimental in the presence of Maria Candida's mournful look and I isolated it, from among so many others, in order to develop a bit of a theory about human relations. When I turned toward Salim, of the dry goods store, the image of Dona Emma sprang into my memory and I tried to think of something else. Let everyone live in his own way and as best he can. Foolish to try to play the moralist. There was no solution for the world's complications. I left Maria Candida with her grief and went to see Emiliana. The night was calm, concealing men's secrets. I thought about the Colonel's death pangs, felt a beginning of remorse, slackened my gait. That diabolic fellow would be capable of dying while I was enjoying her. After all he was one of God's creatures who was hanging on to life for fear of death. That was a matter in which experience repeated itself for everybody. It was disrespectful to violate that anguish of his with moans that did not come from sorrow. I stopped underneath a lamppost, dominated by indecision. Just then beyond a mud wall there broke out the horrible yowling of cats joined together in love. I became startled, then irritated by that shameful behavior, and my indecision disappeared. The figure of the living Emiliana prevailed over that of the dying Colonel.

Now they were coming from his house with the invitation to the funeral. Even long-drawn-out death pangs must come to an end.

"Well, that's it, Bernardo. We have to close early. Colonel Medeiros has handed in his chips."

Aristides' son turns his pimply face toward me in surprise. My merry tone seems out of place to him. He does not understand how the black-bordered letter can arouse such cheerfulness in the notary public. What he does not know is that I shall spend a few hours with Marcoré until the departure of the funeral procession. I'll go home, grab my shotgun, and call out for him to come and pepper with me those Roman pigeons of Tonico Matias that feed in our chicken yard. I won't waste time changing my clothes. Sylvia used to have enough strength to protest, "Please, dear, don't go out to play with Marcoré dressed like that. Put on an older suit."

And Dona Emma won't be there to watch me like a hawk, following me around and looking for reasons to break out into reproofs.

"That child is going to turn out to be a rowdy. He's always got a firearm in his hands. One of these days he'll shoot somebody in the rear. And I won't be to blame. I'm tired of warning."

Nobody will deflect Marcoré's aim at the pigeons. Bernardo cannot understand, he knows nothing about life. He has just recently learned how to handle the books in which the Colonel's name will be entered among the departed. He does not know what it is to have a son, to be able to play with him as an equal. He does not know the greatest happiness in the world and finds it strange that mine at this moment is linked to a man's death.

I give him the facts to be entered in the register, crumple up the death notice and throw it into the wastebasket. The contact with the mournful piece of paper causes me to shudder. I'll need to wash my hands, have them nice and clean to help Marcoré adjust the gun.

Colonel Medeiros has gone, Dona Emma is about to arrive. Two events that are associated and that urge me to be near my son.

Chapter Fourteen

Fifty-two years old, on November 15. I'm afraid my machinery isn't what it used to me, it's slowing down, getting somewhat slack. Lively activity tires me out, and Marcoré won't forgive his father's incipient old age.

"You can't keep up with me any more."

I can't, and I'll be less and less able to. This is true also in my relations with Emiliana. She suspects me of having another woman, when the mere fact is that my former impetuousness has lost its vigor. She still feels hale and hearty and is always ready for love.

"Let's take it easy, my dear. Remember that I'm not a child any more."

She whimpers, her plump arms encircling my neck. I tell her that at my age it's a natural thing, that everybody's strength weakens, that it's necessary to use it with prudence. At first she refuses to accept the arguments I offer impatiently, but she ends up by resigning herself to the situation.

"As long as it isn't because of some other woman . . ."

There was nobody but her, I vowed, swearing by Marcoré's happiness. Her distressed look became serene, her breasts heaved in a sigh. The truth is that I am no longer man enough for Emiliana, or an adequate companion for my son. The demands that each one makes brings on a fatigue that almost kills me. It's evident that the weariness and exhaustion of maturity are arriving sooner than I expected.

I took a long look at myself in the mirror this morning as I was shaving. It was an unpleasant encounter because of the dissatisfaction it provoked. My reflected image seemed to contain a condemnatory accusation. It was vexing to look at it. No comforting or approving gesture, but rather censure and discontent. This morning I read the failure of my life in those eyes refracted against me. I had never penetrated beyond their cold and polished surface. I had never paid much attention to them, and today I surprised a negative message in them. I have passed the half-century mark, I don't know how much farther I'll go. No matter how long I live, however, I'll never forget that mute interview. I learned that it is easy to escape the questioning glances of others, but that it is difficult to face the questions we ask of ourselves.

The truth is that I could have given some utility to my life, by fleeing from pride and dispersion, from my natural inclination toward the easy and the immediate. I would have provided Sylvia

with happy memories only. I would have freed my mother of the sentiments that make her unhappy, I would have made of Dona Emma an almost lovable person. It would have been sufficient to visit my mother once a day, bring her little gifts, let her give me her blessing, simulate the obedience and the homage that her nature requires. My mother-in-law would have been satisfied, for her part, to receive a kiss on the forehead when she came out of her room in the morning and another when she retired at night. She would have liked to have me take her by the arm, when I got home from work, and let her lead me into the back yard to show me her plants, to hear me praise her green thumb. She would have curbed her temper, would not have made herself feared, nor would she have quarreled with any-one over the slightest matters. However, I deliberately had refused to give either of them the affection they expected from me. A gratui-tous refusal, perhaps founded on the weak reason of desiring to see them engaged in disputing an exclusive place in my love, with a kind of authoritarian insistence. It would have required little effort to divide myself between both, to bring them together as an instrument for the common happiness. It would have been beneficial for all, be-ginning with Marcoré, whose growing-up could have taken place with no worries except those natural to his age. I have also remained aloof from my sister Julieta, on purpose and even with a spirit of malice. What I should have done was forget our childhood conflicts and help her solve her more serious problems. Only with respect to Claudia do I feel at ease. I have never refused her anything. On the contrary, I've always given her more than she asked for and I have always been deeply interested in her children's development. I have favored her out of affection, but whenever I outdid myself in gen-erosity I must have been moved by caprice, thinking about poor Julieta. I don't know whether Claudia's death wouldn't grieve me more than that of any other person to whom my life is linked. More than that of Sylvia, more than that of my own mother. Marcoré is be-yond any term of comparison, he has dimensions that do not fit into any normal scale. For him also I could have been more complete. It would have been enough for me not to have gotten upset over Dona Emma's cantankerousness, thus permitting him to have his grand- mother living beside him. But it was precisely for him that I acted senselessly and provoked the division in the family. The image in the mirror is not unaware of my past. It would have been better not to have delved into it. This account-taking has left me with a sensation of emptiness, guilt, instability.

My features are likewise changing. Light but visible lines in my cheeks, my eyes puffy, my hairline receding, a few white strands discreetly scattered here and there. An air of general fatigue, a lassi- tude of body and soul. The notary public is on his way toward re- tirement.

My melancholy state, however, did not originate with this morn- ing's encounter. There is a matter that is more serious and is irreme- diable. Sylvia is approaching the end, we are close to our final separation. She has spent two months in bed, distressed, troubled. At every moment she finds it difficult to breathe, turns purple and lies helpless. Dr. Camargo treats her like a daughter, leaves her only to lend a hand at his office.

"Lie quietly until I return. I'll come back right away and tell you more stories."

In her unhappy eyes there appears a plea for him not to delay. Dr. Camargo knows how to calm her, less with his medicine than by means of oratorical devices. Of a religious rather than a scientific spirit, he keeps diverting her with episodes from sacred history, the lives of the martyrs, the works of the saints, which he knows thor- oughly. That is how he manages to keep Sylvia quiet, to diminish her suffering. When the doctor leaves, Claudia assumes his post. She sings to lull her to sleep and the effect is almost immediate. The room becomes enveloped in a peace so pleasant that I am ready to close my eyes and die also. Leoncia takes care of household matters, often aided by my mother, who frequently comes in the afternoon to see her daughter-in-law. Marcoré has become depressed, Sylvia's deterioration has affected him terribly. He did fairly well on his examinations, was promoted to the eighth grade. He knows that his mother is doomed and he is afraid. He kneels at her bedside, kisses her hand that now consists only of bones, leans his head over her with affection. Sylvia smiles, grateful for her son's love. She no longer weeps, because her body has become shriveled, the springs of her emotion have dried up. But she knows that she will be missed by the boy, her son who cannot stay far away from her, who wants to have his mother always within the sound of his voice so that he can feel secure. She surely remembers that sometimes she used to get annoyed with his excessive insistence on staying close to her, thus limiting her freedom, when he was a little tot who had just taken his first steps. She would leave him playing with his toys and escape with me into the back yard, to go for a stroll hand in hand. It wouldn't be long before the tearful little voice would be calling for her, seeking her near the house.

"Mommeee! Mommeee!"

We would come back, Sylvia slightly vexed:

"The little rascal won't let me go away for a minute."

Dona Emma would observe, "The yoke isn't easy, daughter. I warned you."

His unsteady little steps would come to meet us, a glorious smile on the cheeks where his tears were streaming down. She would take him in her arms.

"Did you lose your wickedness?"

And she would stifle him with kisses.

Now the wickedness would be lost forever. Marcoré would have no one to tell his nightmares to, no one who could pull thorns out of his feet without hurting him, no one for whose protection he would pray at night. The person who meant everything in his life, who was his reason for happiness and sadness, was dying. He would leave the bedroom, go out into the back yard and cry, leaning against the trunk of the hog plum tree.

Dona Emma has not come to see her until today. Leoncia called on her innumerable times on her own, urging her to make peace with her daughter before death separated them forever.

"I won't go, she doesn't need me. I said that I wouldn't set foot there again and I won't. You have the wrong idea about me. Old people keep their word."

She reflected a moment, then proposed, "Only if she should be taken to her mother-in-law's house. Even then I'll think about it for a while first."

Claudia spoke to Father Bento, pleading for his intervention. The vicar shook his head in disbelief, but promised to do something.

It grieves Marcoré to see his mother and grandmother separated. He can't understand how this can happen with two persons of the same blood, one born of the other. It must be the working of what was called in the catechism "a great sin." What would Marcoré understand by "a great sin"? The fact is that he prays in his room endlessly, imperturbably, concentrating with a seriousness that disturbs me because I sense that during those hours he reaches heights that I can not attain. He goes to church, lights candles under the niches, leaves alms in the coffers, takes holy water with his eyes half-closed.

In the month that preceded Sylvia's crisis, Dona Emma moved into the house she had rented. Elisa had left us the evening before, had gone to have lunch ready for her. Leoncia had come to take her place, everything seemed to go on as before. Only Marcoré's habits had changed. After coming out of school he would go first to his grandmother's house. It wasn't long before he would stay there, once in a while, for dinner. Someone would telephone from the bakery.

"They told us to tell you that the boy is having dinner at his grandmother's."

The individual talking would attempt to conceal the fact, but we knew that Elisa was standing beside the phone, whispering the message. Always perceptive, Sylvia observed, "This isn't Mother's doing. It's that imposter who is getting the boy in her clutches."

Dona Carmela is probably also carrying on her wiles. She has transferred her allegiance over there, has seldom come to see Sylvia, and then only in passing.

"It doesn't matter much to me whether that self-centered woman comes to our house or not. Frankly, I'd even prefer that she not come. Now she has taken to helping herself in Mother's kitchen. Well, much good may it do her," Sylvia said in a burst of energy.

In my opinion, the prime mover was probably Dona Emma herself. She knows how to win the boy over with affection, she spoils him. Perhaps the boy felt more at ease in the company of that grandmother whose feelings were so easily hurt but who also could be tenderhearted and solicitous. I even suspect that she attempted to bribe him by giving him small sums that I saw him deposit in a clay bank, kept behind the oratory.

"What do you plan to do with that money, my son?"

He turned toward me in surprise, as if caught in a misdeed. His face blushed and there was a slight tremor in his voice. His embarrassment must have been linked to the origin of the coins.

"Nothing. I'm saving up to buy a Christmas present for Mother."

I have avoided telling him my fear that Sylvia may not last until Christmas. I'm not sure that her strength will hold out three weeks more. Would it be better if it did hold out? It may be inhuman to wish that the slender thread of life that she still possesses should be prolonged that much. Marcoré is saving up as in former years to give her a present that may be her last moment of happiness with us.

I see his picture in the frame—his sturdy body, his muscular legs, a radiant expression on his round face. Sylvia on the other side, in the snapshot made ten years ago. The camera caught her sweet and sentimental air, as if her very soul had posed in complete innocence.

They resemble each other closely, they are beautiful, spiritualized. I feel reduced to the grossest of animality when I capture them in their purity, their trusting eyes turned toward me. My wife and my son. Beings who are part of me, in whom I exist by way of blood, mind, and feeling. The first one is leaving too soon, she will not be able to see her son graduate from school, will not know the grandchildren that will come from him. She will not cross the first bridge he will build, will not see his name cited in government reports. Sylvia, my beloved, what a tremendous boon was conferred upon you, but at what a price! I promise to relate to you some day—if there should be another day for us—the whole story of Marcoré. I shall be at our son's side step by step. I shall make of him the man that you want him to be.

Chapter Fifteen

For the first time I am making an entry in my story while seated at the table around which we gathered together for more than twenty years. Not a sound in the deserted house. The parlor clock has stopped, the fire that was crackling in the kitchen a few hours ago has been reduced to ashes. Leoncia retired after dinner. Outside, the rain has died down, the night wind is entering through the transom and agitating the candle's flame.

I have the distinct impression that, if I perfect my senses, the silence will become audible, almost palpable. The shadows of which it is composed will gain form, the dead whom I most loved will be able to reappear at my side. The door of the large bedroom will open for Camilo, who will look at me for a second, then will go sit at his accustomed place at the head of the table. He will surely take an interest in my notes, will attempt to fill in the minor details that may have escaped me. Sylvia will appear out of the darkness in the hall and will come, effortlessly and tirelessly, to smoothe my forehead and fill it with inspiration. She fears that I may commit some injustice or fail to tell the truth. Honorata will come out of the kitchen, stepping even more lightly, having forgotten the gangrene. She will take Dona Emma's place and by means of discreet gestures or indignant clicks of her tongue will indicate which person is right. The dead can return, for they are more present in me at this moment than my remembrance of the living. I loved my father-in-law, I loved my wife, I loved Honorata, I feel them beside me. Neither fear nor emotion. My sadness leaves me indifferent, insensitive. I shall not raise my eyes so that they will not again retreat into the shadows. I know that they are present, that they are looking at me. Camilo does not cough, Sylvia breathes freely, Honorata's feet do not ache. Death has been good to them, it has liberated them from their ills. I should like to ask them questions that torment me on the days when I am depressed and that I avoid answering myself. Free from passion, perhaps they can answer them better than I can. Sylvia, my dearest, what happened to our love? Why did our lives become fragmented? You can see that grief alone persists in us all, without exception. Were you compensated for your sacrifices? Think back a moment and answer this: without Marcoré, would we be ending our lives side by side? Better with him or without him? I can see you are protesting by rattling the glass in the china closet. Your thoughts reach me in the clear vibration that spreads throughout the room. But you know that I am not uttering any blasphemy, there's no need for you to protest. I am merely attempting to fathom the elements that compose our lives. I adore our son, you know that for him I would be capable of committing any madness. After all, life is a continual questioning, and this evening I have reasons for surrendering to melancholy. I shall not personify the greatest error of our lives in Marcoré—it would be a monstrous thought. But it is true that he was an instrument of discord in our family. He gave consistency, so to speak, to an ambiguous situation that was maintained by means of small artifices. No blame should be placed on him, dearest, but on our love, which gave him life. And was it right to impose a condition on him that we were never certain is a blessing? Tell me, from where you are, is living really worth while? I confess my fear to you that Marco Aurelio has come only to swell the ranks of those who suffer. Again the protest in the china closet. Do not become upset, I shall do everything in my power to prevent that from happening. But I am afraid that the wave of mistakes in our lives may have marked him forever. Mistakes whose origin goes back to the marriage of Camilo and Dona Emma. Of such opposing dispositions, was it right for them to have joined together and borne fruit? We, ourselves, were we right or wrong? With Lauro you might perhaps have had a better fate, and at this hour you could have counted, not only on one child, who cost you so dearly, but on several, and all of normal birth. It is true that the same errors probably occur in the lives of all others. Father Bento is no doubt still lying awake, perplexed by the negative images that come back to him. He is conscious that he has failed in his missionary work, that in his corral it is the black sheep that predominate, that many of his sheep are sick and unhappy. Aristides has probably not yet fallen asleep, worrying over the future of his children. My mother is alone at this moment, sunk in gloomy thoughts. Julieta, her eyes inflamed, allows herself to be torn by jealousy. Even in Claudia, admirable as you know she is, the night that distills the saturated earth can only awaken feelings of frustration and grief. A greater anguish overwhelms the daughters of Major Dario who failed to find husbands in their youth, when their father was still rich. Go, my beloved, enter for a moment into your mother's bedroom. Is she not gnawing her nails, restless, dissatisfied, in the midst of an oppressive void? First pass through Elisa's room and you will note in her features the marks of a lost soul. In your rounds spare only Emiliana, and thus spare yourself, too. You still live in her, she is like your double who has endured for my love. The others, you will visit to conclude that their stories resemble ours, that it is only the costumes that differ from each other. It was this misery that we transmitted to Marcoré in our blindness. Worst of all is that he is becoming alone in the world, fought over by opposing feelings. He is struggling between two poles, unable to decide between them. Had your mother come to say good-by to you, perhaps all would have been settled. My pride is lesser—do me the justice of recognizing that. I would not have resisted the appeal for peace contained in your eyes during your last hours. I would have taken her hand and kissed it. Our feelings of resentment would be forgotten, we would have wept. Marcoré would be saved from his despair, you would smile feebly in the joy that could have preceded your death. She did not come, you had a melancholy end. Reflect and tell me whether my reasoning is correct. Honorata is surely nodding her head in agreement, for I do not hear the disapproving clicking of her tongue. And Camilo, what conclusions can he have reached?

Something like footsteps disappear into the darkness, beyond the pantry. Quiet, gentle footsteps of the dead. I contemplate the empty chairs, the china closet, where the remaining half of the candle projects its trembling light. Its rattling no longer resounds in clear waves. The silence is now the great lord of the house, occupies it entirely, extending it, filling it with mystery. A strange black entity that fails to terrify me. It attempts to oppress me, to expel me from the parlor. It keeps closing in, seems to lean over me to extinguish the candle with one puff. I am not easily intimidated, I guide my pencil over the paper with a steady hand. The dead themselves were present, I received them with naturalness. My decision to extinguish the lights was intentional. I knew that in this way the companions of my life would come back and occupy their places at the table. The silence with its blackness would not succeed in frightening me. It is potent, resembles a dense billow that comes to halt at the edge of the yellowish focus of light. If the candle goes out, it will cave in on top of me and crush me. Yet I'll let it become consumed, I shall continue on my notes until my vision fails.

Perhaps the telephone will ring. "It is Mr. Marco Aurelio, from São Paulo." Sara's voice has aged, but it is still mellifluous. "Oh, my son, I was afraid you wouldn't call me any more." After all, that's why I have stayed at home. Emiliana was expecting me, I seized upon the pretext of the rain, I stood her up. He may call yet, if the storm hasn't interrupted the telephone service. It isn't too late, they must still be awake at Dr. Leandro's house. Leoncia has not wound the cuckoo clock in the parlor since Sylvia's death. Marcilia, I am sure, would not have faced the consequences.

"A clock that has stopped, my boy, slows down the life of the master of the house."

That is what she used to say to me when, as a child, I helped her wind our wall clock, which my mother had inherited from her father. I am no longer counting on slowdowns, my dear Marcilia. Innumerable other clocks have stopped before this one, my share of evil spells must be complete. I would dearly like to hear the voice of my son before I go to bed. I have been waiting for his call for days. He's been away for three weeks. Dr. Leandro had come for the Mass of the seventh day and had taken his godson with him.

"Let's avoid a traumatism," he had said to me seriously. "Make this sacrifice for your son."

The boy had gone away, the days had turned into nights, in a slow and enervating succession. Twice he called me, the normal rhythm of time seemed restored.

"It's really wonderful here, Dad. I have taken some beautiful trips. My godfather is the best in the world."

His mother's expressions, the same enthusiasm, almost the same voice. I primed myself for another wait.

"I'll call you again. I miss you very much."

If he did miss his father, I would be an insanely happy man. I could not believe that he did, nor was I even sure that he missed his dead mother. He had become accustomed for years on end to see her as a semi-invalid, moving about the house with hesitant steps, her mouth half-open in the effort to breathe. He had had the sensation of being an orphan for a long time, as I had had that of being a widower. We lived with a dead woman, whose presence was nevertheless precious to us. A beloved dead woman who kept us suspended between the fear that if she abandoned us our lives would be shattered, and the anguish that if she tarried among us she would know no rest. Marcoré has gone off to enjoy himself in order to forget her. Sylvia herself may have inspired our compadre to invite him to spend his vacation in São Paulo. She wouldn't want her beloved son to be unhappy because of her.

The image of her serene face surrounded by flowers in the coffin comes back to me. The small face of a child, the high cheekbones, the lips distended as if they were going to smile. It was no longer my life's companion that lay inert there. That person had disappeared, days before, when they had cut her hair. Camargo had said, "The heat is frightful. Let's at least give her some relief."

Clemente had come with his bag of instruments, and had sheared off at the nape of her neck those thick tresses with the white strands that lent them dignity. I felt as if they were taking a vital organ from me and I had left the room to keep from crying.

So the dead woman in the coffin had departed, without being my lawful wife. Her bun was missing, they had transformed her into a person who was almost a stranger to me. Her hair clipped under her ears gave her an expression that had never been hers. Clemente had assassinated with his scissors the woman who had most intimately belonged to my life.

The candle has melted to a stump in the silver candlestick. The light is weak, it no longer reaches the china closet. The billow approaches the edge of the table. It is certain that Marcoré will not call. I shall go into the bedroom groping along the walls. I accept the challenge contained in the silence, I refuse to turn on the light. No more than a minuscule flame on the bending wick. The billow presses in on me. I can see the paper in front of me only with an effort. I'll get up and go toward my room. If I cry out, it will be because I have collided with one of my dead.

Chapter Sixteen

I feel fatigue impressed on me like the mark of a rubber stamp. A slowing up of body and soul that makes me uneasy. Parts worn out, emotions saturated. I have thought about taking a trip, seeking contact with strangers. Spending some time in a new environment, brushing off this humble provincial dust. Perhaps that's my trouble. An excess of dust, rusty joints, eyes tired of this immutable landscape that I loved so much as a child. Topplecart Hill covered with goatsbeard, cut by the red strip of road that seemed to me an invitation to mysterious escapades. The solitary cross on top of the station. The magnolias in the square, the church towers, the noisy bandstand on Sundays. Even the swallows have not changed. A need to renew images with a leisurely excursion to faraway places. I would be able to consult doctors who have perfected their auscultation in studies abroad.

Camargo's instruments are poor and antiquated. He won't prescribe without talking to his colleagues first. Impossible for me to leave. Chained to the office, magnetized by Marcoré. It would be madness to leave him in the clutches of his grandmother. That would be to lose him for all time. And Bernardo has not been sworn in, he cannot certify a thing. The remedy is to continue the placid daily rambling around Father Bento's corral.

Emiliana observes my apathy and justly complains, "You are free now to set our lives in order."

She speaks without petulance, moved only by a desire for harmony, for regularity. A legitimate, natural ambition. She would like us to appear in public side by side, as husband and wife. No more than that. I owe her that reparation, but I cannot bring myself to take the necessary steps. I have been going to her house only in the afternoons, and once in a while I have lunch there when Marcoré allows himself to be captured by his grandmother. My evenings now belong to my son. We dine together, go out for a stroll, visit my mother or Claudia. On Saturdays he belongs completely to Dona Emma, until Sunday morning. Emiliana thus has me at her service during that interval. It is not, to be sure, sufficient for her. She has a melancholy expression in her eyes, she sighs sadly.

"I don't know why you don't come to a decision. Can it be that you don't love me any more?"

She is admirably preserved. There are still traces of youth in her face, her dark flesh has remained firm, always ready for love. She vibrates with the intensity of our first hours, but I flee from excessive appeals.

"Let's wait a while longer. Time will tell what we ought to do."

After all, time is the remedy for everything. I have been leaving it up to time to resolve my life with Emiliana, for, to tell the truth, I do not plan to adopt any resolution myself. Time will tell. A shameless subterfuge, which Emiliana nevertheless accepts as she believes it is connected with the duration of Dona Emma's life.

I have never seen the latter again, but I know from Leoncia, and through Elisa, that she was deeply shaken by Sylvia's death.

"It was to be expected, senhor. Nobody could stand having so much remorse. Dona Emma wouldn't listen to anybody, she let the poor thing die without her pardon. Now she is gnawing her nails, eating her heart out."

Maybe she'll gnaw herself up completely, like a scorpion, I thought to myself. She could go to the devil, her grief did not interest me. I had cut her out of my emotional field, I didn't even want to hear her name. Marcoré knows my feelings, not through any admission of mine, but by sensing them from my look. His grandmother must have made the same resolution, for he never talks to me about her, it is as if she had died centuries ago.

My mother keeps expecting that I will call her to keep me company. She counts on seeing me again dependent on her care, submissive to her orders. When I was single, when Marcilia saw my mother taking extra pains to smooth my trousers, she used to say that a man child always holds first place in a mother's love.

"That's not true," she would protest. "I love my daughters just as much. He was my first-born, the one who cost me most pain. He's different."

The pains that I cost her have been repaid with abandonment, almost with forgetfulness. At times I think about taking her into my house, restoring the feeling of possession to her, giving her life a happy ending. However, when I reflect more deeply, I remember Marcoré and my plan disintegrates. I cannot admit her into my house as long as Dona Emma is alive. It would be harmful to my son to be fought over by persons who detest each other. The grandmothers have not spoken to each other since our rupture with Dona Emma.

My mother had written her a letter full of insults in my defense, and had received an answer in kind. They had become mortal enemies. With their grandson in the middle, they would each struggle to destroy the affection he felt for the other. How they would make him suffer!

One afternoon a little before Sylvia's final sickness we were on our way to my mother's house when I heard him utter the question I had always dreaded:

"Dad, why don't my grandmothers get along with each other? I don't understand what the trouble is between them."

I paused for a moment, perplexed, but contained my emotion. It was the first time that he touched on the subject in such an objective way.

"They don't get along because they are obstinate. They had a falling out over a silly matter and have not spoken to each other since. Why do you ask?"

"No special reason. We could all live together, if everybody liked each other. Doesn't Aunt Julieta like you?"

I gave some superficial explanation which, if it didn't convince him, diverted him from the subject. At my mother's house, no sooner did he receive her blessing than he disappeared into the back yard.

He was thus entering, through his own powers of reasoning, into the question of the merit of our family relationships, which were far from excelling in harmony. He was observing the distance at which we lived from each other, the coldness of our treatment of each other, our somber and sullen expressions. To what extent would that observation hurt him?

That same afternoon, on the way home, after some silence he had again taken up the thread of his thought: "The one I like the most, among all our relatives, is Aunt Claudia. If she were alone, she could come to live at our house."

His sentiment pleased me, for it coincided with Sylvia's.

"An extraordinary person," she would say to me. "If I had to be born over again and could choose my mother, I would like to be Claudia's daughter."

She really was extraordinary. Claudia could be the mother of all humanity, and complaints and misunderstandings would then disappear from the world. She has almost supernatural powers of comprehension, a capacity for self-denial that raises her to saintliness. Marcoré knew the worth of his aunt from personal experience. At least once a week from the time he was a child he had become accustomed to eating at her house where he always felt himself treated just like a son.

"Aunt Claudia's cooking is delicious. I've never seen anyone cook like her. Not even Grandma Nena."

"Except Honorata," I corrected him.

But she had departed before Marcoré could judge her virtues.

"Sometimes I have the feeling that I remember her, Dad. I don't know, it's something like a longing. I must have been very fond of her."

"And your grandfather, don't you remember him, son?"

I purposely extended our conversation, for those confessions made me know him better.

"Of course I remember him, Dad. Next to Mother, it was Grandpa Milo that I loved best."

I looked at him half-surprised and half-offended. He blushed, then corrected himself. "Next to Mother and you, of course."

And he tried to cover up his embarrassment: "Marcilia was also good to me. But she wasn't very bright. She believed in so many stupid things . . ."

His acuteness in analyzing persons he felt linked to through association or memory was astounding. The boy was extremely perceptive, he could distinguish the human values that formed his sentimental world. He showed that he possessed a sense of discrimination that could be his best weapon in life.

He is becoming a man, the fuzz on his upper lip is getting more pronounced, his voice is changing. He is almost as tall as I am, his arms and legs are agile and muscular.

While my son gets stronger each day, my strength decreases in exact proportion. It's time to watch my eating habits, avoid drinking. I gave up smoking years ago and I have been avoiding going to excess with Emiliana, not out of virtue but for lack of energy. Marcoré needs a sound father to accompany him through life to wherever it is that destiny may permit.

We placed Sylvia in her grave six months ago, next to Camilo. My companionship with Marcoré has gone along without any problems, in complete understanding. He had come back to me from São Paulo a new person, alert, fluent. I had seen him step down from the train and had been almost speechless with emotion. It was a young man who was in my arms.

"This was the surprise I had for you. My godfather thought I ought to begin to dress like a grownup.

The long pants looked good on him, they gave him an air of propriety that would have delighted Camilo. I had said good-by to a child, received a fine young dandy in return. I had said just that to him, on the way home, in Proença's car.

"Oh, Dad, you forget I'm going to be twelve years old. I can't keep on being a child all my life."

He kept gazing out the window, looking for familiar faces. In three months of absence from his home town he had become astonishingly civilized.

"How come you didn't call Timoteo?" he asked in a low voice.

I told him that Timoteo had sold his car and moved away. His oldest son had taken to stealing, charges were being preferred against him.

"Poor Timoteo. If he hadn't left, I could have learned how to drive from him. Would you have let me?"

The idea frightened me, Marcoré had come back too impetuous.

"It's a bit early for that, son. When you're old enough, we'll see about it."

At home he had regained an awareness of reality: he became conscious of his loss and cried all afternoon long in front of Sylvia's picture.

"Please don't think that I forgot about Mother. I enjoyed myself there only because of my godfather. It would be so wonderful if she were still alive and could see me now!"

The house seems too big and empty to him. Its silence oppressed his expansive nature, and he hastened to seek diversion outside. Sufficient were the long nights that were filled with the images of the dead and recollection of the dissensions of the living. He stayed at home only during the hours when he studied or had his meals, the rest of the time he went out.

"Dad, why is it that you don't go to Mass any more? Everybody has noticed it."

Father Bento's altar boy had come back to life, to express wonder at his father's absence from church. He wanted to know why I had strayed away from God.

"I do not have any desire to go, nor do I feel any need to go, my son. I won't go merely out of a sense of obligation. It would have no value. I accept only the obligation of work, because that is sacred. The rest is human invention."

He had looked at me with surprise, as if disarmed.

"But when Mother was alive you used to go every Sunday."

"I went, not because I felt obliged to go, but to please her. What I did had no value."

A little later he got up dejectedly and went to his room.

Perhaps he thinks I'm a heretic and fears for my salvation. My poor son, he still has so much to learn about life! Indeed, I have yet to tell him almost everything about myself. I need his respect and his confidence to keep me from failing in the task that Sylvia entrusted to me: to make a man of him. Or, rather, an engineer capable of constructing bridges on which his name will be engraved forever.

How can I draw closer to my son when Dona Emma's shadow stands between us? The flower has been well planted, but it will not last for all time. I beg God's pardon for my harshness of soul, for what I desire is to be free to be able to live alone with Marcoré. Let the rest disappear—even Emiliana. I shall go far away, even though it may mean separation from Claudia, never to hear her affectionate voice again.

"I've been missing you so much, my dear brother. Heavens, how old you're getting!"

I'll even move far away from Claudia, even though my mother may weep and implore me to stay. I'll let Marcoré tell me where we should go to live and what we should do with our lives, after the scorpion has bitten off all of its tail. May it destroy itself quickly, out of remorse. I am getting too tired, I won't be able to stand a long wait.

Chapter Seventeen

I haven't written any more in my office or at home at night. Partly because I was waiting for Dona Emma's death to end my story, partly because I was afraid that Marco Aurelio would start wondering what I was putting down on paper. If he asked me—"What is all that, Dad?"—I would be unable to lie to him. I would answer simply, "A summing up of our lives."

Lives of little value, made up of petty, banal episodes. Nothing to distinguish them from ordinary existences. It was as a pastime that I began to set them down in this summary way. And also, perhaps, because of the influence of my occupation. Anyone who has spent so many years certifying—*ad verbum*—documents that pertain to the lives of others would naturally feel tempted to set down a record of his own life.

Marco Aurelio would not have accepted a reason that was basically also puerile.

"Oh, Dad, why waste time on that? There are many things that people should not tell but should try to forget."

I tried to forget them, but there were days when they would come to the surface and agitate me. I would then feel myself going back into the past, examining it with care and stirring up memories that have turned bitter today. I would hasten to set down on paper everything I considered essential to my tale.

The sheets have piled up, the oldest of them having the same age as Marco Aurelio. Many have yellowed with time, on others the writing has faded away almost completely. They will remain buried in my desk drawer until the notary who will take my place some day finds them and has them published in the journal founded by Laurindo, when the people represented here are dead. If it should be Jaime, Claudia's oldest boy, perhaps prudence will prevent him from making them public. They might say that his uncle committed scandalous acts, that he was inhuman, amoral, a slanderer. But whatever they may say about me won't matter, just as what has already been said has never mattered.

The night advances, there is a profound peace in the deserted house. Only memories of its dead populate its gloomy silence. The noises of life that reach me are strange ones, coming from the city that is getting ready to welcome the New Year.

No feeling of revolt or inconformity. My heart is calm, although fatigued by a whole lifetime of mistakes. No contrition either, for I refuse to accept the role that my son has attributed to me. Striking a general balance, I believe that there have been victims only, that there is no possible way of distinguishing the guilty.

Even Dona Emma's name does not arouse any resentment in me. I came close to hating her, I wished for her death so that she would disappear from my world. Today, however, I deplore our childish behavior that permitted pride and distrust to prevail over our other sentiments. She had an uneven temper that was subject to unpredictable variations, but the slightest show of affection made her gentle and submissive. When she was in a good mood she would reminisce about people she knew as a girl, recalling persons and customs that had disappeared. I often heard her reconstructing the world of her adolescence, the nuns' school where she had studied, the dances and the religious celebrations she had participated in. At this moment I recall one of those days that began with laughter at the table. The rest of us always welcomed such days with a kind of delirium. We would do our best to retain and continue them, but the interval of one night was enough to alter the picture of the previous evening. On that particular occasion she had come to lunch holding a handkerchief to her face.

"The devil take it! These things happen only to me! I think I've got a sty in my nose."

Sylvia began to laugh more than was really necessary.

"What an idea, Mother! All you have is a beautiful pimple!"

Camilo and I exchanged delighted glances. If only our lives were always like this!—we said to each other.

Even Honorata had come in from the kitchen.

"I've told the senhora not to eat mangoes. But who ever knew her to listen to anybody?"

Imperturbably, Dona Emma had taken her seat.

"From the pain that I feel it can only be a sty. The nasty thing lost its way."

A day that began like that would end with laughter in the sewing room. She would enclose herself there with Honorata, while the hours would speed by in mutual recollections. They would talk about the town's old-timers, many of whom were still living. They knew the weaknesses those people had, they enjoyed remembering humorous episodes. For reasons I don't know, whenever they had a visitor they liked they rehashed the story of the telegram that Dona Clarinha Medeiros had once received in answer to the letter she had sent to a shop in São Paulo. They wanted to know whether what the lady had ordered was a sample of children or of chiffon.

"She always was a scatterbrain," Dona Emma invariably concluded. "She struts around like a turkey hen but she can't see an inch beyond her nose. I'll bet she actually did order a sample of children, because she had just been married a little while before."

But such moments, which could have occurred with greater frequency in our lives, were on the contrary few and far between. What prevailed was a succession of misunderstandings, suspicions, and insults.

Dona Emma has passed into the ranks of the dead, it is useless now to attempt to weigh the good times and the bad. We surely could have been happy: we possessed the means for it. But the tableau that we formed has broken up into irreparable fragments. I am left without even my son at my side. Lost, separated from me forever more. The portraits distributed around the walls represent all that remains of my past.

My story will soon come to its end. At midnight I shall get up and turn on all the lights in the house. I'll walk through the rooms, stare at the inert pieces of furniture, belabor the reminiscences that persist.

I think back to Camargo's visit to my office, accompanied by Marco Aurelio.

"I must talk to you. The old lady is very ill. I doubt she'll last more than a few days. The time has come to put an end to this foolish enmity."

Let her go, I thought, looking at my son. The time has come all right, but it is the time of our liberation.

The only thing that mattered to me was the proximity of total, exclusive possession. Only with difficulty did I manage to contain my happiness and avoid uttering remarks that would have been out of place.

I called Marco Aurelio over to my chair, while the doctor sat down under the list of marriage banns. I embraced my son, passed my hand over his hair which was as light and smooth as Sylvia's. His dejected look did not surprise me. I attributed it to his grandmother's condition.

"I'll drop by her house later on."

Camargo took his leave.

"Very well. I am relying on you, on your character."

Marco Aurelio didn't stay much longer.

"Grandma needs me. If you only knew how much she has been suffering!"

I didn't hold him back, I let him return to the dying woman's side. She could have the last hours, because all the rest would soon belong to a single master.

I went out after dinner, undecided as to what I should do. Camargo was relying on my character, but he did not know the extent of my pride. I started walking slowly in the direction of Adelino's bakery, but halfway there I turned off into the street by the river. Better to wait until it gets dark, I thought. The conciliatory visit would be less painful. I stopped on the bridge, sat down beside a post. The transparent water flowed past quietly, almost imperceptibly. I seemed to see still reflected in it the image of my little son, leaning over the railing, tossing pebbles that were heaped by his side. I felt a sharp longing to see once again that child who had become a self-assured, impulsive boy. If I could, I would have made the waters flow back until I found that lost treasure again. I would give my life to be able to hold that lively little head in my hands again and sink my face into his hair that smelled like fresh grass. Silence fell over the plain that extended out of sight toward the luminous horizon. It brought the night, with different messages for each one of Father Bento's poor living souls. The evocative moment escaped me, I could not prolong it, sip it like a drink of water. Everything was in motion, in continual flight, at the mercy of an incontrollable impulse. Even the tranquil river, on whose banks mysterious voices began to throb, kept flowing along into the distance, hesitating at backwaters only for a moment. My son had been drawn into the gears and had changed. Honorata had disappeared, her voice would never again be heard in the kitchen scolding Marco Aurelio, a tiny creature, wide-eyed, his hands on his hips.

"Come eat your beefsteak, child. Don't be stubborn. I didn't put any garlic in your food."

Neither would the voice of Camilo be heard protesting when they forced him to take some nourishment.

"I won't drink that milk. It's full of lumps."

Marcilia would not sing any more at the laundry tub in my mother's house. Nor would she narrate to attentive and astonished little faces her story about the cleaning of the world.

Of Sylvia herself, everything is lost. Her love had gone to remain on the other side of the deep river. Impossible to call it back.

Marco Aurelio, despite his alertness, would no longer remember the imaginary companions of his early childhood.

"Daddy, I have to go now to play with Gum and Gim. They are waiting in the back of the yard, in the shade of the mango tree. They're a little brother and sister."

And his imagination went farther.

"Do you know where they live?"

"No."

"In the house of the wind. If I don't hurry, the wind will come and get them."

Dead also and, even more terrible, forgotten forever, were the fictitious creatures created in his mind, in which other symbols were now stirring.

What remained of Dona Emma would soon come to an end. She might not even have enough voice left for a word of peace and pardon.

The river continued to flow amid the descending shadows. The voices in the vegetation along the banks faded away. Tiny beings awoke for another day's journey. Work, love, struggles. Coming from the city, a man riding horseback, wearing a hat with a chin strap and with his hand holding the brim, had crossed the bridge at a half trot. He rode off into the distance at a leisurely pace, the animal's hoofs striking the hardened ground and raising a light wake of dust. I had stared at him for a long time, to retain the memory of a moment that my eyes would never witness again. Everything in my life was like that: fleeting, instantaneous, impalpable.

It had become night, the street lamps had been lit. The waters appeared deeper and more static. But I knew that they continued to move in their divisory function. It was as if the river also flowed through my interior world.

I climbed the slope slowly, a sadness, a tightness in my heart. I headed toward the bakery, walking along without any conviction, uncertain of the consequences of my visit. At the entrance to the house two figures were conversing. I approached and distinguished Claudia and Marco Aurelio.

"How long you took! Grandma is asleep now."

I was surprised by the tone of reproof in his voice. But I did not attach much importance to it, the old lady's condition excused everything.

Claudia, pensive, embraced me.

"I'm afraid Dona Emma won't come out of this. She has declined considerably."

My sister looked different, I hadn't really examined her face carefully for some time. She had put on too much weight, she seemed tired. She had been a pretty girl, with lively gestures and a friendly air. What had happened to the Claudia of my childhood days, my playmate, the confidante of my love affairs? Never again would we fly kites together, never again would we run like cats along the walls, nor would we search for berries in the fields on Topplecart Hill. The river had carried her far away, perhaps Claudia no longer even remembered her childhood.

"It would be better for you to come back tomorrow. But be here early, if you want to see Grandma still alive."

The same impertinent tone, which did not go unnoticed by Claudia. He said good-by and entered the house.

"Don't pay any attention. He has been staying up all night on account of Dona Emma."

It undoubtedly must have been the tension of those last weeks that had upset my son's nerves. He had become his grandmother's nurse, leaving her only to go to school. He was thinner, his hands trembled, his face was noticeably paler.

Claudia had gone on home, I went to the club. I felt indisposed, without the courage to go see Emiliana. I went to bed early. The next morning I was awakened by poundings on my bedroom door. The voice of Leoncia, distressed: "They've sent word that Dona Emma is approaching the end."

I dressed rapidly and hurried there. Camargo was coming out, accompanied to the gate by Marco Aurelio.

"She won't last longer than today. Don't fail to keep your promise."

"I came yesterday but I found her asleep."

"I know that, but you still have time."

I entered, uneasy. It was the first time I had been in that house and I felt a vague fear. Everything clean, neatly arranged. Flowers everywhere, vases filled with maidenhair, the small terrace in front adorned with orchids. I recalled her distant words: "Plants are the only friends I have in this life."

Now she was lying on her deathbed, moaning, taking her leave of the world. Marco Aurelio had gone in to attend to her.

"I'll be right back. I'll see if it's all right for you to go in."

I went to the kitchen, asked Doralice for some coffee. Elisa, seated near the stove, did not even raise her reddened eyes toward me. Her shoulders sagged, she seemed oblivious of everything. I walked over to the door, examined the yard where not a single dry leaf could be seen on the ground. Marco Aurelio's bicycle was in the woodshed, his fishing rod lay across some two-by-fours. It pained me to note that intimacy, my son's belongings, which should have been in our house, stored in enemy territory instead. For at least three months he had lived in closer association with his grandmother than with his father. Only an occasional meal with me, a visit to my office, quick embraces that were not always particularly close.

"I've come to see you for just a second. Grandma is all alone and asked me to come right back. I think she has gotten much worse."

I accepted Dona Emma's condition as a good reason for his haste when he came out to see me and I didn't insist on his staying longer.

"Go ahead, son. She must be needing your help."

From the kitchen I had gone into the other rooms, even into the little sewing room next to Marco Aurelio's bedroom. I felt dizzy, as if I were visiting in real life places I had known only vaguely in dreams. The sewing room, although smaller, was just like the one she used to work in with Honorata. There was the footstool that she used to rest her feet on, the cane seat yellowed but still intact; the machine with seven drawers, with her collection of thimbles, spools, scissors, needles; the iron, small and light, that she sometimes gave to Doralice to play at being an ironing woman with Marco Aurelio. Objects that I had known for more than twenty years, souvenirs of a past that would be extinguished with Dona Emma's death. In the dining room, Camilo's picture had flowers under it—a little pot of violets on an iron stand. I sat down and waited for Marco Aurelio. I wanted him to stay in there a while and come out only in order to tell me that it was too late. There were other persons in the room, for disparate voices were counting beads in a funereal tone. I don't know how much time must have passed before my son came into the room, his countenance agitated.

"Grandma doesn't recognize anybody any more. You should have come yesterday!"

His eyes were red, his voice trembled. I could tell from his breath that he was still fasting.

"But, son, I did come, didn't I?"

He seemed to remind himself, after a moment's reflection: "You came very late. I was so disappointed! Grandma wanted so much to talk to you."

He went back into the bedroom almost weeping.

To tell the truth, I didn't believe that the old lady had wanted to talk to me. She was a hard woman, she was not one to soften up even in the face of death. All that must have been her grandson's doing, probably with Claudia's support. It could not be a spontaneous gesture by a person who had sworn never to forgive me, either in heaven or in hell, for having thrown her out of her own house.

I had let myself remain there a while longer. Adelino's wife and daughters came and went, on tiptoes. They all wore expressions of fear rather than of grief. Claudia had appeared with Josefina, Dona Carmela's unmarried daughter. Her old friend was also ailing, she no longer went out, even to go to church.

In a short while the house had filled up. I noticed the strained manner with which people greeted me, I became bored waiting and got up to leave. Marco Aurelio, his eyes moist, had come out to meet me.

"Aren't you going to see her at least for a moment?"

I felt he was being insolent and answered, "No. It won't do any good now. I'm going home."

And I left, with a scowl on my face.

At one o'clock they telephoned from the bakery to tell me that

Dona Emma had died. I felt a great relief, I began to breathe deeply. Nothing could prevent Marco Aurelio any more from remaining forever dependent on me. I was free to live with him wherever I wanted to, without anyone coming between, without any shadow watching our steps.

She was buried the next morning. I accompanied her to the cemetery, held one of the handles of the coffin two or three times during the funeral procession. No movement any more in that body that had been so active, no word, no gesture. No miracle would revive her to upset my plans.

When we left the cemetery Marco Aurelio told me that he was very tired and needed to rest.

"You're right, son. We'll go straight home."

We kept walking side by side, in silence, avoiding the groups that went ahead of us along the sidewalk.

"But I won't be going with you. Today and tomorrow I must look after some things that Grandma left."

He spoke without looking at me, in a grief-stricken voice that suited the occasion. My first impulse was to order him to come with me, for I was irritated by the thought that even when dead Dona Emma should continue to interfere in my life. I held my temper, however, and left him at the door of the little house with its blue windows. The following day he came to my house, dressed up as if he were going to some ceremony. He found me in my bedroom, still in my pajamas. I went up to him to take him into my arms, but he drew back.

"I've come to say good-by. I'm leaving in a little while for São Paulo. I'm going to stay at my godfather's house and study there."

I sat down on my bed, stunned.

"What's the matter with you, son?"

His face became red, he avoided my eyes.

"I don't want to live with you any more."

I got up, enraged, and seized him by the shoulders.

"You mean, I've waited so long to have you with me and now you're talking such nonsense to me?"

He freed himself from my hands in a sudden movement.

"Well, if you must know, I am ashamed of you and your hard heart and your lack of decency! Ever since I was eight years old I've known about the kind of life you've been leading. You killed Mother by causing her grief, you threw Grandma out of the house. You are a wicked man, a heretic, a man with no morals . . ."

His screams had turned into sobs. I felt myself stagger as if I had been struck on the head. I went toward him, my hand raised to slap him. Above his head, however, Sylvia's picture, hanging on the wall, came into my field of vision. Her serene look interceded. I hesitated a moment, my attack of anger abated. Marco Aurelio gave me a last glance of fear in the face of my threat of aggression, then disappeared out the door.

I sat down on the bed again, a sharp pain in my breast, my heart racing. I could accept anything except having my son insult me in that way, then abandon me. I felt that, for me, Marco Aurelio was dead.

If it is true that every man must weep at least once in his life, my turn had come. The closet mirror reflected a shape that was shaken by sobs and whose features I could not distinguish through my blurred eyes. My grief increased, a strange, disintegrating sort of grief that seemed to tear me apart. I felt faint and dropped onto my bed. Tears streaked down my cheeks, my arteries throbbed rapidly. I could not coordinate my ideas, I was completely confused and agitated. But in all that tangle of emotions, the feeling of loss predominated. It was as if something had pierced my life and had separated me from my son. I saw him draw farther and farther away, without saying good-by to me, running desperately, not even looking back. Overcome by exhaustion, I believe I fell asleep.

When I came to, Claudia was at my side, sitting on the edge of my bed. Calm and capable of reflecting now, I took her hand.

"Imagine what happened to me, Claudia. I don't know what will become of me without him."

An outburst I could not repress and which moved her by its sincerity. So great was my feeling of abandonment that I did not try to hide from her how much I had wept. On the contrary, I let her dry my eyes, my mouth, and my cheeks, and straighten my hair with her fingers.

"He came by my house and told me everything. He also cried a lot and held me tight. I think that later on he'll change his mind and will come back to you."

I tried to hang on to that hope, but the image of Dona Emma appeared and frightened it away. I came back to reality.

"No, Claudia, he won't ever come back. He has his grandmother's blood in his veins."

"In that case you will have to go to him."

"I don't know if I'll have the courage to face another humiliation."

We talked together for some time, in short phrases that were broken by intervals of silence. She tried to comfort me, declaring that it had just been an incident that would not have any serious consequences and that had come about only because of the conditions of my life. Time would fix everything, I only had to wait and see. I thought I noticed a slight tone of censure in her voice, even though it was affectionate, when she pronounced the word "conditions." I considered telling her about my intimate life with Sylvia, about the motivation that had led me into that irregular arrangement. But I felt it would be tedious and irksome to stir up the past again, so I let her continue on with her explanations.

She had taken lunch with me and had then left, certain that she had convinced me about the transitory nature of the situation.

A little later my mother came in, out of breath.

"You didn't come to see me, son, but I know how you must be suffering. I made a great effort to come here. Now you see how sad it is to be left alone."

"Don't worry about me. What's done is done. I'll get along all right by myself."

She appeared not to have heard me and went on, without looking at me.

"When I told you that that other woman was going to ruin your life, you thought it was none of my business. Now you see the result."

She always used to insist on demonstrating the accuracy of her predictions, and that must have been the only reason for her visit. Her gesture was not one of solidarity, but rather of censure and complaint. I was sorry, for both of us, that she had come.

"Don't blame Emiliana. It would only compound the confusion," I said to her in a harsh voice.

She looked at me coldly, as if she considered it disrespectful of me to mention that name in her presence. She turned around and then began to inspect all the rooms, one by one. She opened the drawers, counted the sheets and bedspreads, went into the kitchen and the pantry, examined the canned goods. She cast a long glance into the back yard, saw hog plums rotting on the ground, guavas that had been pecked at by birds. She passed in review all of the things that she had dreamt for years of possessing. Knowing that I was alone now, she had hurried over, thinking that finally her turn had come. The reception she got from me disillusioned her and she asked me to call a cab, as she felt too tired to walk home.

From my front terrace I saw her leave, alone and unhappy. Her white hair moved me, I considered telling her to stay. She slowed her steps down, as if she were expecting me to call her back. At the same time the thought occurred to me that Marco Aurelio might come back some day and that her presence might not please him. I let her continue on her way. She reached the gate, turned her sad eyes toward me for a moment.

"May God be with you, son."

She got in the car and left.

I suffered like a wounded animal and wept frequently during the weeks that followed. Sylvia's picture and the mirror are the only witnesses of my new weaknesses. I spent hours going through old family albums, I kissed all the snapshots of my son. I caressed Sylvia's face, tried to take Camilo's fleshless hands in mine. I raved, I gnawed at my wrists, I sobbed like a lost soul. What had happened to that world that had seemed so peaceful, in which everyone smiled with such confidence? It had become reduced to cardboard, like a jigsaw puzzle.

With my eyes blurred I have looked through his school notebooks, in which his pothooks gradually took on a definitive and personal form. A glorious little voice seemed to rise up out of the ruled sheets.

"Dad, I already know what a prime number is!"

I have read and reread, until I have learned them by heart, all of Dr. Leandro's letters. In all of them, the same advice: trust time to find a solution to the problem. Time, indeed. Claudia had said the same thing. But how long can I endure waiting? I felt that I had aged a lifetime during those days. Even now, two months later, I feel a formless inertia that incapacitates me for human contacts. A process of disintegration has begun in me and I don't know to what extremes I will be carried by it.

On this last night of the year I most feel the weight of solitude. My mother is far away just now, she went with Sabino to spend some time at the shore. Her feeling of having been abandoned can't be as painful as mine. I remember once finding her at home without Marcilia.

"All alone, Mother?"

She seemed offended.

"Alone? No; with God!"

She appeared to be aware of some permanent presence that brought a sense of security into her internal order. She complained about the daily routine, felt that she had been forgotten by her children, but the unfathomable part of her being maintained a kind of alliance that must have been her reason for living.

She is far away at this moment, I can't give even her my conventional embrace. To tell the truth, I feel relieved of an unpleasant obligation.

Marco Aurelio, also far away, probably does not have a single kind thought about me. "I wonder what Dad is doing at home alone now." Maybe he wouldn't even use the word "Dad." He would just say "he."

As for Emiliana, she moved away a few days ago. Ermelinda had found a job in São Paulo and took her mother with her. Emiliana had a hurt look in her eyes when she announced her decision to me, "I'm going away with my daughter. I learned too late that I was just a kind of prop in your life. My God, how blind I was!"

I had wanted to bind her to me in the formal union that she desired so badly and that she undoubtedly had a right to expect. I was afraid of losing her, but I didn't have the strength to do the right thing. My good intentions were nullified by the hope that Marco Aurelio would come back to me.

"I always hoped to be able to join my life to yours, to provide you with children, to give you the peace that you never had. Now that we are completely free and still have time to put our lives in order, you become even more attached to a child who has rejected you."

Emiliana was wrong. We were not as free as all that, and I can't admit that there has ever been anyone completely free. Not even Paulo, whom I admired so much. He came back to this city not long ago, worn-out, white-haired, with a distant and unhappy expression on his flaccid face. He had come to see me at my office on the day he arrived, had dropped wearily on the bench under the banns. He had left town as a young man in order to seek his fortune and had come back beaten, without the self-assurance he used to have, even though he was well-dressed, with a pearl stickpin in his tie. Where in the world had he been, to have come back thus destroyed? It comforted me to ponder over his downfall.

While I looked at him slouched in a corner of the bench, my memory suddenly recalled the figure of Timoteo, skinny, with sad, sunken eyes. One of his sons was a fugitive from the law; Timoteo had come to my office to say good-by. He had sat down in the same place, and it seemed I could still hear his words.

"I don't know what harm I ever did to God for my life to become ruined like this. I have to leave this town. My wife is wasting away day by day. She says it's from shame."

And sighing deeply: "This world is a madhouse. Everybody has a cross to bear."

A madhouse, no doubt. There was Paulo to confirm it.

"I made plenty of money, had as much fun as a drunken sailor. But I'll tell you one thing: life isn't worth a damn."

I had agreed with him, without inquiring into his reasons. My reason was a recent one, although it had old roots, and it gave me a feeling of helplessness.

I thought about Gloria, hard-working, busy with the children and the household chores.

"How's your family?"

"As well as anyone could expect. I'm the one who doesn't feel so good. I don't know what the trouble is with me that keeps me from finding a resting place. I've come back to look for a little peace here where we spent our childhood."

He soon realized that he had come knocking at the wrong door. I couldn't give him any comfort. He stared at me for a long while, then shook his head.

"Damn if you haven't been reduced to a hulk yourself. It's just like I said. Life is just a stupid affair."

And on his way out, "I'm going to see if I can buy the place that my parents used to own. Maybe I'll feel better living there. You can start getting the deed ready."

Paulo, whom I used to consider a strong guy, had come back an empty shell. And Emiliana talked to me about being free. Nobody is free in this world.

It's a few minutes before midnight. Camilo's clock ticks away on the table, it's the only company I have left. When the hands meet, I'll turn on all the lights in the house and scare away, at least for a few moments, the darkness that surrounds me.

I don't know what I'll do the rest of my night. I won't go to the club, or to Claudia's house. I know very well that in both places I would only be like an undesirable shadow. Should I go to see Aristides and make a clean breast of things to him? I would only get a reprimand.

"Compadre, I always told you that everything must come to an end in this world, everything except the love of God."

Should I heed the call of Father Roque's bells? I long ago stopped listening to those of his predecessor, despite Sylvia's pleas for me never to fail to take the sacraments. Father Bento, secluded in his little room at the parish house, will perhaps remember this impenitent recluse in his prayers. He must be distressed over the knowledge that disorder prevails in the corral from which old age has separated him. Disorder that is not external but in the hearts of his poor flock.

The hubbub outdoors is increasing. The clamor of groups on their way to church. The factory whistle will blow very soon.

The town square must be full of people. Hours ago snatches of band music reached my ears, carrying me back to the days when I loved so much to stroll along the sandy lanes. They no longer retain my footprints, and the musicians are not the same. If I went there, they would look at me as if I were a stranger.

I can't count on sleep getting me through the night. I am certain now that my son will not phone. I have stayed at home since the afternoon in the hope that he would call. Dr. Leandro would be on the phone first, to make the necessary introduction: "We have a surprise for you." A pause, and then the voice that means everything to me would come over the wires: "Hello, Dad . . ." For hours I have rehearsed our meeting. I reached the point of asking his forgiveness for my errors, to beg him to let us start a new life together. Useless. The telephone will not ring.

In a short while I will go outside, I'll walk around aimlessly under the moonlit sky. Perhaps I'll stroll down to the bridge, sit down beside one of the posts. I'll look at the quiet, deep water, may lean on the railing and toss pebbles into the stream. Among the waves that will appear, no larger than a child's face, perhaps there will appear the image of Marco Aurelio when he was small, saying to me: "Daddy, Daddy, don't be sad over your little boy. I am living down here at the bottom of the water with Gum and Gim. That's why I can't come to you." I'll stay there until dawn, I may even fall asleep, never to awaken again. Because I don't know what to do with the day that is about to dawn, or with all the days to come, in this grief I feel in having outlived my loved ones.

The hands of the clock have met. Outside, the bells have begun to ring in a wild gaiety. The riotous vibrations dominate the night, I feel the urge to cry out to them to take pity on me, to make my son remember me.

I weaken, my hope springs up again in the midst of my tears that the telephone will yet ring. The clamor of the bells envelops me like an omen. I'll turn on all the lights and I'll keep waiting. I can't go on living without Marcoré.